"McBain still is fresh with his observations, and his prose is as sturdy as ever."
Washington Post Book World

"The kind of adrenalin rush that has carried this series through 35 novels."
Des Moines Register

"One of the best McBain novels so far."
Houston Chronicle

"Tight, compelling and suspenseful."
Newsday

Also by Ed McBain
Published by Ballantine Books:

THE MUGGER

KILLER'S CHOICE

HE WHO HESITATES

EIGHTY MILLION EYES

DOLL

WHERE THERE'S SMOKE

RUMPELSTILTSKIN

HEAT

AN 87TH PRECINCT MYSTERY

McBAIN

BALLANTINE BOOKS • NEW YORK

This is for Annie and Syd Solomon

A portion of this book appeared originally in *Playboy* in different form.

Library of Congress Catalog Card Number: 81-65263

ISBN 0-345-34597-5

This edition published by arrangement with The Viking Press

Manufactured in the United States of America

First Ballantine Books Edition: March 1983
Twelfth Printing: January 1990

The city in these pages is imaginary.
The people, the places are all fictitious.
Only the police routine is based on established
investigatory technique.

ONE

The five-year old, unmarked sedan Steve Carella was driving to the scene was fitted with an air conditioner that had been repaired last summer and that now—when it was desperately needed—had perversely decided to malfunction. The windows front and back were open, but the air that flowed through the car was sodden and hot, the humidity in this city frequently accompanying the soaring temperature like a leaden ballet dancer lifting a fat partner. Bert Kling sat suffocating in silence beside Carella as the car moved uptown and crosstown.

The initial call had been received by Communications on High Street at 8:30 a.m., an Emergency 911 call that had been routed immediately to a dispatcher who'd radioed car Eight-Seven Frank to the scene. The responding patrolmen weren't at all surprised to find a corpse: the woman who'd called 911 had reported that she'd just come home to find her husband dead in their apartment. The dispatcher had ended his radio message with "See the lady," and the lady had

1

indeed been waiting for the police in the lobby of the building. But they had not called back to the station house with a request for detectives until they'd entered the sixth-floor apartment and seen for themselves that there was, in fact, a body on the living-room floor.

The building was in a section of the precinct that was rather more elegant than many of the others, sitting in a semicircle of apartment houses that partially surrounded Silvermine Oval and overlooked Silvermine Park, the River Highway, and the river itself beyond. The buildings themselves had succumbed to the onslaught of the graffiti writers, a visual attack as numbing as a blackjack blow, but there were still doormen in livery here, and the security was presumably tight. A trio of radio motor patrol cars and an Emergency 911 van were all angle-parked in front of the building as Carella nosed the unmarked sedan into the curb. It was then that Kling, who had been silent all the way from the station house, said, "Steve, I think my wife is playing around with somebody"

One of the patrolmen who'd responded to the dispatcher's call was standing at the curb, waiting for the detectives. He recognized the faded maroon car as Carella cut the ignition, and then he recognized Carella and Kling as well, and moved toward the car as the doors on either side opened. Carella was staring at Kling over the roof of the car. Kling, his head ducked, began walking toward the patrolman. He had, until just recently, been the youngest man on the squad, blond and blue-eyed, with a boyish, clean-shaven face and an innocent gaze that belied his line of work. He was slightly taller than Carella, and broader in the shoulders; he was wearing a lightweight jacket, darker slacks, a white shirt, and—in keeping with the lieutenant's recent dictum—a tie. Carella, a stunned look still on his face, came around the side of the car and stepped onto the curb. He walked with the casual stride of an athlete, a man with dark hair and dark eyes peculiarly slanted downward to give his face a somewhat Oriental look. The tropical suit he'd put on at a quarter to seven that morning had already wilted; it resembled an insulted dishrag.

"Where is it?" he asked the patrolman.

"Upstairs, apartment 6B. My partner's in the hall outside. Lady's in the lobby, with the doorman there. Came home and found the spouse dead."

The lady was a tall brunette, her hair cut in the wedge an ice-skating star had made famous, looking fresh and cool in a cotton print dress and high-heeled pumps. Her face was narrow, almost lupine, dominated by startlingly green eyes and a wide mouth. She had been crying; her eyes still glistened with tears, and mascara was running down her cheeks. Carella hesitated before approaching her. This was the part he hated; this was the part that was always most difficult. He took a deep breath.

"I'm Detective Carella," he said, "Eighty-seventh Squad. I'm sorry, ma'am, but I have to ask you some questions."

"That's all right," she said. Her voice was low and throaty. She seemed numb as she blinked back the tears and nodded.

"Can you tell me your husband's name, please?"

"Jeremiah Newman."

"And your name?"

"Anne. Anne Newman."

"I understand you came home to—"

"Yes."

"When was that, Mrs. Newman?"

"Just before I called the police."

"What time was that?"

"Around eight-thirty."

"And you were coming *home,* did you say?"

"Yes."

"Do you work nights?"

"No, no. I've been away. I came here directly from the airport."

"Away where?"

"Los Angeles. I caught the Red Eye last night at ten-thirty and was supposed to get here at six-thirty this morning. But the plane was late, and we didn't land till almost seven-thirty."

"Is that when you left the airport?"

"As soon as I'd picked up my luggage, yes."

"And came immediately here?"

"Yes."

"When you went upstairs, was the door locked?"

"Yes."

"Did you touch anything in the apartment?"

"Nothing."

"Not even the telephone?"

"I called from downstairs in the lobby. I couldn't have stayed in that apartment another minute."

The apartment was a malodorous oven.

The moment the detectives opened the door, they were assailed with a blast of heat and an accompanying stench that caused them to back off at once. Covering their noses with their handkerchiefs, they moved into the apartment as though it were the lair of a foul, fire-breathing dragon, and walked directly into the living room. The dead man lay on his back on the rug, his body cavities, tissues and blood vessels bloated with gas, the skin on his hands, face, and throat—where it showed in the open neck of his bathrobe—discolored a brown that was almost black. The internal gaseous pressure had protruded his lips and forced his tongue out between his lips. His eyes were bulging. His nose had bled, and the blood was now caked beneath his nostrils and on his upper lip, where it had merged with a greenish fluid. He smelled of bacterial invasion and vomited stomach contents and expelled fecal matter.

"Jesus, let's open some windows," Kling said.

"Not till the techs get here."

"Then how about the air conditioner?"

"The M.E.'ll want the temperature the way we found it."

"So what do we do?"

"Nothing."

There was, in fact, nothing they *could* do till the rest of the team arrived. It was almost a full hour before the Mobile Laboratory technicians finally dusted the apartment for latent prints, but even then Carella would not open any of the windows till the Medical Examiner got there. The assistant M.E., who'd been stuck in traffic on his way uptown, got there at twenty minutes past ten. He winced when he stepped into the apartment and then automatically checked the thermostat on the wall, and said to Carella, "If this thing's right, the temperature in here is a hundred and two degrees."

"Feels like a hundred and *ten*," Carella said. "Can we turn on the air conditioner?"

"Not till I'm through," the M.E. said, and knelt beside the body and went to work.

Anne Newman was waiting in the corridor outside. There were two expensive suitcases alongside the wall, apparently where she'd dropped them before unlocking the door. Her eyes were dry now, and she had wiped her face clean of the mascara stains. She still looked amazingly cool in her cotton print dress.

"If you feel up to it," Carella said, "I'd like to ask a few more questions."

"Yes, certainly," she said.

"Mrs. Newman, can you tell me when you left for California?"

"On the first."

"A week ago today?"

"Yes."

"Just in time to miss the heat wave."

"It was hot the morning I left."

"What time would that have been?"

"I caught a ten o'clock plane."

"What time did you leave the apartment here?"

"At about a quarter to nine."

"Was your husband here when you left?"

"Yes."

"I have to ask this, Mrs. Newman. Was he alive?"

"Yes. We had breakfast together."

"What time would that have been?"

"At eight o'clock, I would guess."

"Is that the last time you saw him alive?"

"When I left the apartment, yes."

"What was he wearing?"

"I don't remember."

"Was it the robe he has on now?"

"No, I don't think so."

"Did you speak to him at any time after you got to California?"

"Yes, I called him last Friday, after I checked into the hotel. And I spoke to him again on Tuesday."

"That would've been . . ."

"This past Tuesday."

"The fifth. Three days ago."

"Yes."

"What'd you talk about?"

"Which time?"

"The last time you spoke."

"I called to tell him I'd be catching a late plane out on Thursday night, and would be home this morning."

"How did he sound?"

"Well . . . it was sometimes difficult to tell with Jerry."

"What do you mean?"

"He was an alcoholic. He had his ups and downs."

"Did he sound as if he'd been drinking when you talked?"

"He sounded depressed."

"What time was this, Mrs. Newman? When you made the call?"

"It was after dinner, around nine California time."

"That would have made it midnight here."

"Yes."

"Was he awake when you called?"

"Yes. He told me he'd been watching television."

"How old was he, Mrs. Newman?"

"Forty-seven."

"Can you tell me *your* age?"

"I'm thirty-six."

"How long had you been married?"

"Fifteen years. Well, it would've been fifteen years in October."

"Was this a first marriage for both of you?"

"No. Jerry was married before."

"Would you know his first wife's name?"

"Yes. Jessica."

"Jessica Newman, would it be?"

"I don't know if she's still using her married name."

"Would you know her maiden name?"

"Jessica Herzog."

"Does she live here in the city?"

"I believe so."

"Did your husband have any living relatives?"

"His mother. And a brother in San Francisco."

"Can you tell me *their* names?"

"Susan and Jonathan."

"Both Newman?"

"Yes."

"Does your mother-in-law live here in the city?"

"Yes."

"I assume you have her address."

"Yes."

"I'd like it before we leave, if you don't mind."

"Not at all."

"Mrs. Newman, can you tell me where you were staying in Los Angeles?"

"The Beverly Wilshire."

"Were you there on business or pleasure?"

"Business."

"What sort of work do you do?"

"I'm an interior decorator. There was a trade show out there this week."

"Did you call your brother-in-law while you were out there?"

"Jonathan? No. He's in San Francisco."

"Well, that's relatively close to Los Angeles, isn't it?"

"I didn't call him."

"When did the show start?"

"What?"

"The trade show."

"Oh. Monday."

"But you went out the Friday before."

"Yes. I thought I'd relax a bit over the weekend."

"Mrs. Newman, you told me the door was locked when you got home. . . ."

"Yes, it was."

"Would anyone but you or your husband have a key to the apartment?"

"No."

"Do you have a housekeeper?"

"A cleaning woman. But she doesn't have a key."

"Do you know where I can reach her?"

"She's in Georgia just now, her mother—"

"When did she leave for Georgia?"

"The middle of July. Her mother's very sick."

"Can you tell me her name, please?"

"Bonnie Anderson."

"Where does she live?"

"I don't know her address. Someplace in Diamondback."

"Do you know her phone number?"

"It's in the book. Bonnie Anderson."

"You the investigating detective?" a voice at Carella's elbow asked.

He turned to find a pair of uniformed cops, their hands on their hips, and he knew before seeing their arm patches that they were Emergency 911 cops. There was something about this all-volunteer arm of the Police Department that telegraphed itself from miles away: a swagger, a bravado, an attitude that told all other cops they were only mere mortals.

"Carella," he said, nodding. "The Eight-Seven."

"I hear we got a real blob inside there," the 911 cop said. "You want us to bring up a body bag?"

"This is the man's wife," Carella said.

"Nice to meet you," the 911 cop said obliviously, and then gallantly touched the peak of his cap. "Yes or no?"

"I think we'll need one," Carella said, and turned away from him.

Tears were forming in Anne Newman's eyes again.

"Where will you be staying tonight?" Carella asked gently.

"I thought with my mother-in-law. She doesn't know about Jerry yet, I'll have . . . I'll have to call her."

"If you'd like someone to take your bags downstairs, and hail a taxi . . ."

"Yes, I'd appreciate that, thank you," she said.

"Just one other thing, Mrs. Newman. If we find any good latents in the apartment—"

"Latents?"

"Fingerprints, we'd want to compare them against your husband's, and yours, and your cleaning woman's when she gets back from Georgia. Have you ever been fingerprinted? I'm certain there's no criminal record in your past. . . ."

"None."

"But have you ever held a governmental position? Or were you in the armed forces?"

"No."

"Then I wonder if I could ask you to stop in at the station house, at your convenience, when you've had a chance to—"

"I don't understand."

"It'll just take a few minutes, the stuff washes off with soap and water, and it'll be a great help to us."

"I still don't understand."

"I'm sorry, ma'am, but we're required to investigate any apparent suicide exactly like a homicide."

"Oh."

"Yes, ma'am. Before we can close it out."

"Oh. Well, then, certainly."

"Thank you," Carella said.

He asked the patrolman on duty outside the apartment to take the lady's bags down for her, and then—as they walked together toward the elevator bank—turned to examine the lock on the front door. It was a double-cylinder deadlock, which meant that it could only be unlocked by key on either side, inside or out. Anne Newman had just told him that only she and her husband had keys to the apartment. He could see no visible jimmy marks on the outside cylinder or doorjamb. He was still studying the lock when Kling and one of the lab technicians came out of the apartment.

"Better take a look at this," Kling said. "Found it on the bathroom floor."

"I was just about to tag it," the tech said. He was wearing white cotton gloves, and holding a small plastic bottle in his right hand. There was only one gelatin capsule in the bottle. He held it up so that Carella could read the label:

AMBROSE PHARMACY
Phone: EX 2-1789
3712 Jackson Circle - - Isola

No: C - 11468 Dr.: James Brolin

ANNE NEWMAN   7/29

One capsule before retiring, as needed for sleep.

SECONAL

Carella jotted down the name and telephone number of the dispensing pharmacy and beneath that the name of the doctor. He was putting his notebook back in his pocket when the M.E. came out of the apartment.

"You can ventilate whenever you want to," he said.

"What've we got?" Carella asked.

"No visible wounds, cause of death'll have to wait till we open him up."

"Fucking temperature in there," the tech said, "I wouldn't be surprised he died of *heat* stroke."

It was almost noon when they started back for the station house. In this city, homicides and suicides were treated in exactly the same way, and so—still lacking evidence of either—they had made their drawings of the scene, and talked to the other tenants on the sixth floor and the doorman on duty in the lobby, and had learned only that Anne Newman had indeed left for *someplace* on the first of August, and that no one had seen her husband, Jerry, for the past week or so. According to the tenants and the doorman, this wasn't particularly unusual: Jerry Newman was a free-lance commercial artist who worked out of his own apartment and who sometimes locked himself in for days while trying to meet an illustration deadline.

The car windows were open, the heat ballooned around the two men as Carella edged the vehicle through the heavy lunch-hour traffic. He glanced sidelong at Kling, who was staring straight ahead through the windshield, and then said, "Tell me."

"I'm not sure I want to talk about it," Kling said.

"Then why'd you bring it up?"

"'Cause it's been driving me crazy for the past month."

"Let's start from the beginning, okay?" Carella said.

The beginning, as Kling painfully and haltingly told it, had been on the Fouth of July, when he and his wife, Augusta, were invited out to Sands Spit for the weekend. Their host was one of the photographers with whom Augusta had worked many times in the past. Carella, listening, remembered the throng of photographers, agents, and professional models, like Augusta, who had been guests at their wedding almost four years ago. He preferred not to dwell too often on that day because it had culminated in the abduction of Augusta by a lunatic who'd fanatically followed her career over the years and who had made a virtual shrine of the apartment in which he'd kept her captive for three days.

". . . on the beach out there in Westphalia," Kling was saying. "Beautiful house set on the dunes, two guest rooms. We went out on the third, and there was a big party the next day, models, photographers . . . well, you know the crowd Gussie likes to run with. That was when I got the first inkling, at the party."

He had never felt too terribly close to his wife's friends and associates, Kling said; they had, in fact, had some big arguments in the past over what he called her "Tinsel Crowd." He supposed much of his discomfort had to do with the fact that as a Dectective/Third he was earning $24,600 a year, whereas his wife was earning $100 an hour as a top fashion model; the joint IRS return they'd filed in April had listed their combined incomes as a bit more than $100,000 for the previous year. Moreover, most of Augusta's friends were *also* earning that kind of money, and whereas she felt no qualms about inviting eight or ten of them for dinner at any of the city's most expensive restaurants and signing for the tab afterward ("She keeps telling me they're business associates, it's all deductible," Kling said), he always felt somewhat inadequate at such feasts, something like a poor relative visiting a rich city cousin, or—worse—something like a kept man. Kling himself preferred small dinner parties at their apartment with friends of his from the police force, people like Carella and his wife, Teddy, or Cotton Hawes and any one of his dozens of girl friends, or Artie and Connie Brown, or Meyer Meyer and his wife, Sarah, people he knew and liked, people he could feel relaxed with.

The party out there on the beach in Westphalia, some hundred and thirty miles from the city in Sagamore County, was pretty much the same as all the parties Augusta dragged him to in the city. She'd get through with a modeling job at four, five in the afternoon, and if he'd been working the Day Tour, he'd be off at four and would get back to the apartment at about the same time she did, and she'd always have a cocktail party to go to, either at a photographer's studio or the offices of some fashion magazine, or some other model's apartment, or her agent's—always someplace to go. There were times he'd be following some cheap hood all over the city, walking the pavements flat and getting home exhausted and wanting nothing more than a bottle of beer, and the place would be full of flitty photographers or gorgeous models talking about the latest spread in *Vogue* or *Harper's Bazaar,* drinking the booze Augusta paid for out of her earnings, and wanting to know all about how it felt to shoot somebody ("Have you ever actually *killed* a person, Bert?"), as if police work was the same kind of empty game modeling was. It irked him every time Augusta referred to herself as "a mannequin." It made her seem as shallow as the work she did, a hollow store-window dummy draped in the latest Parisian fashions.

"Well, what the hell," Kling said, "you make allowances, am I right? I'm a cop, she's a model, we both knew that before we got married. So, okay, you compromise. If Gussie doesn't like to cook, we'll send out for Chink's whenever anybody from the squad's coming over with his wife. And if I've just been in a shoot-out with an armed robber, the way I was two weeks ago when that guy tried to hold up the bank on Culver and Third, then I can't be expected to go to a gallery opening or a cocktail party, or a benefit, or whatever the hell, Gussie'll just have to go alone, am I right?"

Which was just the way they'd been working it for the past few months now, Augusta running off to this or that glittering little party while Kling took off his shoes, and sat wearily in front of the television set drinking beer till she got home, when generally they'd go out for a bite to eat. That was if he was working the Day Tour. If he was working the Night Watch, he'd get home bone weary at nine-thirty in the morning, and *maybe,* if he was lucky, catch breakfast with her before she ran off to her first assignment. A hundred dollars an hour was not pumpkin seeds, and—as Augusta had told him time and again—in her business it was important to make hay while the sun was shining; how many *more* years of successful modeling could she count on? So off she'd run to this or that photographer's studio, rushing out of the apartment with a kerchief on her head and her shoulder bag flying, leaving Kling to put the dishes in the dishwasher before going directly to bed, where he'd sleep till six that night and then go out to dinner with her when she got home from her usual cocktail party. After dinner, *maybe,* and nowadays less and less frequently, they'd make love before he had to leave for the station house again at twelve-thirty in the morning. But that was only on the two days a month he caught the Night Watch.

In fact, he'd been looking forward to going out to Sands Spit, not because he particularly cared for the photographer they'd be visiting (or *any* of Augusta's friends, for that matter) but only because he was exhausted and wanted nothing more than to collapse on a beach for two full days—his days off. Nor was he due back at work till Saturday afternoon at 1600— and that's where the trouble started. Or, at least, that's where the *argument* started. He didn't think of it as trouble until later that night, when he got into a conversation with a twerpy little blonde model who opened his eyes for him while their photographer-host was running up and down the beach touching off the fireworks he'd bought illegally in Chinatown.

The argument was about whether or not Augusta should stay at the beach for the entire long weekend, instead of going back to the city with Kling on Saturday. They'd been married for almost four years now; she should have realized by this time that the Police Department respected no holidays, and that a cop's two successive days off sometimes fell in the middle of the week. He was lucky this year, in fact, to have caught the Glorious Fourth and the day preceding it, and he felt he was within his rights to ask his own *wife*, goddamn it, to accompany him back to the city when he left at ten tomorrow morning. Augusta maintained that the Fourth of July rarely was bracketed by an entire long weekend, as it was this year, and it was senseless for her to go back to what would be essentially a ghost town when *he* had to go to work anyway. What was she supposed to do while he was out chasing crooks? Sit in the empty apartment and twiddle her thumbs? He told her she was coming *back* with him, and *that* was that. She told him she was *staying*, and that was *that*.

They barely spoke to each other all through dinner, served on their host's deck overlooking the crashing sea, and by the time the fireworks started at 9:00 p.m., Augusta had drifted over to a group of photographers with whom she'd immediately begun a spirited, and much too animated, conversation. The little blonde who sat down next to Kling while the first of the fireworks erupted was holding a martini glass in her hand, and it was evident from the first few words she spoke that she'd had at least *four* too many of them already. She was wearing very short white shorts and an orange blouse Kling had seen in *Glamour* (Augusta on the cover) the month before, slashed deep over her breasts and exposing at least one of them clear to the nipple. She said, "Hi," and then tucked her bare feet up under her, her shoulder touching Kling's as she performed the delicate maneuver, and then asked him in a gin-slurred voice where he'd been all afternoon, she hadn't seen him around, and she thought sure she'd seen every good-looking man there. The fireworks kept exploding against the blackness of the sky.

The girl went on to say that she was a junior model with the Cutler Agency (the same agency that represented Augusta) and then asked whether he was a model himself, he was so good-looking, or just a mere photographer (she made photographers sound like child molesters) or did he work for one of the fashion magazines, or was he perhaps that lowest of the low, an agent? Kling told her he was a cop, and before she could ask to see his pistol (or anything else) promptly informed her that he was here with his wife. His wife, at the moment was ooohing and aaahing over a spectacular swarm of golden fish that erupted overhead and swam erratically against the sky, dripping sparks as they fell toward the ocean. The girl, who seemed no older than eighteen or nineteen, and who had the largest blue eyes Kling had ever seen in his life, set in a pixie face with a somewhat lopsided chipmunk grin, asked Kling who his wife might be, and when he pointed her out and said, "Augusta Blair," the name she still used when modeling, the girl raised her eyebrows and said, "Don't shit me, man, Augusta's not married."

Well, Kling wasn't used to being told he wasn't married to Augusta, although at times he certainly felt that way. He explained, or *started* to explain that he and Augusta had been married for—but the girl cut him off and said, "I see her all over town," and shrugged and gulped at her martini. She was just drunk enough to have missed the fact that Kling was a cop, which breed (especially of the detective variety) are prone to ask all sorts of pertinent questions, and further too drunk to realize that she didn't necessarily have to add, "with *guys*" after she'd swallowed the gin and vermouth, two words which—when coupled with her previous statement and forgiving the brief hiatus—came out altogether as "I see her all over town with guys."

Kling knew, of course, that Augusta went to quite a few cocktail parties without him, and he also knew that undoubtedly she *talked* to people at those parties, and that some of those people were possibly *men*. But the blonde's words seemed to imply something more than simple cocktail chatter, and he was about to ask her what she meant, exactly, when a waiter in black trousers and a white jacket came around with a refill, apparently having divined her need from across the wide expanse of the crowded deck. The blonde deftly lifted a fresh martini glass from the tray the waiter proffered, gulped down half its contents, and then—compounding the felony—said, *"One* guy especially."

"What do you mean, exactly?" Kling managed to say this time.

"Come on, what do I mean?" the blonde said, and winked at him.

"Tell me about it," Kling said. His heart was pounding in his chest.

"Go ask Augusta, you're so interested in Augusta," the blonde said.

"Are you saying she's been seeing some guy?"

"Who *cares?* Listen, would you like to go inside with me? Don't fireworks bore you to death? Let's go inside and find someplace, okay?"

"No, tell me about Augusta."

"Oh, *fuck* Augusta," the blonde said, and untangled her legs from under her bottom and got unsteadily to her feet, and then said, "And you, *too,"* and tossed her hair and went staggering into the house through the French doors.

The last time he saw her that night, she was curled up, asleep in the master bedroom, her blouse open to the waist, both cherry-nippled breasts recklessly exposed. He was tempted to wake her and question her further about this *"one* guy especially," but his host walked into the room at that moment, and cleared his throat, and Kling had the distinct impression he was being suspected of rape or at least sexual molestation. The blonde later disappeared into the night, as suddenly as she had materialized. But before leaving the next day (Augusta stayed behind, as she had promised, or perhaps threatened) Kling asked some discreet questions and learned that her name was Monica Thorpe. On Monday morning he called the Cutler Agency, identified himself as Augusta's husband, said they wanted to invite Monica to a small dinner party, and got her unlisted number from them. When he called her at home, she said she didn't know who he was, and didn't remember saying anything about Augusta, who was anyway her dearest friend and one of the sweetest people on earth. She hung up before Kling could say another word. When he called back a moment later, she said, "Hey, knock it off, okay, man? I don't know what you're talking about," and hung up again.

"So that's it," Kling said.

"That's it, huh?" Carella said. "Are you telling me . . . ?"

"I'm telling you what happened."

"*Nothing* happened," Carella said. "Except some dumb blonde got drunk and filled your head with—"

"She said she saw Augusta all over town. With *guys*, Steve. With *one* guy *especially*, Steve."

"Uh-huh. And you believe her, huh?"

"I don't know *what* to believe."

"Have you talked to Augusta about it?"

"No."

"Why not?"

"What am I supposed to do? Ask her if there's some guy she's been seeing? Suppose she tells me there *is*? Then what? Shit, Steve . . ."

"If I were in a similar situation, I'd ask Teddy in a minute."

"And what if she said it was true?"

"We'd work it out."

"Sure."

"We would."

Kling was silent for several moments. His face was beaded with sweat, he appeared on the verge of tears. He took a handkerchief from his back pocket and dabbed at his forehead. He sucked in a deep breath, and said, "Steve . . . is it . . . is it still good between you and Teddy?"

"Yes."

"I mean—"

"I know what you mean."

"In bed, I mean."

"Yes, in bed. And everywhere else."

"Because . . . I, I don't think I'd have believed a word that blonde was saying if, if I, if I didn't already think something was wrong. Steve, we . . . these past few months . . . ever since June it must be . . . we . . . you know, it used to be we couldn't keep our hands off each other, I'd come home from work, she'd be all over me. But lately..." He shook his head, his voice trailed.

Carella said nothing. He stared through the windshield ahead, and then blew the horn at a pedestrian about to step off the curb against the light. Kling shook his head again. He took out his handkerchief again, and again dabbed at his brow with it.

"It's just that lately... well, for a long time now... there hasn't been anything between us. I mean, not like before. Not the way it used to be, when we, when we couldn't stand being apart for a minute. Now it's... when we make love, it's just so... so cut and dried, Steve. As if she's... *tolerating* me, you know what I mean? Just doing it to, to, to get it *over* with. Aw, shit, Steve," he said, and ducked his face into the handkerchief, both hands spread over it, and began sobbing.

"Come on," Carella said.

"I'm sorry."

"That's okay, come on."

"What an asshole," Kling said, sobbing into the handkerchief.

"You've got to talk to her about it," Carella said.

"Yeah." The handkerchief was still covering his face. He kept sobbing into it, his head turned away from Carella, his shoulders heaving.

"Will you do that?"

"Yeah."

"Bert? Will you talk to her?"

"Yeah. Yeah, I will."

"Come on now."

"Yeah, okay," Kling said, and sniffed, and took the handkerchief from his face, and dried his eyes, and sniffed again, and said, "Thanks," and stared straight ahead through the windshield again.

TWO

The neighborhood had changed.

He hadn't expected it to look the same, not after twelve years, but neither had he expected so overwhelming a transformation. He got off the elevated train at Cannon Road, and then came down the steps onto Dover Plains Avenue, called simply and familiarly "the Avenue" when he was still living here. The area then had been a peaceful mix of Italians, Jews, Irish, and blacks, but as he walked up toward Marien Street, he noticed with a fleeting pang that time had passed him by, all the familiar landmarks were gone.

What had once been an Italian *latticini* was now a Puerto Rican *bodega*. What had once been a kosher butcher shop was now a billiard parlor; through the open door of the place, he could see clusters of teenage Puerto Ricans holding pool cues. The pizzeria on the corner of Yardley was now a bar and grill, and Harry's candy store—where he used to take the kids for ice-cream sundaes—was now a shoe store, a huge sign lettered

Zapatería across the front of it, a plate-glass window replacing the open counter over which Harry used to pass his egg creams. All gone, he thought. My two youngest kids living in Chicago with Josie's mother now, and my eldest, my daughter—ah, my daughter.

He was back here today to find his daughter.

He had last seen this neighborhood when he was twenty-seven years old. A young man. Twenty-seven. He would be forty in November, twelve years of his life blown in prison. Moira had been six when they sent him away, she'd just turned eighteen this past June, he hadn't seen her in all that time. He wondered if she would recognize him. He was a tall man— they didn't *shrink* you up there at Castleview, though they did just about everything *else* to you—and still muscularly built, thanks to workouts in the prison gym, never missed a day of lifting those weights, except that time he was in solitary for a month, that was after the stabbing that cost him a sure parole and an additional two years of time.

He'd been away for twenty-to-life on a Murder One conviction, which meant he'd have been eligible for parole in ten if it hadn't been for D'Annunzio starting in about his nose, greeting him every morning with "Hey, Schnoz, how's it going?" or "How's the Schnozzola today?" Trapped up there where you can't avoid somebody who's bugging you, man keeps calling attention to the fact you got a big nose, there's only so much of that shit you can take. Grabbed a fork off the mess hall table one night after D'Annunzio made some crack about guys with big noses having tiny little cocks—which was wrong, anyway, it was supposed to be the other way around, a big nose meant a *big* cock—and went at his face with it, tore D'Annunzio's face to ribbons with the fork, would've blinded the son of a bitch if three of the pigs hadn't clubbed him to the floor. Spent a month in solitary and then heard the good news that his parole request was being denied. Later, the state added two years to the obligatory ten he had to serve. The pigs were fond of saying "If you can't do the time, don't do the crime." He had done his time—twelve long years of it—and now he was out.

And now he wanted to see his daughter again.

This was Saturday, the neighborhood seemed drowsy and peaceful in the blistering midday sun. He walked up Marien to the house they used to live in, a two-family, clapboard-and-

brick building with a low picket fence around it. The house
and fence used to be painted white; the new owner had painted
them green. There were two mailboxes side by side at the curb,
one with the name JOHNSON on it, the other with the name
GARCÍA. A black man was in the big front yard, hunkered over
an azalea bush, pulling weeds from around it. Halloran stood
staring at the house for a moment, remembering, and then
turned and walked back toward the Avenue again.

He had never been a drinking man, even before the trouble,
and drinking was one habit you couldn't pick up in stir. But
his lawyer had told him that his daughter had come back from
Chicago and was living someplace in the old neighborhood,
and Halloran hadn't been able to find a listing for her in the
Riverhead directory, so he figured maybe the best place to start
was one of the bars, ask if anybody knew where Moira Halloran
was living these days. Puerto Rican and black neighborhood
like it was now, an Irish girl had to stand out, right? Irish girl
with blond hair and blue eyes like her mother's—Ah Jesus,
Josie, I never meant to do it.

He went into the bar that used to be a pizzeria. Made good
pizza back in the days before he got sent away, used to take
Josie and the three kids there all the time. Used to think a lot
about Josie up there at Castleview. In bed alone at night, he
thought about Josie. Even later on, when he found himself a
punk who'd do whatever he was *told* to do or *else*, it was Josie
he thought about during the sex act. Always Josie. Josie he
thought about, Josie he imagined. Josie who he'd killed with
a hatchet.

The jukebox was playing a Spanish song, whole damn world
was going Hispanic, more of them up there in Castleview than
you could flush out of a field of sugar-cane. The spic behind
the bar was humming along with the tune, polishing a glass,
tossing his head in time to the Latin rhythms. The bar was empty
otherwise. Halloran took a stool near the bartender and asked
him for a beer. The bartender seemed annoyed that somebody
was interrupting his little spic jam session. Scowling, he put
down the glass he'd been polishing, and went to draw the beer.

"Thanks," Halloran said.

"*De nada*," the bartender said.

"You live in this neighborhood?"

"Why? You police?"

Halloran thought that was very funny. He smiled and shook his head. "No," he said, "I'm not police."

"You look like police," the bartender said, and shrugged.

"My name's Jack Halloran, I'm up here looking for my daughter."

"Your daughter, huh?"

"That's right."

"Halloran, huh?" the bartender shook his head. "Nobody name Halloran come in here. Your daughter, huh?"

"My daughter. Blond girl, eighteen years old. Moira Halloran."

"I don' know nobody by that name. You want to pay for the beer, please?"

"I'm not a cop, and she's not in any trouble," Halloran said, reaching for his wallet. "I'm just trying to find her, is all."

"I don' care if she's in trouble or what she is," the bartender said. "I don' know her. Tha's seventy-fi' cents."

Halloran paid for the beer without touching a drop of it, and then went out onto the Avenue again. The elevated tracks overhead cast a shadow on this side of the street, and he was grateful for the respite from the sun. Otherwise, there wasn't a breeze, not a breath of fresh air in this damn suffocating heat. He went from bar to bar asking if anybody knew his daughter, Moira Halloran. He did not hit pay dirt until the fifth bar. The bartender there, like all the *other* bartenders, was a Puerto Rican with an accent you could slice with a machete.

"Moira Halloran?" he said. "No Moira Halloran. Only Moira *Johnson.*"

"Johnson?"

"Johnson, *sí*. Tall blon' girl, dee age you say, eighteen, nineteen, like that."

"Johnson, huh?"

"Johnson. She's marry to Henry Johnson, they live on Marien Stree, you know Marien?"

"I'm familiar with it, yes."

"So tha's where," the bartender said.

He remembered the mailboxes in front of the old house, the names Johnson and García on them. Had his daughter come back to live again in that house? His lawyer had told him the place was up for sale, but Jesus, had his daughter and her husband bought it? Were they maybe living in the same apartment the family had lived in twelve years ago, the downstairs apartment, renting the smaller upstairs one to the spic García, the one he'd seen weeding in the front yard, some of these spics were blacker than African niggers.

Halloran paid for the beer and walked out. It was hotter in the street now, and suddenly he was sweating. Now that he was closer to finding her, now that it was proving easier than he'd ever *dreamed* it could be, he found himself sweating, and a little short of breath, his heart pounding in his chest as he made the familiar turn onto Marien, and walked past half a dozen little Puerto Rican girls skipping rope, and then stopped in front of the clapboard-and-brick house he'd once lived in with Josie and the kids before he'd had to kill her, the *same* house—his daughter Moira was living here in the same house he'd shared with Josie for seven years. The black African spic, García, was still out front, weeding.

"Hey!" Halloran called.

The man looked up.

"You speak English?" Halloran asked.

"You talking to me?" the man said. He looked to be in his early twenties, a thin guy wearing a tank-top undershirt and cut-off blue jeans. He was holding a claw-shaped gardening tool in his right hand.

"Yes, I'm talking to you," Halloran said. "I'm looking for Moira Johnson, do you know her?"

"I know her," the man said. "What do you want with her?"

"She's my daughter," Halloran said.

"Well, well," the man said.

"What's *that* mean, 'Well, well'?"

"They decided to let you out, huh?"

"Who the hell are *you?*" Halloran asked.

"Henry Johnson," the man said. "Moira's husband. Why don't you get lost? Moira don't want nothin' to do with you, man."

"Look, punk," Halloran said, and opened the gate in the picket fence, and hesitated when he saw Johnson's hand tighten on the claw tool.

Locked up in prison, you learned to sense when it was wise to shout a man down, and when it was best to leave him alone. You saw it in the eyes. D'Annunzio should've seen it in *his* eyes the night he started in about a big nose, he should've seen

Halloran's eyes narrowing and should've known right then that his face was going to be hamburger. There was something in this nigger's eyes now (Moira married to a *nigger*, his daughter married to a *nigger!*) that told Halloran he could be dangerous. He hesitated just inside the gate, and then tried a tentative smile, and then said, "I've come a long way to see her, son."

"Don't give me no 'son' bullshit," Johnson said. "I'm no more your son than she's your daughter anymore."

"I'd like to see her," Halloran said quietly.

"She ain't home. Take off, before I call the cops."

"She's my daughter, and I want to see her," Halloran said in a steady monotone. "I want to see what my daughter looks like now that she's grown up, I'm not leaving here till I see her, I've waited twelve *years* to see her, and I'm *going* to see her, have you *got* that, I'm going to *see* her, son."

There must have been in his eyes the same look D'Annunzio should have seen there an instant before the fork plunged into his face, the same look Halloran thought he'd detected in young Johnson's eyes just a few minutes ago. He saw the grip on the gardening tool loosen, saw Johnson taking his measure, a veteran street fighter the way all the niggers up at Castleview were, a bad-ass cat who could recognize trouble when it was coming down the pike, and who wanted no part of it when the man's eyes were signaling mayhem.

"She *still* ain't home," Johnson said, but all the bluster had gone out of his voice.

"When *will* she be home?" Halloran asked.

"She's out marketing," Johnson said.

"That doesn't answer my question."

"What is it, Hank?" a woman's voice behind him said.

He turned.

She was standing just outside the picket fence, a tall slender blonde wearing sandals, white slacks, and a tomato-red tube top, clutching a brown paper bag in each arm, holding them close to her breasts. Even from this distance, he could see the startlingly blue eyes, and for a moment he thought he was looking at Josie, thought he was looking at his dead wife, and told himself that this beautiful woman was his daughter, his—

"Moira?" he said.

She must have recognized him, she remembered him, Jesus,

she *remembered* him! She kept staring at him over the low picket fence, and then she said, "What do you want here?"

"I came to see you."

"Okay, you've seen me."

"Moira—"

"Hank, tell him to get out of here."

"Moira, I just want to say hello, that's all."

"Then say it. And leave."

"I never did anything to you," he said plaintively, and spread his arms wide in supplication, the fingers on both hands widespread.

"You didn't, huh? You killed my *mother*, you son of a bitch! Get out of here!" she said, screaming now. "Get *out* of here, leave me alone, get out, get *out!*"

He looked at her a moment longer, and then lowered his arms and walked silently through the open gate, and past her where she stood shaking with rage on the sidewalk. Their eyes met for only an instant before he turned away from the hatred in them and began walking swiftly toward the Avenue.

At a little past three that Saturday afternoon, Kling called the Medical Examiner's Office to ask what was delaying the autopsy report. The man he spoke to was the one who'd been at the scene the morning before. His name was Joshua Wright, and the first thing he said was, "Hot enough for you?"

Kling grimaced, moved a pad into place, and prepared to write. At his desk near the filing cabinets, Carella was on the telephone with someone at Ambrose Pharmacy. He had earlier called the number listed for Bonnie Anderson, the Newmans' cleaning lady, and had learned from her brother that she had indeed been in Georgia since the twelfth of July; he was now touching second base. The squad-room windows were wide open, but no breeze filtered through the wire-mesh grilles that covered them. A standing electric fan was going in one corner of the room, but all it did was rearrange the heat. Both men were in their shirt-sleeves, their collars open, their ties pulled down, their sleeves rolled up. Across the room, Hal Willis, who liked to think of himself as dapper, was wearing a tan tropical suit with a gold-and-brown silk-rep tie neatly tacked to his shirt. He was sitting at his desk, talking to a man whose jewelry store on the Stem has been held up three times in the past month.

There were six detectives working the Day Tour that Saturday, but three of them were out of the office. Artie Brown was downtown at the Criminal Courts Building, trying to get a search warrant that would allow him to enter the premises of a man suspected of dealing in stolen goods. Meyer Meyer and Cotton Hawes were at the moment on Ainsley Avenue, talking—once again—to the night clerk of a hotel where, four days ago, a young prostitute had been found dead in a bathtub, her throat slit. In this precinct, seventy-five homicides had been committed since January and through the month of July, up sixteen percent from the same period the year before. Of those seventy-five, forty had already been closed out, there were good leads on another eleven, and the remaining two dozen were as cold as last night's leftovers. If statistics held, the precinct detectives would solve only eighty percent of the murders they investigated this year. This meant that by the end of December, twenty out of a hundred killers would still be out there roaming the streets. If the homicide rate kept rising—well, no one at the Eight-Seven liked to think about that.

"It's a little difficult to determine the postmortem interval on this one," Wright said, and them—assuming Kling was as dumb as half the detectives he dealt with—immediately translated the medical terminology for him. "The time of death, that is."

"Yeah," Kling said. "What was the *cause*, can we start with that?"

"Barbiturate poisoning," Wright said. "Congestion of the viscera and brain, edema of the lungs, fluid blood in the heart cavities. Stomach contents revealed a substantial residue of a barbiturate we were able to isolate as Seconal."

"Seconal," Kling said, writing.

"Which is a short-acting barbiturate that's absorbed very rapidly."

"How rapidly?"

"Within minutes after ingestion. The medicinal dose is zero point two grams."

"And the fatal dose?"

"Anywhere from five to ten grams."

"How many would you say the victim had ingested?" Kling

asked, figuring he'd impress Wright with a little medical terminology of his own.

"Impossible to tell. But certainly five grams at least. That would be twenty-five capsules."

"How about *when* he ingested them?"

"That's what I meant earlier," Wright said. "About the postmortem interval. As I told you, Seconal is absorbed within minutes, and an overdose would have brought on rapid coma and death. Was the man a heavy drinker?"

"Why do you ask?"

"Our alcohol findings were positive, with values well into the intoxicated range. Since ingested alcohol will decrease in value during putrefaction, it's safe to say that at the time of death our man was in an intoxicated state possibly *greater* than that indicated by the percent of alcohol recovered."

"His wife told us he was an alcoholic," Kling said.

"That certainly would be in keeping with our findings. You've got to remember, too, that alcohol is a depressant, and that its ingestion would have worked on the central nervous system in sympathy with the toxic action of the Seconal."

"So when did he die?"

"Well, considering the intense heat in the apartment—are you familiar with how we determine the postmortem interval?"

"Not entirely," Kling said. He had stopped writing, and was listening intently.

"The loss of body heat is one of the determining factors. But in a circumstance such as this one, where the temperature in the apartment was a hundred and two degrees, the temperature of the flesh had in fact *risen* rather than dropped, even though rigor mortis was complete. Do you know what rigor mortis is?"

"Well, yes," Kling said uncertainly.

"It's a muscle stiffness that occurs after death," Wright said.

"Well, sure," Kling said.

"To make it simple, *before* death the muscle protoplasm is alkaline, and *after* death it becomes acid, usually within six hours, at which time the muscles of the face, jaw, neck, arms, legs, and trunk—in that order—begin to stiffen. The process is reversed when the muscle protoplasm changes to alkaline again—usually anywhere between twelve and forty-eight hours—causing the rigor to disappear. Which brings us back to the temperature in that apartment."

"What do you mean?" Kling asked.

"Heat speeds up the rigor mortis process as *well* as its reversal."

"So you're saying—"

"I'm saying rigor is of no help to us here. Neither is the postmortem decomposition. The bacterial agents we isolated were *Clostridium welchii*, which can invade the body very soon after death, and also *Escherichia coli* and *Proteus vulgaris* . . . are you writing this down?"

"Well . . . no," Kling admitted.

"Good, because you don't need to. All these bacteria can be found in the earliest postmortem stages, but we also found *Micrococcus albus* and *Bacillus mesentericus*, which normally will not invade until several days after death. In other words, because the heat in the apartment caused such advanced putrefaction, it would be impossible to estimate a time of death on the basis of decomposition alone."

"So then . . . are you saying you can't tell me when he died?"

"I'm saying we're unwilling to hazard such an estimate. I'm sorry. It's the goddamn *heat*, you see."

"But it *was* an overdose of Seconal?" Kling said.

"Definitely. Something in excess of five grams."

"About twenty-five capsules."

"Or more," Wright said.

"Well, thank you," Kling said. "Will you send the written report to us, please?"

"Will do," Wright said, and hung up.

Kling put the receiver back on its cradle and looked at his notes. He underlined the word "Seconal," and then picked up his pad and walked to where Carella was just ending *his* telephone conversation.

"What've you got?" Carella asked.

"It was Seconal. Something more than five grams."

"How many capsules would that have been?" Carella asked at once.

"Twenty-five."

"Figures."

"How so?"

"I was just talking to Mr. Ralph Ambrose, who runs the

Ambrose Pharmacy on Jackson Circle. Asked him how many Seconal capsules were in that prescription he filled for Mrs. Newman on July twenty-ninth. He checked his files, and said the prescription called for a month's supply, thirty capsules."

"Must've stocked up for her trip to California, huh?" Kling said.

"Then why'd she leave the bottle home?" Carella asked.

"Good point, we'll have to ask her."

"Yeah," Carella said, and nodded.

"Only one left in that bottle," Kling said.

"Only one. So let's say she took one every night from July twenty-ninth to August first, when she left for California. That'd be three capsules right? Thirty-one days in July, right?"

"Three capsules, right." Kling said.

"Plus one left in the bottle makes it four."

"That puts twenty-six inside of him."

"One more than he needed to kill him."

Both men were silent for several moments.

"She said he sounded depressed when she talked to him," Kling said.

"Yeah, but no suicide note," Carella said.

"They don't all leave notes."

"No, not all of them. How'd the M.E. make out with a time of death?"

"No help there, Steve. The heat is working against us."

"Why would a guy turn off the air conditioner during the hottest summer in ten years?" Carella asked.

"Guy about to kill himself doesn't *care* how cool the room is," Kling said.

"So let's say he went in the bathroom, and found his wife's pills, and swallowed twenty-six of them, and then went out to the living room to die, okay? Would he have *first* turned off the air conditioner?"

"Well . . . no, that doesn't seem likely."

"Then who turned off the air conditioner?" Carella asked.

"The M.E. says he was drunk," Kling said. "Maybe he didn't even *realize* the air conditioner wasn't running."

"The heat wave started Friday morning, the day his wife left for California," Carella said. "She spoke to him the following Tuesday. Are you telling me he was drunk all that time, with the windows closed and the air conditioner *off?*"

"No, maybe just that night. The night he decided to kill himself."

"Went to turn off the air conditioner first, huh?"

"No."

"No," Carella said.

"No," Kling said again. "But maybe it was broken or something. Maybe he didn't realize—"

"I turned it on the minute the techs were through with it yesterday. It was working fine."

"Yeah," Kling said.

"With this heat, the air conditioner should have been *running*, damn it."

Both men were silent again. Across the room, Willis began typing. On the street outside, an ambulance went by, its siren blaring.

"I think we ought to talk to Anne Newman again," Carella said, and looked up at the wall clock. It was almost three-thirty, a half hour before the Evening Tour would relieve. "Want to hit her now, or have you made other plans?"

"No," Kling said. "No other plans."

"Have you talked to Augusta yet?"

"Not yet."

"You promised . . ."

"Tonight," Kling said. "When I get home tonight."

"Then maybe you want to go straight home now. I can see the Newman woman alone, be no problem."

"No, it'll wait," Kling said.

THREE

═══════════════

Susan Newman, the mother of the dead man, lived just off Condon Square, where the big statue of General Richard Joseph Condon reminded the city's sometimes jaded populace that during the Civil War there had lived an Army officer of unsurpassed wit, style, and grace. Covered with pigeon shit now, the smile on the general's face nonetheless beamed out in bronzed splendor, causing responding smiles from any passersby who chanced to look up. In this city, not many people looked up, perferring instead to study the sidewalks for souvenirs of its vast dog population. General Condon pressed on undaunted, his sword raised high above his head, his smile undiminished after all those years of standing out in the cold, the rain, the snow, and the heat.

They parked the car two blocks from the address Anne Newman had given them at the scene, and then walked past the statue, smiling up at it, and around the corner to number twelve Charlotte Terrace. A doorman asked them to identify themselves, and then phoned upstairs to inform Mrs. Newman that a Mr. Cappella and a Mr. Kling were downstairs in the lobby. He listened for a moment, and then told the detectives they could go right on up, it was apartment 3G.

Mrs. Newman was a woman in her late sixties, wearing a flowing caftan designed to obscure her plumpness. She was perhaps five feet three inches tall, Carella guessed, with an apple-dumpling face and neatly coiffed white hair, folds of flesh hanging on her jowls and on her arms, where they were exposed by the three-quarter-length sleeves of the caftan. She had told them on the telephone that her daughter-in-law would be back from the funeral home by four, but it was now four-fifteen and she apologized for Anne's delay, saying she had phoned not a moment before to say she'd be a little late. The flesh around her eyes were puffy, and the eyes themselves were streaked with red; it was obvious she'd been crying before the detectives arrived.

"We'll be burying him tomorrow morning, you know," she said. "Anne is making all the funeral arrangements." She took a handkerchief from the single pocket of the caftan, and dried the tears that were forming in her eyes again.

"Mrs. Newman," Carella said, "I know this is a particularly difficult time for you, and I apologize for intruding on your grief this way."

"That's all right," Mrs. Newman said, "I know you have a job to do."

"Would it be all right, then, if we asked you some questions?"

"Yes, I told you on the phone it would be all right."

"I appreciate your generosity," Carella said. "Mrs. Newman, your daughter-in-law told us she left for California on the first of August, is that right?"

"Yes."

"She also said she'd spoken to your son this past Tuesday night. . . ."

"I wouldn't know about that, I'm sorry."

"What I was wondering . . . had you spoken to him anytime this past week?"

"No."

"Was it his normal habit to call you every so often?"

"Yes, once or twice a month."

"When did you speak to him last, Mrs. Newman?"

"I really couldn't say. A few weeks ago, I would guess."

"How did he sound at that time?"

"Well, he . . ."

"Yes?"

"My son was an alcoholic, you see."

"Yes, we know that."

"And when he called . . . well, usually he was drunk when he called."

"Was he drunk when you spoke to him that last time?"

"Yes."

"What did you talk about, Mrs. Newman?"

"The usual."

"Which was what?"

"His father. Jerry would get drunk, and then he'd call me and talk about his father." She paused. "My husband died two years ago," she said.

"How did he die, Mrs. Newman?"

"He . . . killed himself. He committed suicide."

"I'm sorry," Carella said, and Mrs. Newman looked at him, and nodded, and then dabbed at her eyes with the handkerchief again. "And this was what your son usually talked about when he—"

"Yes. He was the one who . . . who found him, you see. Jerry. I was working at the time. I'm a registered nurse, I only stopped working last year. I was at the hospital the night . . . the night it happened. Jerry had been calling the apartment . . . he was very close to his father, you see . . . and when he kept getting no answer, he thought something might be wrong, and he went right over. My husband was a painter, you see. An abstract expressionist, quite well known, Lawrence Newman. He normally worked at home, in the apartment we lived in on Jefferson, had his studio in a large room overlooking the avenue, the northern light, you see. So when Jerry got no answer, he . . . he automatically figured something was wrong. He got the doorman there to open the door with a passkey, and when he went in he . . . he found his father."

"How did he kill himself, Mrs. Newman?"

"With a pistol. He put the barrel of the pistol in his mouth and . . . pulled the trigger. In the . . . the studio. Where he used to work."

"I'm sorry," Carella said again.

"I asked him constantly to get rid of that gun, but he said in this city a man *had* to keep a gun if he hoped to survive. I don't believe that, Mr. . . . Carella, is it?"

"Carella, yes."

"I don't believe people *need* guns. Nobody keeps a gun unless he plans to use it, isn't that so? On another human being."

"That's been our experience," Carella said.

"I read someplace—this was before Larry killed himself, I used to use it as an argument whenever I was trying to convince him to get rid of the gun—I read that a very large percentage of people who keep guns will sooner or later use that gun on *themselves*. Is that true?"

"The handgun suicide rate is very high, yes."

"I told him. But, of course, he wouldn't listen. Said he needed to *protect* himself. Against *what?* I asked. Wild Indians? There are no wild Indians on this island anymore, gentlemen. There are only wild Indians in a person's head." She sighed, took a deep breath, and then said, "I shouldn't have left him alone that night. He'd been working on a particularly difficult concept, and simply couldn't find a solution. He'd done the painting a dozen times over and he *still* wasn't happy with it. He was working on that same painting when I said good-bye to him for the last time. I told him it was a fine painting. I knew he didn't believe me." She sighed again, and looked away, toward the windows and the magnificent view of the River Dix and its bridges beyond. "And so he found a solution at last in that studio room streaming northern light, with a pistol in his mouth and his finger on the trigger." She drew a deep, tortured breath and then expelled it on a sigh. "My son was devastated," she said. "Jerry. That was when he began drinking so heavily. When his father took his own life."

"This was two years ago, you say?"

"May the twelfth, two years ago. I'll never forget that day as long as I live."

"And when your son called you . . ."

"Yes, that was what he talked about. He was drunk, of course, there was hardly a time he *wasn't* drunk, and he talked about his father, yes, and relived again that day in May when he'd walked in and found him with the . . . the back of . . . of his head..." She turned away again. Carella waited. Kling was looking down at his shoes. "Forgive me, it's still very painful. I'm getting to be an old woman now, but I haven't forgotten what it was like to love someone more than life itself. And now...now this. Now Jerry. Almost as though he—" She shook her head, and brought the handkerchief to her eyes again. "Forgive me," she said.

"Mrs. Newman, did your son ever give any indication that he might be contemplating suicide?"

"Do they ever?" she asked. "Did my husband? People get depressed, you accept that as a normal human condition. If they keep their troubles bottled inside, how can anyone know what they're contemplating? Do you realize what pain a human being must be feeling even to *think* of taking his own life? I can't conceive of such monumental suffering. The will to live is so great, it seems unimaginable that anyone would—" She shook her head again. "Unimaginable," she said.

"Do you think your son committed suicide, Mrs. Newman?"

"I don't know what to think."

"Did he have any enemies that you might know of?"

"He never mentioned any."

"Would you know if he'd ever received any threatening letters or telephone calls?"

"You'd have to ask Anne about that."

"How did he get along with her?"

"As well as could be expected. Considering."

"Considering what?"

"The drinking. It was a problem, of course. But they were very much in love when they got married—it was Jerry's second marriage, you know—and I think Anne was behaving admirably, considering the circumstances. In fact, she's been an absolute *saint* these past two years. I'm very fond of that girl."

"How about your son's first wife? Jessica Herzog, is it?"

"Yes, that was her maiden name."

"Have you seen her since the divorce?"

"No. She's quite a nice person, actually, and I wouldn't have minded continuing our relationship. But one tends to side with flesh and blood in any divorce situation and...well, unfortunately, we lost contact. It's a pity, really."

"Mrs. Newman, from what I understand, you have another son . . ."

"Yes, Jonathan."

"Who lives in San Francisco, is that right?"

"Yes."

"How did he and Jerry get along?"

"As well as could be expected, considering the distance involved." She looked Carella directly in the eye, and said, "Forgive me, Mr. Carella, but you sound . . . do you suspect that someone might have *killed* my son?"

"In any traumatic death," he said, "we're compelled to consider all the possibilities."

"I see."

"Mother?" a voice said, and they turned toward the entrance foyer, where Anne Newman was extricating a key from the lock on the door. She was wearing a black-and-white striped blazer over a white cotton-knit sweater and black skirt. As she had yesterday, she looked exceedingly cool, and Carella envied a metabolism that seemed to render her immune to the heat. She put the key on the hall table and came into the living room, her hand extended.

"I'm sorry I'm late," she said, shaking first Carella's hand and then Kling's. "There were so many things to attend to. Would you care for something to drink? Mother, have you offered them something? A soft drink perhaps? Some iced tea?"

"No, thank you," Carella said.

"Thank you, ma'am," Kling said, shaking his head.

"I'd love a gin and tonic, would anyone mind? Mother, could you fix me one while we talk, please?"

"Yes, darling," Mrs. Newman said, and immediately left the room.

"What is it you'd like to know?" Anne asked. "This heat is brutal, isn't it? Is it cool enough in here for you?"

"Yes, it's fine, thank you," Carella said. "Mrs. Newman, Detective Kling here was the one who spoke to the Medical Examiner just a little while ago, would you mind if he asked the questions?"

"Not at all," she said, turning to Kling. "What did they find?"

"Conclusive evidence that he was killed by an overdose of Seconal," Kling said.

"Ah," she said.

"Mrs. Newman, we found a prescription bottle . . ."

"Yes, that must've been it," Anne said.

". . . on the bathroom floor," Kling said. "One Seconal capsule in it."

"One? Oh my God! There were *thirty* capsules in that bottle when I left for California."

"Then you hadn't taken any between the time you filled the prescription on July twenty-ninth—"

"No, I still had some left from last month, half a dozen or so. I took those with me to California."

"Does your doctor regularly prescribe Seconal for you? Dr. Brolin, is it?"

"Yes, James Brolin. I have difficulty sleeping and the stuff you can buy over the counter wasn't working for me. Dr. Brolin saw no danger in prescribing a barbiturate."

"How long have you been taking Seconal?" Kling asked.

"Ever since . . . well, it's been several years now."

"Ever since what, Mrs. Newman?"

"Ever since Jerry began drinking so heavily. Living with an alcoholic isn't an easy task, I'm afraid."

"Did you take the drug every night?"

"No, not every night."

"Was the prescription a refillable one?"

"No, that's forbidden by law in this state. Too many refillable prescriptions were falling into the hands of addicts."

Kling felt mildly reprimanded. He plunged ahead regardless. "Then Dr. Brolin wrote a prescription for you each and every month, is that right?"

"Sometimes less frequently. Depending on how low my supply was."

"And it was low just before you left for California."

"Yes. As I say, I had six or seven capsules left, something like that. I'm the sort of person who doesn't like loose ends hanging. I try to tidy things up before going away anyplace. So I asked Dr. Brolin for a new prescription."

"Do you go away frequently?"

"Only occasionally. When there's a show I feel I must see. I never miss the one in Chicago, for example, and the one in Los Angeles this year promised to be particularly good."

"Mrs. Newman, the Medical Examiner's report indicates

that your husband was intoxicated at the time of his death. When you—"

"I'm not surprised," Anne said.

"When you spoke to him last Tuesday, did he sound drunk?"

"It was sometimes difficult to tell. He'd very often be drinking steadily and still manage to sound quite lucid."

"Did he sound lucid the night you spoke to him?"

"He sounded . . . normal. Depressed, but normal. Then again, depression had become almost a normal state with him in recent months."

"Did he ever discuss suicide with you?"

"Well . . . I'm reluctant to admit this because it might sound callous."

"In what way?"

"You may wonder why I left him to go to California when I knew how he was feeling."

"How was he feeling, Mrs. Newman?"

"He told me . . . he said he'd had enough."

"Of what?"

"Of living. Of life."

"When was this?"

"The day before I left."

"That would've been a Thursday . . ."

"Yes, Thursday night."

"July thirty-first."

"Yes."

"He told you he'd had enough of living?"

"He was drunk, of course, I . . . he'd told me the same thing many times before."

"That he was thinking of taking his own life?"

"Not in those exact words."

"What were his exact words?"

"He said his father had the right idea."

"Meaning . . ."

"He was referring to his father's suicide. His father killed himself two years ago."

Mrs. Newman came back into the room. She had cut a lime in the kitchen, and a slice now floated in the tall glass containing Anne's gin and tonic. She overheard the last of her daughter-in-law's words, and said, "I've already told the gentlemen about that, darling. Here you are."

Anne accepted the drink, said, "Thank you," and then said to the detectives, "Are you sure?"

"We're on duty, ma'am," Kling said.

"Ah, yes, of course. Cheers," she said, and took a sip of the drink. "Oh, that's good," she said. "I find this heat insufferable, don't you?"

"Regarding the heat," Carella said, "I'd like to ask you some questions about the air conditioning in your apartment."

"The air conditioning?" Anne said, looking surprised.

"Yes, ma'am. I'm sure you noticed how hot the apartment was . . ."

"Yes, of course."

"Well, the windows were all closed, and the air conditioner was turned off, and I was wondering—"

"We always had trouble with the air conditioning," Anne said, and sipped at her drink again.

"What kind of trouble?"

"We were constantly calling the super to have it repaired."

"Well, it was functioning properly, ma'am. I know because I personally turned it on after the techs were through with it. The point is, it was turned to the *off* position, and I'm wondering whether it was in that position when you left the apartment on Friday morning."

"I really don't know," Anne said. "I mean, the apartment seemed cool enough, I simply didn't check to see whether the air conditioner was on or not."

"But the apartment *did* seem cool."

"Yes, definitely."

"When you spoke to your husband on Tuesday night, did he mention anything about the heat?"

"He said the temperature had hit ninety-eight that day."

"But he didn't say the *apartment* was unusually hot, did he? He didn't say the air conditioner had been malfunctioning, anything like that?"

"No, he didn't."

"Or that anyone had been there to look at it."

"No."

"I'm trying to account for that switch being in the off position, you see. If someone had *worked* on the unit, then perhaps it was left off by accident."

"No, Jerry didn't mention anyone coming in to look at it."

"Uh-huh," Carella said. "Bert?"

"Just a few more questions," Kling said, "and then we'll let you go. I'm sorry we're taking so much of your time."

"Not at all," Anne said.

"Can you tell me what you remember of your conversation the night before you left for California?"

"Not in exact detail, I didn't think it was that important at the time."

"As much as you can remember."

"Well, Jerry had been drinking, and he told me again—this was a usual complaint—about what a poor artist he was in comparison to his father. Jerry was an illustrator, you have to realize, and his father was quite a well-known artist, and Jerry felt he could never live up to his father's high achievement. He idolized him. . . . Well, isn't that true, Mother?"

"Yes, it is," Mrs. Newman said.

"And . . . well . . . I sometimes felt he wanted to be like him in *every* way possible. I suppose I should have taken his constant threats of suicide more seriously, given the past circumstances. But I didn't. When he began talking again about how it was all so meaningless, so pointless, I . . . I hate to admit this, but I cut him sort. I had a long trip ahead of me, and this was close to midnight, and I had to get some sleep. I told him we'd talk about it when I got back. I didn't know I'd be seeing him for the last time at breakfast the next morning."

"How did he seem then? At breakfast, I mean."

"Hung over."

"Mrs. Newman, did your husband know you were taking Seconal?"

"Yes, he did."

"Did he know where you kept the drug?"

"We kept *all* our drugs in the bathroom medicine cabinet."

"And that was where you kept the Seconal?"

"Yes."

"Is that where you put the new prescription you'd had filled?"

"Yes."

"The bottle containing thirty capsules?"

"Yes."

"When did you do that?"

"The day I had the prescription filled."

"That would've been the twenty-ninth of July."

"Yes."

"And your husband knew this? He knew you'd put that bottle of Seconal in the medicine cabinet?"

"I assume he did."

"Thank you. Steve? Anything?"

"No, that's it," Carella said. "Ladies . . . thank you for letting us talk to you. We're sorry for the intrusion, you've been very gracious with your time."

"Not at all," Mrs. Newman said.

"Please keep us informed," Anne said.

In the corridor outside, as they waited for the elevator, Kling asked, "What do you think?"

"I don't know," Carella said. "I want to check with the Beverly Wilshire out there, see how long she talked to him last Tuesday night. Might help us in establishing the time of death."

"What'll *that* get us?" Kling asked.

"Who the hell knows?" Carella said. "But the *heat* in that goddamn apartment still bothers me. Doesn't it bother you?"

"Yes."

It was almost five-thirty. They said good-bye on the sidewalk outside, Carella walking to where he'd parked his car, Kling walking toward the kiosk on the corner and the subway ride home to his wife, Augusta.

The note, tacked with a magnet to the refrigerator door, read:

Bert--
I waited for you till six
o'clock and then had to leave
for the party at Bianca's. She
will probably be going on to
dinner later, so I'll see you
around ten. Fix yourself something
from the fridge.
                    Love ya,
                    A.

She did not get home until almost eleven.

He was watching the news on television when she came into the apartment. She was wearing a pale green, silk chiffon jumpsuit, the flimsy top slashed low over her naked breasts, the color complementing the flaming autumn of her hair, swept to one side of her face to expose one ear dotted with an emerald earring that accentuated the jungle green of her eyes, a darker echo of her costume. As always, he caught his breath at the sheer beauty of her. He had been tongue-tied the first time he'd seen her in her burglarized apartment on Richardson Drive. She had just come back from a skiing trip to find the place ransacked; he had never been skiing in his life, he'd always thought of it as a sport for the very rich. He supposed they were very rich now. The only problem was that he never felt any of it was really his.

"Hi, sweetie," she said from the front door, and took her key from the lock, and then came to where he was sitting in front of the television set, a can of warm beer in his hand. She kissed him fleetingly on top of his head, and then said, "I have to pee, don't go away."

On the television screen, the newscaster was detailing the latest trouble in the Middle East. There was always trouble in the Middle East. Sometimes Kling thought the Middle East had been invented by the government, the way the war in Orwell's novel had been invented by Big Brother. Without the Middle East to occupy their thoughts the people would have to worry about unemployment and inflation and crime in the streets and racial conflict and corruption in high places and tsetse flies. He sipped at his beer. He had eaten a TV dinner consisting of veal parmigiana with apple slices, peas in sea-soned sauce, and a lemon muffin. He had also consumed three cans of beer; this was his fourth. The thawed meal had been lousy. He was a big man, and he was hungry again. He heard her flushing the toilet, and then heard the closet door in their bedroom sliding open. He waited.

When she came back into the living room, she was wearing a wraparound black nylon robe belted at the waist. Her hair fell loose around her face. She was barefoot. The television newscaster droned on.

"Are you watching that?" she asked.

"Sort of," he said.

"Why don't you turn it off?" she said and, without waiting for his reply, went to the set and snapped the switch. The room went silent. "Another scorcher today, huh?" she said. "How'd it go for you?"

"So-so."

"What time did you get home?"

"Little after six."

"Did you forget the party at Bianca's?"

"We're working a complicated one."

"When *aren't* you working a complicated one?" Augusta asked, and smiled.

He watched as she sat on the carpet in front of the blank television screen, her legs extended, the flaps of the nylon robe thrown back, and began doing her sit-ups, part of her nightly exercise routine. Her hands clasped behind her head, she raised her trunk and lowered it, raised it and lowered it.

"We had to go see this lady," Kling said.

"I told you this morning about the party."

"I know, but Steve wanted to hit her this afternoon."

"First twenty-four hours are the most important," Augusta said by rote.

"Well, that's true, in fact. How was the party?"

"Fine," Augusta said.

"She still living with that photographer, what's his name?"

"Andy Hastings. He's only the most important fashion photographer in America."

"I have trouble keeping them straight," Kling said.

"Andy's the one with the black hair and blue eyes."

"Who's the bald one?"

"Lamont."

"Yeah. With the earring in his left ear. Was he there?"

"*Everybody* was there. Except my husband."

"Well, I do have to earn a living."

"You didn't have to earn a living after four p.m. today."

"Man dies of an overdose of Seconal, you can't just let the case lay there for a week."

"First twenty-four hours are the most important, right," Augusta said again, and rolled her eyes.

"They are."

"So I've been told."

"You mind if I turn this on again?" he asked. "I want to see what the weather'll be tomorrow."

She did not answer. She rolled onto her side, and began lifting and lowering one leg, steadily, methodically. He put the beer can down, rose from where he was sitting in the leather easy chair, and snapped on the television set. As he turned to go back to his chair, the auburn hair covering her crotch winked for just an instant, and then her legs closed, and opened again, the flaming wink again, and closed again. He sat heavily in the leather chair and picked up the beer can. The female television forecaster was a brunette with the cutes. Smiling idiotically, bantering with the anchorman, she finally relayed the information that there was no relief in sight; the temperature tomorrow would hit a high of somewhere between ninety-eight and ninety-nine ("That's normal *body* temperature, isn't it?" the anchorman asked. "Ninety-eight point six?") with the humidity hovering at sixty-four percent, and the pollution index unsatisfactory.

"So what *else* is new?" Augusta said to the television screen, her leg moving up and down, up and down.

"Marty Trovaro is next with the sports," the anchorman said. "Stay tuned."

"Now we get what all the baseball teams did today," Augusta said. "Can't you turn that off, Bert?"

"I like baseball," he said. "Where'd you go after the party?"

"To a Chinese joint on Boone."

"Any good?"

"So-so."

"How many of you went?"

"About a dozen. Eleven, actually. *Your* chair was empty."

"On Boone, did you say?"

"Yes."

"In Chinatown?"

"Yes."

"All the way down there, huh?"

"Bianca lives in the Quarter, you know that."

"Oh, yeah, right."

The television sportscasters in America all had the same barber. Kling had thought the distinctive haircut was indigenous only to this part of the country, but he'd once gone down to Miami to pick up a guy on an extradition warrant, and the television sportscaster there had his hair cut the same way, as if someone had put a bowl over his head and trimmed all around it. He sometimes wondered if every sportscaster in America was bald and wearing a rug. Meyer Meyer had begun talking lately about buying a hairpiece. He tried to visualize Meyer with hair. He felt that hair would cost Meyer his credibility. Augusta was doing push-ups now. She did twenty-five of them every night. As the sportscaster read off the baseball scores, he watched her pushing against the carpet, watched the firm outline of her ass under the nylon robe, and unconsciously counted along with her. She stopped when he had counted only twenty-three; he must have missed a few. He got up and turned off the television set.

"Ah, blessed silence," Augusta said.

"What time did the party break up?" he asked.

Augusta got to her feet. "Would you like some coffee?" she asked.

"Keep me awake," he said.

"What time are you going in tomorrow?"

"It's my day off."

"Hallelujah," she said. "You sure you don't want any?"

"I'm sure."

"I think I'll have some," she said, and started for the kitchen.

"What time did you say?" he asked.

"What time what?" she said over her shoulder.

"The party."

She turned to him. "At Bianca's, do you mean?"

"Yeah."

"We left about seven-thirty."

"And went across to Chinatown, huh?"

"Yes," she said.

"By cab, or what?"

"Some of us went by cab, yes. I got a lift over."

"Who with?"

"The Santessons," she said, "you don't know them," and turned and walked out into the kitchen.

He heard her puttering around out there, taking the tin of coffee from the cabinet over the counter, and then opening one of the drawers, and moving the percolator from the stove to set it down noisily on the counter. He knew he would have to discuss it with her, knew he had to stop playing detective here, asking dumb questions about where she'd been and what time she got there and who she'd been with, had to ask her flat out, *discuss* the damn thing with her, the way he'd promised Carella he would. He told himself he'd do that the moment she came back into the room, ask her whether she was seeing somebody else, some other man. And maybe lose her, he thought. She went back into the bathroom again. He heard her opening and closing the door on the medicine cabinet. She was in there a long time. When finally she came out, she went into the kitchen and he heard her pouring the coffee. She came back into the living room then, holding a mug in her hand, and sat cross-legged on the carpet, and began sipping at the coffee.

He told himself he would ask her now.

He looked at her.

"What time did you leave the restaurant?" he asked.

"What *is* this?" she said suddenly.

"What do you mean?" he said. His heart had begun to flutter.

"I mean . . . what *is* this? What time did I leave *Bianca's*, what time did I leave the *restaurant*—what the hell *is* this?"

"I'm just curious."

"Just curious, huh? Is that some kind of occupational hazard? Curiosity? Curiosity killed the cat, Bert."

"Oh? Is that right? *Did* curiosity . . . ?"

"If you're so damn interested in what time I *got* someplace, then why don't you come *with* me next time, instead of running around the city looking for pills?"

"Pills?"

"You said Seconal, you said—"

"It was capsules."

"I don't give a damn *what* it was. I left Bianca's at seven twenty-two and fourteen seconds, okay? I entered a black Buick Regal bearing the license plate . . ."

"Okay, Augusta."

". . . double-oh-seven, a license to *kill*, Bert, owned and operated by one Philip Santesson, who is the art director at . . ."

"I said okay."

". . . Winston, Loeb and Fields, accompanied by his wife, June Santesson, whereupon the suspect vehicle proceeded to Chinatown to join the rest of the party at a place called Ah Wong's. We ordered—"

"Cut it out, Gussie!"

"No, goddamn it, *you* cut it out! I left that fucking restaurant at ten-thirty and I caught a cab on Aqueduct, and came straight home to my loving husband who's been putting me through a third-degree from the minute I walked through that door!" she shouted, pointing wildly at the front door. "Now what the hell is it, Bert? If you've got something on your mind, let me know what it is! Otherwise, just shut up! I'm tired of playing cops and robbers."

"So am I."

"Then what is it?"

"Nothing," he said.

"I *told* you about the party, I *told* you we were supposed to..."

"I know you—"

"...be there at six, six-thirty."

"All right, I know."

"All right," she said, and sighed, her anger suddenly dissipating.

"I'm sorry," he said.

"I wanted to make love," she said softly. "I came home wanting to make love."

"I'm sorry, honey."

"Instead..."

"I'm sorry." He hesitated. Then, cautiously, he said, "We can still make love."

"No," she said, "we can't."

"Wh...?"

"I just got my period."

He looked at her. And suddenly he knew she'd been lying about the party at Bianca's and the ride crosstown with the Santessons and the dinner at Ah Wong's and the cab she'd caught on Aqueduct, knew she'd been lying about all of it and putting up the same brave blustery front of a murderer caught with a smoking pistol in his fist.

"Okay," he said, "some other time," and went to the television set and snapped it on again.

FOUR

If every cop on the force had the same days off, then there'd be nobody out there in the streets on those days, and the bad guys would run amok. That was only logical. That was why cops had different days off on a rotating schedule. That was why Kling's two successive days off did not always coincide with Carella's. A Police Department duty schedule looked like a scroll dredged from the Dead Sea. Night Watch only complicated matters; Night Watch was a footnote, in Sanskrit, to an already complicated chart. The amazing thing about the schedule was that any cop giving it even a casual glance could tell you in a minute exactly which days off he had in any given month. It was considered a stroke of extreme good fortune when a cop's two days off fell on a Saturday and a Sunday, like any *normal* human being's. This happened only once a month. This week, Kling had been off on Monday and Tuesday, and now it was Sunday, and he was off again. So was Augusta. That is to say, she was off visiting a model named Consuela

Herrera, who had come down with hepatitis and who was at
the moment languishing in the city's posh Physicians' Pavilion.
Kling didn't mind; he planned to work today anyway.

The work he had in mind was detective work of a sort, but
it had nothing to do with the Eighty-seventh Squad. The moment Augusta left the apartment, Kling opened the Isola telephone directory and searched out an address for a restaurant
called Ah Wong's. Wearing blue jeans, loafers, and a blue T-
shirt with the numeral thirteen across its back, a souvenir of
the interdepartmental baseball game in which he'd represented
the Eight-Seven as a second baseman last summer, he went
downstairs, hailed a taxi, and told the driver to take him to 41
Boone Street, down in Chinatown. The moment the cabbie
threw his flag, Kling looked at his watch. It was precisely
eleven minutes past noon.

"Hot enough for you?" the cabbie asked.

Kling grimaced.

"I hear it's gonna be the whole week," the cabbie said.

"I hope not," Kling said.

"The whole fuckin *week*," the cabbie said. "You know
where my wife and kids are today? They're at the *beach* today,
that's where they are. You know where *I* am today? I'm pushin
a fuckin hack is where *I* am today."

"Yeah," Kling said.

The traffic on a Sunday—especially on a Sunday in August
when those people who weren't away on vacation were most
certainly out at the beaches with the cabbie's wife and kids—
was so light as to be almost nonexistent. Augusta had told him
that the cab ride to Ah Wong's last night had taken a half hour;
she'd left the restaurant at ten-thirty and did not walk into the
apartment until eleven. That had been Saturday night, though,
the busiest night of the week, and given the number of people
out on the town howling, and the attendant vehicular congestion, Kling figured he'd have to add maybe ten, fifteen minutes
to however long it took him to get downtown now.

The cabbie dropped him off in front of the restaurant at
exactly twelve twenty-six by Kling's watch. Fifteen minutes.
So okay, it *could* have taken Augusta a half hour last night.
On the other hand, with him or without him, she'd probably
taken taxis to and from Chinatown at least a dozen times this
year; she knew how long the trip took, she wouldn't have come

up with something absurd like ten minutes on a Saturday night. Kling paid and tipped the cabbie, and then walked toward the front door of the restaurant.

Ah Wong's was sandwiched between a Chinese five-and-ten and the station house for the Chinatown Precinct, one of the oldest in the city, in fact about to celebrate its centennial this year. He was tempted to stop inside, say hello to Frank Riley, who'd gone through the Academy with him and who was now a Detective/Second working out of the squad room on the second floor of the ancient building. Instead, he stood for a moment on the pavement outside the restaurant, and looked up the street, trying to visualize it as it had been last night, when Augusta said she was here.

Silken banners lettered in Chinese hung lifelessly on the leaden air, crossing the street at intervals overhead, fastened to the buildings on either side. The street was thronged with restaurants similar to Ah Wong's, their neon signs dead in the brilliant sunshine; last night, the street would have been alive with oranges, blues, and greens. It was almost deserted now, the garbage cans overflowing into the sidewalks in front of the restaurants, green plastic bags squatting beside them like bulky sentinels. A meter maid's motor scooter was chained to one of the metal posts flanking the steps to Ah Wong's basement. Kling thought it ironic that even the *cops* had to chain up their bikes in this city, outside their own damn station house.

Even so, the Chinatown Precinct was not an "A" house, like the Eight-Seven or some of the other high-crime houses in the city. It encompassed The Straits of Napoli (as the Italian section of the precinct was called) as well as the city's mile-long strip of sleazy hotels and shabby bars (known familiarly as The Vineyard, for its collection of vagrant winos), and its boundaries also enclosed several pockets of blacks and Hispanics, mostly in the Governor James L. Grady Housing Project bordering the River Dix and in that end of the precinct where The Stem joined Dallas Avenue. The biggest crime in the precinct these days was the extortion committed by the Chinese youth gangs, many of whom were suspected of having connections with the older Chinese who ran the basement gambling houses, where Mah-Jongg was the favored game. The gamblers, tired of getting ripped off by itinerant holdup artists, had only several years back begun hiring these kids to protect their premises. The minute the kids tipped to how much money was being wagered at the tables, they began demanding higher fees and threatening mayhem if the demands weren't met. From the gambling dens, they had branched out to the restaurants and stores, and now held the honest merchants in terror of their organized power.

There were no whorehouses, as such, in the precinct and no massage parlors, either, an oddity in a city that for the past ten years had been sprouting them like venereal lesions. But there was a large contingent of streetwalkers (none of them Chinese) working the area between Aqueduct and Clancy, and occasionally a pimp would decide to exercise his authoirty by slashing a breast or a pretty face, and—even more often—a visiting fireman in search of a cheap thrill would get mugged and rolled and left in an alley that stank of stale urine and sour wine. The continuing feud between the Dominicans and the Puerto Ricans up around Dallas was a headache to the cops, and since the Criminal, Family, Municipal, and City Court buildings were clustered within the precinct, farther downtown on High Street, there was a steady parade of offenders moving through the precinct to and from the corridors of the law. But for the most part, the precinct was a quiet one.

Riley, who had once worked out of the Marine Tiger Precinct in Riverhead, named after the ship that presumably had carried the first Puerto Ricans here from San Juan, had described his new job as "a month in the country," this despite the twenty or so homicides committed here annually, and a fair share besides of burglaries, robberies, and grand larcenies. But Riley had come from a precinct where the life of an unpartnered foot-patrol cop wasn't worth a plugged nickel. The Chinatown Precinct wasn't a cop-killing precinct like either the Marine Tiger or the city's notorious Vale Street Precinct. Nor was its crime rate as high as the Eight-Seven's, where, thank God, the populace had not yet taken to stoning policemen. Kling thought he might have liked working here; he loved Chinese food.

He realized how hungry he was the moment he stepped into the restaurant and a swarm of exotic aromas assailed his nostrils. He took a table near the wall, ordered a gin and tonic and an assortment of fried shrimp, egg rolls, barbecued spare ribs, dumplings, and then—still hungry—ordered the moo goo gai pan, with which he drank a bottle of Heineken beer. When the waiter came back to the table to ask him if there would be anything else, Kling debated flashing the tin before asking his questions, and decided against it.

"That was delicious," he said. "My wife told me about this place—she was here last night with some friends."

"Yes?" the waiter said, smiling.

"Big party. About a dozen people."

"Ah, Miss Mercier party," the waiter said, nodding.

Miss Mercier was Bianca Mercier, who only last month had adorned the cover of *Harper's Bazaar,* a dark-haired beauty with a Nefertiti look that was currently driving the city's fashion editors wild.

"Yes, that's the one," Kling said.

"But no dozen," the waiter said. "Only ten."

"Eleven, I guess," Kling said.

"No, ten. Only one big table here," he said, pointing to a round table across the room. "Seat ten people. Was only ten last night, Miss Mercier party."

"My wife thought it was eleven," Kling said.

"No, only ten. Which one your wife?"

"The redhead," Kling said.

"No redhead," the waiter said.

"Tall redhead," Kling said. "Wearing a green jumpsuit."

"No redhead," the waiter said again, shaking his head. "Only three lady. Miss Mercier, black hair, another lady black hair, and one lady yellow hair. No redhead."

"Did you serve the party?" Kling asked him.

"I am Ah Wong," he said, drawing himself up proudly. "Miss Mercier very good customer, I wait on her myself last night."

"This wouldn've been around eight o'clock, maybe a little earlier," Kling said.

"Reservation for eight o'clock," Ah Wong said, nodding. "Ten people. But no redhead."

"What time did it break up?"

"Late."

"How late."

"Finish eat, sit around drink. Leave here eleven o'clock."

"Eleven o'clock," Kling said. Eleven o'clock was when

Augusta had walked into their apartment. "Well, listen, thanks," he said, "that was really delicious."

"Come back soon," Ah Wong said.

Kling paid the check and left the restaurant. The meter maid's scooter was gone; its chain was still wrapped around the iron post and locked with a huge padlock. He debated going crosstown and uptown to where Bianca Mercier lived in The Quarter, ask her whether Augusta had indeed been at that pre-dinner cocktail party last night. He decided against it. Whether she'd been there or not was a matter of small concern. She'd left their apartment uptown at 6:00 p.m. (or so the note on the refrigerator door had said) and had presumably been at Bianca's party till a little before seven-thirty. ("I left Bianca's at seven twenty-two and fourteen seconds, okay?") An hour and a half didn't matter too much when there were a missing *three* hours to account for—the time between when she *said* she'd left Bianca's and, later on, the restaurant. Three hours, Kling thought. He had known Augusta to climax in three *minutes*.

He took a deep breath and walked toward the subway kiosk on Aqueduct.

The hooker who picked up Halloran in a bar near Playhouse Square, farther uptown, told him she was from Minnesota. She wasn't really from Minnesota, she was from the city's Calm's Point section, and the distinctive way in which she abused the King's English should have informed Halloran of that fact in a minute. But Halloran was drunk for the first time in his life, and the girl's story went down without a ripple. She had been telling prospective customers she was from Minnesota ever since the hookers from that state started getting so much free publicity in the papers and on television. To be from Minnesota meant you were a helpless victim in the clutches of an evil black pimp, selling yourself against your will, corn-fed and wholesome before the big bad city corrupted you. Men liked to think they were sticking it in some kind of technical virgin, and all those innocent-looking hookers from Minnesota were *stars* in this city.

Kim—whose real name was Louise Marschek—had been a blonde since she was fifteen, when a white pimp took her under his wing and turned her out with promises of unimagined riches and glamour, meanwhile buying her a three-dollar bottle of commercial bleach. It was he who suggested she change her name, professionally, to Kim—"You look a lot like Kim Novak," he told her. With the new blond hair, she *did* in fact believe she looked a lot like Kim Novak, except with smaller breasts. For the past year or so, ever since she'd begun telling customers she was from Minnesota, she'd been bleaching herself below as well, the better to promote the image of country-girl inviolability. The first words she said to Halloran when she took the stool next to his at the bar, were, "Hi, I'm Kim—from Duluth, Minnesota." She did not have the faintest idea where Duluth was, or even where *Minnesota* was, for that matter. Neither did Halloran, so they were even.

Sitting beside him, Kim thought how thrilled he probably was to have someone who looked so much like Kim Novak putting her widespread hand on his thigh and asking "Want to have a party?" Halloran had begun drinking at noon, when the city's bars were allowed to open after everybody got out of church (and *headed* for the bars) and by one-thirty, when she sat down beside him, he had consumed three whiskey-sodas and was feeling a bit sick, to tell the truth. He was Irish, and the Irish were supposed to be big drinkers, but his grandfather had died young of cirrhosis of the liver, and his father had never touched a drop in his life, and he'd have beaten Halloran silly if ever he'd caught him lifting so much as a beer. He was just sober enough to recognize that the girl sitting there beside him with her hand close to his groin was maybe seventeen, eighteen years old, and he was drunk enough, *more* than enough, to think she looked just like his wife, Josie, when she was that age, or his daughter, Moira, the way she'd looked yesterday when she'd given him his walking papers. He said to the girl on the stool beside him, "You shouldn't have done that, Moira."

"Let's go have a party, huh?" she whispered in his ear, her hand moving closer to his groin.

Halloran had been in prison for twelve years, and he wouldn't have understood the expression even if he'd been sober enough to hear it correctly. He simply nodded.

"Okay?" she said. "Let's go, okay? Pay for your drinks, and let's get out of here."

He said, "Sure," and nodded again, and took a ten-dollar bill from his wallet, and put it on top of the bar. Kim noticed that there was a sheaf of greenbacks in the bill compartment of the wallet. She had already noticed that he was bombed out of his mind, and she figured if she played her cards right this big jerk could be the only trick she'd have to turn this afternoon. Throw him a quickie, walk off with the billfold, thanks a lot, mister. The money in the wallet, minus the ten-dollar bill, actually totaled a hundred and sixty dollars, all that Halloran had left of the two hundred he'd managed to borrow from an old friend who used to work at the telephone company with him. That was before the trouble, when Halloran had been one of the best linemen in the city. He got off the stool now, and the girl looped her arm through his. Together, they went out of the air-conditioned bar and into the afternoon blaze of the street outside.

By the time they got to the hotel on one of the side streets off Lassiter, he realized that the girl wasn't his daughter, Moira, nor was she his wife, Josie, either, which she *couldn't* have been anyway since Josie had been dead for a long time now, he had killed Josie with a hatchet twelve years ago. He realized, too, that the girl was a hooker, but he thought, What the hell, so what? It had been a long time since he'd been with a woman. In prison, your women were the young boys. You put a shank to a kid's throat, some dumb fish just inside the walls, you told him what you wanted and he either gave it to you or his pretty little face got messed up. If he went to The Man to complain about it, you got him alone someplace, more places to ambush a man in prison, and this time a *dozen* guys put it to him, and then he was yours forever, walked by your side, shaved his legs for you if that was what you wanted, let you paint tits on his back, that's what it was like in prison. Take or be taken. If you can't do the time, don't do the crime.

"You live here?" he asked her.

"No, no, just rentin' a room for now," Kim said.

"What's this gonna cost me?" he asked.

"We'll talk about that upstairs, okay?" she said, and winked at the clerk behind the desk when he handed her the key.

The room was on the fourth floor, a shabby cubicle that looked like a cell at Castleview, bed against the wall, dusty venetian blinds hanging crooked on the single window, scarred dresser against the other wall, open door leading to a toilet where somebody's vomit had dried on the bowl. He closed the door to the toilet, and then parted the slats on the blinds and looked down to the street below. Everybody was walking like in a slow-motion movie, afraid to exert any energy in this goddamn heat. The room was stiffling. He raised the blinds, and opened the window. When he turned, the girl was sitting on the bed.

"What'd you say your name was?" he asked.

"Kim."

"Sure," he said.

"Don't you like that name?" she asked, smiling.

"Yeah, it's fine," he said.

"You think I look like Kim Novak?"

"Now that you mention it," he said. She looked about as much like Kim Novak as he did.

"People say I look a lot like Kim Novak."

"Yeah, you do. So what's this gonna cost me?" he asked.

"How about fifty?" she said.

"How about we go back to the bar?" he said.

"Forty?"

"Twenty-five."

"Okay," she said. She was still smiling. She was thinking of all those bills she'd seen in his wallet. "But I have to take it now, okay? Before we start, I mean. That's a general rule."

"Sure," he said. He took his wallet from his pocket, and handed her two tens and a five.

"Thanks," she said.

"How old are you, anyway?" he asked.

"Seventeen," she said. She was twenty-two, and she'd been hooking for seven years, and she had a heroin habit as long as her arm. "People say I look even younger, though."

"Yeah, you do," he said. Now that he was beginning to sober, he thought she looked twenty-eight or nine.

"So what'll it be?" she asked.

"Let's talk a little first, okay?"

"Sure," she said, "whatever you like."

She was still thinking about the money in his wallet, and wondering whether she could talk him into sending down for a bottle. The room clerk would find somebody to go out for a bottle if you tipped him a couple of bucks. She didn't like the way he seemed to be sobering up so fast. Only way she could get at that wallet was to have him as drunk as he'd been just a little while ago.

"Would you like me to get us something to drink while we talk?"

"I don't drink," he said.

"Oh-ho," she said, "he doesn't drink."

"I mean it."

"You don't look like a man who doesn't drink," she said, "big man like you?" and allowed her glance to drop shyly to the front of his trousers.

"That was the first time in my life I ever had any hard liquor," he said. "This afternoon. First time. Hit me like a ton of bricks."

"I'll bet," she said.

"It's the truth."

"*I* never drink, either," she said, figuring she'd give him a bit more of the Lily-White Virgin routine. "Back in Minnesota, drinking is considered a sin."

"Yeah, Minnesota," he said.

"Duluth," she said.

"Where's that?"

"In Minnesota," she said.

"This is the first time I've been with a woman in twelve years," he said.

"Really? Then I've got something good coming, huh?"

"First time I've even really *talked* to a woman in all that time."

"How come? You been on the wagon or something?"

"No, I—"

"You give it up for Lent or something?" she said, and laughed the way she thought Kim Novak laughed, from way back in her throat, deep and husky.

"I've been in jail," he said.

"Oh?" she said, and shrugged. Half the people she knew had spent at least some time behind bars. Even her old man, the one who'd first told her she looked like Kim Novak, had once done two years for Promoting Prostitution, a Class C felony.

"Up there at Castleview," he said. "You know Castleview?"

"I heard of it. Listen, are you sure you wouldn't like me to send out for a bottle? The room clerk—"

"No, I don't want anything else to drink."

"'Cause, you know, we could sort of take it easy, talk awhile, drink awhile, do whatever you'd like, you know?"

"What I *don't* want to do is drink any more," he said.

"Okay, whatever you say," she said, and in that instant lost all interest. If she couldn't get him drunk again, then all she wanted was to get it over with fast. "So what'll it be?" she said. There was a harder tone to her voice now, a business edge he missed entirely.

"Spent twelve years up there," he said, "twelve long years."

"Listen," she said, "if you don't mind, I'd really like to—"

"Went to see my daughter yesterday," he said. "She's eighteen now, married to a nigger. All I wanted to do was *see* her, you know? *Talk* to her a bit." He shook his head. "Told me to get lost. Sent me on my way."

"Yeah, kids," she said, hoping that would be the end of it. "Mister, what is it you'd like? Because, you see I'm—"

"It's not her I blame," he said.

But neither could he blame *himself* for what he'd done twelve years ago, when he'd learned that Josie was having an affair with another man. Arguing in the living room of the Marien Street house, his two young sons asleep in the end bedroom, his daughter, Moira, in the room closest to where he and Josie were yelling at each other, Josie finally shouting that it was true, yes, she *was* seeing another man, she *was* in love with another man, and naming him, hurling the name at him, and then bursting into tears.

"—a working girl, you know?"

"What?" he said.

"I said I'm a working girl. So what do you say? What'll it be?"

"You know what I did time for?"

"No, what?" she said, and sighed.

"Murder," he said.

She looked at him.

"I killed my wife," he said.

She kept looking at him.

"With a hatchet," he said.

He used to keep the hatchet on a shelf just inside the basement door, above the steps, he remembered moving away from her wordlessly, and opening the basement door, and taking the hatchet from where it was resting on the shelf, and then going back into the living room and hitting her with it, hitting her repeatedly, opening her skull and her face, and continuing to hit her even after she was dead and gushing blood onto the pale-green living-room rug.

"It wasn't my fault," he said, and turned to look at the girl where she was still sitting on the bed, watching him.

She studied him silently, trying to figure out whether or not he was putting her on. Lots of guys tried to impress you with their big macho bullshit, tried to show you what *men* they were—some kind of *men*, all right, who had to pay to get laid. He was maybe six feet three inches tall, something like that, weighing more than two hundred, she guessed, bigger than her old man, broad shoulders and thick forearms and huge hands. He had black hair and dark-brown eyes and a big nose, and he was frowning now, his thick eyebrows pulled into a scowl. She had never in her life been afraid of any john. Hooking for seven years now, and never been afraid, even with the real weirdos who sometimes you got stuck with even though you tried to spot them in advance and steer clear of them. But all at once, when it sank in that she was in this room alone with a man who'd maybe *really* killed somebody, she was afraid.

"Listen," she said, "maybe we oughta just forget it, you know what I mean?"

He kept staring at her. She wondered if she should yell for help. She wondered if she should try to get past him to where she'd put her bag on the dresser. There was a single-edged razor blade in her bag, insurance against situations like this one. He seemed not to know she was in the room with him. He kept staring at her, but not seeing her.

"I mean, I . . . really, I'm a working girl, you know? I . . ." She wet her lips. Her hands were beginning to shake. "It's just . . . you know . . . we've been here awhile now. If you . . . if you're not interested, you know, in *doing* anything, then why don't I just give you back the twenty-five, no hard feelings, and I can—"

"No, you can keep it," he said.

"I don't want to take money for something I didn't—"

"*Keep* it!" he said.

"Well . . . well, okay, thanks, but I feel rotten taking your money when I—"

"Just get out of here, okay? Just leave me alone."

"Well, okay," she said, getting off the bed quickly and moving toward the dresser. She picked up her bag. "Will you be here awhile or what?" she asked. "'Cause what I do, the clerk lets me have the room for a half hour, you know? I give him five for a half hour. So if you're gonna be longer than that . . ."

"That's all right," he said.

"That's only, like you know, just another fifteen minutes or so."

"That's all right," he said again.

"I'm sorry about your daughter," she said, and opened the door.

He did not answer her.

"Well . . . so long," she said, and went out, closing the door behind her.

He went to the bed, and sat on it where she'd been sitting, sat there for a long while without moving, and then lay back against the pillow, his hands behind his head, and stared up at the ceiling.

The night he'd killed her (well, it hadn't been his fault) he'd driven downtown afterward to search for the man Josie had named. Found him standing outside a sleazy hotel on Culver Avenue, chased him down the street with the bloody hatchet in his hand, finally caught up with him and yanked him to the sidewalk and was about to do to him what he had already done to Josie when a car pulled up to the curb, and a young guy in plainclothes jumped out waving a gun and yelling.

Staring at the ceiling, tears forming in his eyes, burning there with anger and regret and a sense of loss that made him feel powerless ("Big man like you," and her eyes dropping to his crotch), he remembered that son of a bitch coming out of the car, waving his pistol in the air, "Police! Stop or I'll shoot!" remembered telling him stupidly and in tears all about what had happened in the clapboard-and-brick house on Marien Street, "It wasn't my fault." And the cop had answered, the son of a bitch had answered, "It's never anybody's fault, is it?" Those words echoed in his head for twelve long years—"It's never anybody's fault, is it?"—as if a man was supposed to ignore the fact that his wife was fucking somebody else, as if it was the *man's* fault instead of . . .

That son of a bitch, he thought.

Twelve years in prison, he thought.

Twelve years of making love to young boys instead of Josie. You son of a bitch.

The tears running down his face, his fists clenched, he knew whose fault it was, all right, never mind it never being anybody's fault, never mind *that* fucking shit! Knew just who was responsible for all those years in prison, knew who to blame for the way his only daughter had treated him yesterday, exactly who to blame for all of it ("It's never anybody's fault, is it?").

Detective Third/Grade Bertram A. Kling, he thought.

And nodded grimly.

Detective Third/Grade Richard Genero was Carella's partner that Sunday. It could have been worse; Carella *could* have been partnered with Andy Parker. Genero, after months of trying, had finally given up on the spelling of "perpetrator." In coping with that enormously difficult word and its accomplice "surveillance," Genero had imaginatively come up with spellings like "perpetuater" and "sirvellance," which sounded like the name of a medieval French knight, and "survillance" and even "perpitraitor," which sounded like someone who *might* logically commit a crime of heinous proportion. He had settled for typing the abbreviations "perp" and "surv" in all of his reports, a practice that had since gained common currency in the squad room, elevating Genero to the celebrity of a pacesetter.

Like a messenger working in the garment center, Genero never went anywhere without his portable radio. While he typed all those perps and survs in triplicate, his radio sat on the corner of his desk, blaring the latest rock and roll tune. Lieutenant Byrnes had informed him that the squad room was not a ballroom ("This is not a *ballroom* up here, Genero, we are not *ballroom* dancers up here, Genero") and had warned him that he would be back in uniform, walking a beat in Bethtown, if he did not get rid of that "noisy piece of nonregulation equipment forthwith." But Lieutenant Byrnes was off today, and Genero's radio, tuned to the rock station Carella's ten-year-old twins listened to, was going full blast as Carella dialed the Beverly Wilshire Hotel in Los Angeles.

The assistant manager who spoke to him was courteous, polite, and eager to assist. Out there in Los Angeles, everybody tried to be as courteous, polite, and eager to assist as were the LAPD cops themselves. Carella could visualize an armed robber and a uniformed cop out there, bowing from the waist to each other before shooting it out in one of the canyons.

"I'm calling about a recent guest of yours," Carella said.

"Yes, sir?"

"A woman named Mrs. Jeremiah Newman, she may have registered as Anne Newman. That would've been on August first, according to our information."

"Yes, sir," the assistant manager said. "Could you hold one moment while I check with Reservations?"

"I need some other information as well," Carella said. "I might be saving you time if I gave it all to you up front."

"Yes, sir, happy to help."

"I'll want to know when she checked in—I'd like you to confirm that August first date for me—and also when she checked out. And then I'd like to know whether she made any long-distance telephone calls, the number she called, and the dates and duration of those calls."

"I'd have to transfer you to the Cashier's Office on the calls, sir," the assistant manager said. "But let me check with Reservations first."

"Thank you," Carella said.

There was a click on the line; he hoped he had not been cut off. Across the room, Genero's radio was spewing a song with the repeated lyric "If I love you, how come you don't love me?" He wondered why Genero didn't get himself one of those little things you stuck in your ear. He would suggest it to him, as soon as he got off the phone.

"Mr. Carella?" the assistant manager said.

"Yes, I'm here."

"I have those dates for you, sir. We do indeed show an Anne Newman registering on the first of August and checking out late Thursday night, August seventh."

"Thank you," Carella said. "Could you put me through to someone who'd know about the phone calls?"

"It might take a few minutes for them to find the charge slips," the assistant manager said. "Would you like us to call you back?"

"No, I'll wait, thanks," Carella said.

"Fine, it shouldn't take too very long. Please hold on, won't you?"

There was another click on the line. Carella waited. The rock singer still wanted to know how come the recipient of his lament didn't love him. "Genero?" Carella called over the din.

"What?" Genero called back.

"Can you hear me?"

"What?" Genero said. He was a wiry man with curly black hair, dark-brown eyes, and a strong Neapolitan nose. He sat hunched over his typewriter, pecking at the keys with the forefingers of both hands.

"I said, can you *hear* me?" Carella shouted.

"Of *course* I can hear you," Genero said, "I'm not deaf," and then immediately added "Sorry" when he remembered Carella's wife was a deaf-mute.

"Why don't you get one of those little ear things?" Carella said.

"What do you mean, one of those little ear things?"

"One of those little things you stick in your ear. So you can hear the radio without the *rest* of us having to listen."

"No, they're no good," Genero said. "They distort the sound. The acoustics in this room are very good, I like to get the full acoustics."

"You know what'll happen if the Loot walks in, don't you?"

"No, he's at the ball park," Genero said.

"How do you know that?" Carella asked, surprised, and thinking maybe Genero was a better detective than he realized.

"He told me he had two tickets for today's game."

"Well, could you *lower* it a little, please?"

"I don't want to tamper with the acoustics," Genero said.

"Mr. Carella?" a woman on the phone said.

"Yes, this is Detective Carella."

"This is the Cashier's Office," she said, "I have those telephone charges. Would you like to jot them down?"

"Yes, go ahead," Carella said.

"I have four long-distance calls charged to Anne Newman's account during her stay with us. She made one at eight p.m. on the night she checked in, that was August first, the call was made to 765–3811 in Isola, and it lasted for three minutes and seventeen seconds."

"Go ahead," Carella said, writing.

"The second call was made on Monday afternoon, August fourth, at four-thirty p.m., to 531–8431, also in Isola. She spoke for twenty-seven minutes and twelve seconds."

"Go on, I'm listening."

"She called the 765 number again on Tuesday night, August fifth, at nine-twelve p.m. and spoke for—"

"That would be the 765–3811 number?"

"Yes. She spoke for twelve minutes and seven seconds."

"And the last call?"

"To 332–0295, also in Isola, on August seventh, at five p.m."

"Would all those times be local?"

"Yes, sir, California time."

"Thank you very much," Carella said.

"Have a nice day," the woman said, and hung up.

"Genero, turn off that *radio!*" Carella shouted. "I have some more calls to make."

"Why don't you get one of those little things you stick in your ear?" Genero said. "Those little rubber things that block out sound."

"Genero . . ." Carella said warningly.

"Italians are supposed to *like* music," Genero said, but he turned off the radio.

Only one of the telephone numbers sounded familiar to Carella, and only because he'd called it yesterday, before going to visit Anne Newman at the apartment she was presently sharing with her mother-in-law. He checked his notebook just the same, and verified that the 332–0295 number was indeed Susan Newman's and wondered why Anne had called her just before she'd left California last Thursday night.

The 765–3811 number was undoubtedly Anne's home phone number; she'd told Carella that she'd called her husband on Friday night when she checked in, and again on Tuesday night, both calls corroborated by the Beverly Wilshire, *if* that was the number. He checked the Isola directory and found a listing for Jeremiah R. Newman on Silvermine Oval; the number checked out.

But the last number was still a mystery.

He looked over his notes again.

She had called 531–8431, here in the city, on Monday afternoon, August the fourth, and had spoken to someone there for twenty-seven minutes and twelve seconds. Carella pulled the phone to him and dialed "O" for operator. When she came on the line, he said, "This is Detective Carella at the Eighty-seventh Squad, I need assistance on a police matter, the call-back number is 377–8024, extension four. Can your supervisor get back to me, please?"

"In a moment, sir," the operator said.

He hung up. He would have to call Mrs. Newman to ask what she and her daughter-in-law had talked about on the night of the seventh. It seemed odd to him that the last call Anne Newman had made before leaving the Coast was to her mother-in-law. She had already phoned home on the fifth to tell her husband she'd be catching the Red Eye back on the seventh, so why *another* call East? The phone rang. He snatched the receiver from its cradle.

"Eighty-seventh Squad, Carella," he said.

"Yes, Detective Carella, this is Marjorie Phillips, telephone company."

"How do you do, Miss Phillips? I need assistance on a telephone listing. I have the number, and I'd like the name and address of the subscriber, please."

"Here in the city, is it?"

"Yes. It's an Isola listing."

"And the number?"

"531–8431."

"Just a moment, please."

Carella waited. Canned music floated from the earpiece. If it wasn't Genero, then it was the goddamn phone company. A shlock orchestra was playing a string arrangement of "Penny Lane" designed to cause any listening rock fan to jump up and down in rage.

"Mr. Carella?"

"Yes, Miss Phillips."

"I have that listing for you. Have you got a pencil?"

"Right here in my hand."

"The number—that's 531–8431—is listed to a Dr. James Brolin at 493 Courtenay Plaza in Isola."

"Thank you," Carella said. "Miss Phillips, while I have you on the line, I wonder if you can help me with another matter?"

"Yes, what is it?"

"I'd like a record of all the telephone calls made from—"

"I'm sorry," Miss Phillips said, "you'd have to call the Business Office for that."

"Yes, but this is Sunday, and I—"

"They'll be open at eight tomorrow morning."

"No way you can help me meanwhile?"

"I'm afraid not. I wouldn't have such records here. I'm sorry."

"Okay, thanks anyway," Carella said.

"Glad to be of assistance," Miss Phillips said, and hung up.

Dr. James Brolin, Carella thought, and opened his notebook again. Beneath the name of the pharmacy that had dispensed the Seconal capsules to Anne Newman, he had jotted the name of the doctor who'd written the prescription: Dr. James Brolin. He picked up the receiver again, and dialed the number. A woman answered the phone.

"Dr. Brolin, please," he said.

"Who's calling, please?"

"Detective Carella of the Eighty-seventh Squad."

"Just a moment," she said, "I'll see if he's in."

Which in English meant he was very definitely in and she was checking to see if he wanted to talk to a detective. Carella waited. He heard muted voices in the background, and then the receiver being picked up from wherever it had been dropped.

"Hello?" a man's voice said.

"Dr. Brolin?" Carella asked.

"Yes?"

"This is Detective Carella of the Eighty-seventh Squad. I'm investigating an apparent suicide, and I wonder if I may ask you some questions, sir."

"Yes, certainly."

"Have you got a few moments?"

"Well, we have guests just now. . . ."

"This won't take long."

"Certainly," Brolin said.

"Dr. Brolin, you *are* the physician who prescribed a month's supply of Seconal capsules for Anne Newman, are you not?"

"I am."

"Is that usual, Dr. Brolin? Such a large supply of barbiturate, I mean?"

"Mrs. Newman is an insomniac. As part of her treatment,

I've been prescribing Seconal. There's nothing unusual about the quantity of the drug, no."

"She came to see you on July twenty-ninth, is that correct? The date on the prescription..."

"Was that a Tuesday?" Brolin asked.

"Yes, sir, I believe it was."

"Then, yes, she was here. I see her every Tuesday, Wednesday, and Friday."

"Sir?" Carella said. "Every...?"

"I'm a psychiatrist," Brolin said.

"Oh, I see," Carella said, and nodded.

"Yes," Brolin said.

"And you're treating her for insomnia, is that it?"

"Insomnia is one of her symptoms, yes. I don't feel I'm obliged to discuss the exact nature of her problem, Mr. Carella."

"Of course not," Carella said. "Dr. Brolin, did Mrs. Newman call you from California last Monday night?"

"Yes, she did."

"For what reason?"

"She'd missed her Friday session because of the trip. She was suffering a severe attack of anxiety out there, and she wanted to talk to me."

"How long did you talk, Dr. Brolin, would you remember?"

"Twenty minutes? A half hour? I really couldn't say."

"Did she call you at any time after that?"

"No, she did not."

"That was the last time you spoke to her."

"Yes. I'll be seeing her this Tuesday, of course."

"Every Tuesday, Wednesday, and Friday, you said."

"Yes."

"Dr. Brolin, did you know *Mr.* Newman?"

"No, I did not."

"Did you know he was found dead last Friday morning, by Mrs. Newman when she returned from California?"

"Yes, I did."

"How did you learn about his death, sir?"

"Mrs. Newman informed me."

"Oh, I thought you hadn't spoken to her since—"

"I'm sorry, I thought you meant from California. She called

me yesterday. She was quite upset, we had a long talk on the phone."

"I see. Well, Dr. Brolin, I know you have guests. I won't keep you. Thanks for your time."

"Good-bye then," Brolin said, and hung up.

Across the room, Genero was standing with his hands on his hips, looking at the street below through the metal grille covering the open window.

"Come look at these two," he said.

"I'm busy," Carella said, and picked up the receiver again.

"Tits out to here," Genero said.

Carella dialed Susan Newman's home. She picked up the phone on the third ring. "Hello?" she said.

"Mrs. Newman? This is Detective Carella, how are you?" he asked.

"We just got back from the cemetery," Mrs. Newman said. "All things considered, I suppose I'm all right."

"Is this an inconvenient time for you?"

"There are people here," she said. "But, please, what is it?"

"Mrs. Newman, from what I've been able to learn, your daughter-in-law called you from California last Thursday night, is that correct?"

"Yes, she did."

"The call was placed at five p.m. in Los Angeles, that would've made it eight o'clock here. Can you tell me what you talked about?"

"Well . . . yes. But why do you want to know?"

"Just as a matter of course."

"I'm not sure what that means, 'a matter of course.'"

"There are certain avenues we're obliged to investigate in any traumatic death."

"Traumatic?"

"Yes, ma'am. Such as a suicide or a homicide."

"I see. Then you *do* suspect my son's death was a homicide."

"I don't suspect anything, Mrs. Newman. I'm simply assembling the facts so I can make an informed judgment."

"And what does Anne's call to me have to do with this *informed* judgment?"

"She'd spoken to her husband . . . your son . . . on Tuesday night. So far as I can tell, she didn't speak to him again after that. But she called *you* on Thursday, just before she left for home. I'm curious as to why."

"Do you suspect Anne had something to do with Jerry's death?"

"No, ma'am, I'm not saying that."

"Then I'm not sure what the purpose of your call is, Mr. Carella."

Carella looked up at the wall clock. He had been on the phone with her for close to three minutes already, and she *still* hadn't told him why her daughter-in-law had called on Thursday night. Normally, he would have had nothing but respect for such tight familial security. But considering the circumstances—Tell her about the *heat* in that apartment, he thought. Tell her there's something mighty fishy about an apartment with the air conditioner turned off when the temperature outside is in the nineties. Tell her, *yes,* goddamn it, I'm *not* eliminating the possibility of homicide.

"Mrs. Newman?" he said.

"Yes?"

"You're under no obligation to reveal the contents of the telephone conversation you had with your daughter-in-law. I was hoping, however—"

"Anne had nothing to do with my son's death."

"How do you know that?"

"Because you don't kill someone you're planning to divorce, Mr. Carella."

"Was she planning to divorce your son?"

"That's what she called about Thursday night."

"To discuss divorce?"

"To tell me she was going to ask for a divorce as soon as she got back East."

"I see. Did your son know this?"

"No."

"She hadn't mentioned it to him, is that it?"

"She was going to tell him when she got home. She called to ask my advice."

"What did you tell her?"

"I told her to go ahead and do it. My son became a worthless drunk the moment my husband killed himself. I'm a registered nurse, you know, he'd call me every time he'd had too much to drink, ask me to come over and take care of him. I sat through more nights with him, helping him to ward off his imaginary bats and mice . . . well, a mother is supposed to do that, I guess. But I was amazed that Anne was able to bear it as long as she did."

"What was her mood when she called?"

"Troubled, concerned. She was in tears all the while we talked."

"And when the conversation ended?"

"Determined. She planned to tell him the next morning. I believe I gave her the courage to go ahead with it. And then, of course, when she got home . . ."

"It was too late."

"Yes, she found him dead."

"Why were you so reluctant to tell me this, Mrs. Newman?"

"Simply because it's none of your business, Mr. Carella."

"Maybe it isn't," he said. "Thank you. I appreciate your candor."

"He killed himself, that's the long and the short of it," Mrs. Newman said. She hesitated, and then added, "It runs in the family, you see," and hung up.

FIVE

The first call Carella made on Monday morning was to the telephone company's Business Office. He identified himself as a detective working out of the Eight-Seven, and was beginning to tell the woman on the other end what he was looking for when she said, "What number are you calling from, sir?"

"377–8024," he said. "But—"

"Is that a business or a residence?"

"Neither," Carella said.

"Sir?"

"It's a police station."

"Well, that's a business, I suppose," she said.

He had never thought of criminal investigation as a business, but maybe the lady was right. "In any event," he said, "I need—"

"Is this a billing matter, sir?"

"No, it's a police matter."

"What is it you wish, sir?" the woman said.

"I need a record of calls made from a number here in Isola . . ."

"What number is that, sir?"

"Just a moment," Carella said, and consulted his notebook, his finger traveling down the page. "That's 765–3811, the phone is listed to Jeremiah R. Newman, at 74 Silvermine Oval."

"Yes, sir, and *what* was it you wished, sir?"

"A record of calls made from that number, starting on the first of August and continuing through the eighth."

"Then this *is* a billing matter, isn't it?"

"No, it's a police matter."

"The only reason we keep a record of calls is for billing purposes. And those are only long-distance calls. The local calls . . ."

"Well, fine, whatever. Can you get me a . . . ?"

"You'd want a duplicate *bill*, isn't that it?"

"No, all I want is whatever record you've got of the calls made . . ."

"That would be on the *bill*, sir. Let me pull that file, can you hold a moment, please?"

He held.

"Hello?" the woman said.

"Yes, I'm here."

"Sir, we don't bill to that number until the seventeenth of the month."

"I don't *want* a bill," Carella said. "All I want is a record of the calls made from—"

"Yes, that would be on the bill, sir."

"Are you looking at the bill now?"

"No, sir, the bill won't be mailed till the seventeenth. It'll be *prepared* on the fourteenth, and it'll include all calls made up to and including that date."

"Today's the eleventh," Carella said.

"That's right, sir,"

"I can't wait on this till the fourteenth," Carella said. "I need—"

"The *seventeenth*, sir. The bill won't be mailed to Mr. Newman till the *seventeenth*."

"Mr. Newman—"

"Why don't you simply check with him when he receives the bill?"

"He's not *going* to receive the bill," Carella said. "He's dead."

"In that case, sir, I don't know how I can help you."

"You can help me by putting on your supervisor," Carella said.

"Yes, sir, just a moment, please."

Carella waited.

"Good morning, Miss Schulz here," a cheery voice said.

"Good morning, this is Detective Carella of the Eighty-seventh Squad here in Isola. I've just had a less than satisfying conversation with—"

"Oh, I'm sorry, sir."

"I need a record of calls made from 765–3811 between the first of August and the eighth of August, and I've just been told—"

"Yes, Miss Corning filled me in," Miss Schulz said. "We bill to that number on the seventeenth."

"I understand that. But this is a police matter, and time is of the essence, and I'd like a copy of that record as soon as possible."

"Mm," Miss Schulz said.

"So if you don't mind, if someone can make a photocopy for me, I'll have it picked up sometime later to—"

"I'm not sure we're authorized to release a record of calls to anyone but the subscriber, sir."

"I'm a policeman," Carella said.

"Yes, I realize that. But you see, sir, an individual's privacy—"

"The individual is *dead*," Carella said. "Listen, what *is* this? I'm making a routine request, and I'm getting a runaround like I've never—"

"I'm sorry you think it's a runaround, sir."

"Yes, that's *just* what I think it is," Carella said. "When can I pick up that record? Or do I have to get a goddamn court order for it?"

"Don't curse, sir," Miss Schulz said.

"When can I pick it up?"

"Just a moment, please," Miss Schulz said.

Carella waited. One of these days, he thought, the people of the United States are going to declare war on the telephone company. Tanks will go rolling up the avenue to the business off—

"Mr. Carella?"

"Yes?" he said.

"I can mail that to you sometime tomorrow."

"No, I don't *want* it mailed," Carella said. "I want to send a *messenger* for it."

"I was told it would be mailed, sir."

"Who told you it would be mailed?"

"My superior, sir."

"Well, you tell your superior it will *not* be mailed, you tell your superior I'll be sending a patrolman to the business office—What's your address there, give me your address."

"Sir—"

"Give me your goddamn address!"

"Please don't curse, sir."

"What's the *address* there?"

"384 Benedict."

"384 Benedict, right," Carella said. "A patrolman will be there at two p.m. sharp, Miss Schulz, and he'll ask for you personally, and I suggest you let him have a record of those calls, for which he will properly sign a receipt, because if he doesn't get it, the next step is to go before a magistrate to ask for a court order to—"

"Just a moment, please," Miss Schulz said.

Carella waited again.

He kept waiting.

"Hello?" Miss Schulz said.

"Yes, I'm still here," Carella said.

"We'll need a written request," Miss Schulz said.

"Okay, forget it. I'll go downtown myself, I'll get a goddamn court order—"

"Please sir, I wish you wouldn't curse," Miss Schulz said. "If you can send someone down with a written request, I can have a transcript of those calls ready for pickup tomorrow morning. I'm sorry I can't do it sooner than that, but we're computerized, sir, and this would mean—"

"Tomorrow morning will be fine," Carella said.

"But we'll need your written request today."

"A patrolman will hand-deliver it."

"Thank you, sir," Miss Schulz said. "Have a nice day."

When the call from the Hack Bureau came not ten minutes later, Carella expected more trouble. Make a simple request in this damn city, you got involved with all kinds of bureaucratic bullshit that made your job impossible to do. But the woman he spoke to there told him they had run a routine check on their licensed taxi drivers' call sheets for the first of August, when Anne Newman said she'd left for Los Angeles, and the eighth of August, when she'd returned. Sure enough, the records showed an August 1, 8:45 a.m. pickup at 74 Silvermine Oval for a passenger going to the city's international airport, and an August 8, 7:30 a.m. pickup at the airport for a passenger the driver dropped off at 74 Silvermine Oval.

There was no way of ascertaining that the passenger had indeed been Anne Newman, but given the corroborating evidence Genero had garnered (after calling three of the airlines flying to Los Angeles, and finally learning from a *fourth* airline that their manifests for those dates showed an Anne Newman traveling to and from that city), it seemed certain she'd been in California at the time of her husband's death. Despite the nagging air-conditioner problem—and maybe Kling was right, maybe Newman *had* been dead-drunk when he swallowed those capsules—Carella was about to close out the case as a suicide.

The radio on Genero's desk was silent, but that was only because Lieutenant Byrnes was back at work and in his office. The squad room was thronged besides on that Monday morning with four other members of the squad who were at the moment planning a raid on a Culver Avenue shooting gallery. Ever since January, and on direct orders from the Commissioner himself, the cops of the Eight-Seven (and indeed every *other* precinct in the city) had been putting the heat on narcotics dealers; the gallery on Culver had been under surveillance since late February. It was now a known fact that junkies of every persuasion marched in and out of that doorway at 1124 Culver; the cops had parked a van purporting to be a bakery truck just across the street from the building, and they had home movies of virtually every known addict in the precinct. A bust would have been a simple thing. Trot up there to the third floor, round up all the junkies and the small-time pusher doling out the daily fixes, take them all to court, and get the meager sentences for what the cops were certain would be only small quantities of dope.

But at least once a month, the stream of junkies stopped entirely, the gallery upstairs apparently closed for business on those days. Or so the cops believed until their movies revealed certain foreign individuals of French extraction coming and going on the days the junkie traffic trickled off. It was their guess that on those days huge quantities of heroin or cocaine were exchanged for similarly huge quantities of dollars. In effect, the shotting gallery was a cover for a much bigger operation, the bad guys hoping the cops wouldn't be interested in any penny-ante shit, and hoping further that the big-time dealing would go unnoticed in the rush of daily hand-to-mouth trade. Lieutenant Byrnes found it impossible to believe that a shooting gallery operating virtually in the open could be a cover for a multimillion-dollar narcotics operation. But Detective Meyer Meyer—who was in charge of the surveillance and the impending raid—figured the bad guys had only taken their cue from the CIA. Meyer maintained that no professional intelligence agency could be as blunderingly stupid as the CIA. The CIA *had* to be a cover for America's *real* intelligence agency.

In much the same way, the guys buying narcotics from their Gallic cousins, must have figured that a small-time mom-and-pop dope store would be allowed to flourish unmolested when the cops had bigger fish to fry. The bigger fish, the cops now firmly believed, could be hooked on the third floor of 1124 Culver Avenue once a month, every month of the year. The raid was set for this Wednesday night, the thirteenth of August. The detectives were working out their strategy when the woman came up the iron-runged steps leading to the second floor of the station house, and paused just outside the slatted-rail divider that separated the squad room from the corridor outside.

"Yes?" Carella said. "May I help you?"

She was a woman in her late thirties, he guessed, dressed entirely and suitably in summertime white—a white dress and white high-heeled pumps, a white shoulder-slung leather bag, a white carnation in her jet-black hair. She was tall and superbly tanned, her eyes the color of anthracite in a sharp-nosed Mediterranean face that could have belonged to a Spaniard or an Italian, a generous mouth with a beauty spot near the tapered corner of her lips.

"I am looking for the policeman investigating the death of Jeremiah Newman," she said. She spoke with a distinctive foreign accent Carella couldn't quite place. She appeared calm and unruffled, as though walking into a police station did not have the same disquieting effect on her that it had on most citizens, innocent *or* guilty.

"I'm Detective Carella," he said. "I'm handling that case."

"May I come in?" she asked.

"Yes, please," he said, and rose from his desk, and came around the green filing cabinets to open the gate in the railing for her. Across the room, Genero looked up from where he was typing and scanned her head to toe, his eyes lingering on legs Carella now noticed were beautifully proportioned. She sat in the chair beside his desk, crossing her legs, and Genero could not resist a long low whistle. The woman seemed not to have heard it. At his own desk, surrounded by detectives listening to his game plan, Meyer looked up and glared at Genero, who shrugged and went back to his typing.

"I am Jessica Herzog," the woman said. "I was once married to Jeremiah."

"How do you do?" Carella said, and waited. Jessica looked around the squad room, as though wanting to make certain of her surroundings before committing herself to anything further. Across the room, Genero looked up from his typing, studying her breasts this time, firm and full in the scoop-necked top of the white dress. A moment later, he picked up an eraser.

"I received a call from my brother on Saturday. He wanted to tell me about the funeral the next day," Jessica said. "He thought I might want to attend. I could not, of course, attend. We have been divorced now for almost sixteen years it will be. I meant no disrespect, but clearly it would have been impossible."

"Why do you say that, Miss Herzog?"

"Well, because of Anne, don't you see?"

"I'm not sure I understand."

"It was for Anne that he left me all those years ago. I think it would have been an uncomfortable situation, don't you think? To be there at his funeral? With his present wife, I mean?"

"Yes, I can see where—"

"So of course I said I could not go. I hope Martin understood."

"Martin?" Carella said.

"Yes, my brother. He is the one who introduced me to Jeremiah when I first came here."

"Excuse me, Miss Herzog, but where *are* you from originally?"

"Israel," she said.

"Ah," he said.

"I still have a terrible accent, I know."

"No, no," he said.

"Yes, I know, do not lie, please. I am here for nineteen years now and my English is still so bad. I came to sell bonds for my country, I was at the time a captain in the Israeli Army," she said, and Carella remembered the way she had reconnoitered the squad room just a few moments earlier, as though scouting for high ground. "Well, that was a long time ago, I was only twenty-two at the time. I have been living here since, but I go back every now and again to Tel Aviv. My mother still lives in Tel Aviv. All my friends are here now," she said, "and of course my brother. It would be difficult to return there to live."

"And you say you met Mr. Newman through your brother?"

"Yes, at a bond rally. And we fell in love and got married. Two years later, he met Anne, and he asked me for a divorce. Well, that is how it is sometimes, you know."

"Yes," Carella said, and wondered why she had come to the squad room. He waited.

"My brother mentioned to me that Jeremiah had died of sleeping pills. He had taken too many sleeping pills."

"Yes, that's what the autopsy revealed."

"Yes, but that is impossible, don't you see?"

"Impossible? Why?"

"Well, I was only married to him for two years, you understand, but you come to know a person very well when you are living with him, and I can tell you Jeremiah would not have taken even *one* sleeping pill, never mind how many he is *supposed* to have taken."

"Twenty-nine," Carella said.

"Impossible," she said. "Not Jeremiah."

"I still don't understand."

"He had a terrible fear of drugs, do you see? He would not even take an aspirin if he had a headache. It was from when he was a teenager, and a doctor gave him penicillin tablets and he had a severe reaction and almost died. Believe me, Jeremiah would not have swallowed voluntarily any kind of pill. I know. I lived with him. Even an *aspirin*, believe me. He would rather have suffered through the night than take an aspirin. He told me it would make him throw up. So how can a man with such fear take so many pills to kill him?"

"It's supposed to be a painless death, Miss Herzog. Barbiturate poisoning—"

"Not to Jeremiah. Not taking any kind of pill. That would not have been painless to him. He would have died of fright first."

"I see," Carella said.

"I was talking about this to Jonathan only last week," she said, "about his brother's fear of drugs. We used to laugh about it when we were still married, you know, the way Jeremiah would go pale if you even *mentioned* any kind of medication. Well, his brother, Jonathan, remembered, of course. In fact, I'm surprised *he* hasn't been here to see you. Has he been here to see you?"

"No, he hasn't."

"I'm surprised."

"Well, he lives in San Francisco, you know...."

"Yes, of course, but he is here."

"What do you mean?"

"Jonathan. He is here."

"In the city, do you mean?"

"Yes, of course."

"Did he fly in for the funeral, is that it?"

"From *before* the funeral. He has been here almost two weeks now."

Carella looked at her.

"I thought you understood, when I said I had been talking to him—"

"I thought you meant on the telephone."

"No, he is here. He called me when he arrived, we had lunch together one day. He is a nice man, Jonathan."

"I'm surprised his mother didn't mention—"

"Well, so many things on her mind. The funeral, you know."

"Yes. Would you know where he's staying?"

"At the Pierpont. Do you know this hotel?"

"Yes, I do."

"Downtown, near Farley Square?"

"Yes, I know it."

"You should go to see him," Jessica said, "before he leaves. He will tell you how Jeremiah felt about drugs. He will tell you it would have been impossible for him to have taken those pills." She nodded emphatically. "Impossible," she said.

Kling should have realized his marriage was doomed the moment he began tailing his wife.

Carella could have told him that in any marriage there was a line either partner simply could not safely cross. Once you stepped over that line, once you said or did something that couldn't possibly be taken back, the marriage was irretrievable. In any good marriage, there were arguments and even fights— but you fought fair if you wanted the marriage to survive. The minute you started hitting below the belt, it was time to call the divorce lawyers. That's why Carella had asked him to *discuss* this thing with Augusta.

Instead, Kling decided he would find out for himself whether she was seeing another man. He made his decision after a hot, sleepless night. He made it on the steamy morning of August 11, while he and Augusta were eating breakfast. He made it ten minutes before she left for her first assignment of the week.

He was a cop. Tailing a suspect came easily and naturally to him. Standing together at the curb outside their building, Augusta looking frantically at her watch, Kling trying to get a taxi at the height of the morning rush hour, he told her there was something he wanted to check at the office, and would probably be gone all day. Even though this was his day off, she accepted the lie; all too often in the past he had gone back to the station house on his day off. He finally managed to hail a taxi, and when it pulled in to the curb, he yanked open the rear door for her.

"Where are you going, honey?" he asked.

"Ranger Photography, 1201 Goedkoop"

"Have you got that?" Kling asked the cabbie through the open window on the curb side.

"Got it," the cabbie said.

Augusta blew a kiss at Kling, and the taxi pulled away from the curb and into the stream of traffic heading downtown. It took Kling ten minutes to find another cab. He was in no hurry.

He had checked Augusta's appointment calender while she was bathing before bed last night, when he was still mulling his decision. It had showed two sittings for this morning: one at Ranger Photography for nine, the other at Coopersmith Creatives for eleven. Her next appointment was at two in the afternoon at Fashion Flair, and alongside this she had penned in the words *Cutler if time*. Cutler was the agency representing her.

Goedkoop Avenue was in the oldest section of town, its narrow streets and gabled waterfront houses dating back to when the Dutch were still governing. The area lay cheek by jowl with the courthouses and municipal buildings in the Chinatown Precinct, but whereas the illusion was one of overlap, the business here was neither legal nor administrative. Goedkoop was in the heart of the financial district, an area of twentieth-century skyscrapers softened by the old Dutch warehouses and wharves, the later British churches and graveyards. Here and there in lofts along the narrow side streets, the artists and photographers had taken up residence, spilling over from the Quarter and the more recently voguish "Hopscotch" area, so-called because the first gallery to open there was on Hopper Street, overlooking the Scotch Meadows Park. Standing across the street from 1201 Goedkoop, where he had asked the cabbie to let him out, Kling looked around for a pay phone, and then went into a cigar store on the corner of Goedkoop and Fields, where he looked up the phone number for Ranger Photography. From a phone booth near the magazine rack, he dialed the number and waited.

"Ranger," a man's voice said.

"May I speak to Augusta Blair, please?" he said. It rankled every time he had to use her maiden mame, *however* damn professionally necessary it was.

"Minute," the man said.

Kling waited.

When she came onto the line, he said, "Gussie, hi, I'm sorry to break in this way."

"We haven't started yet," she said. "I just got here a few minutes ago. What is it, Bert?"

"I wanted to remind you, we're having dinner with Meyer and Sarah tonight."

"Yes, I know."

"Oh, okay then."

"We talked about it at breakfast," she said. "Don't you remember?"

"Right, right. Okay then. They're coming by at seven for drinks."

"Yes," she said, "I have it in my book. Where are you now, Bert?"

"Just got here," he said. "You want to try that new Italian joint on Trafalgar?"

"Yes, sure. Bert, I have to go. They're waving frantically."

"I'll make a reservation," he said. "Eight o'clock sound okay?"

"Yes, fine. 'Bye, darling, I'll talk to you later."

There was a click on the line. Okay, he thought, she's where she's supposed to be. He put the phone back on the hook, and then went out into the street again. It was blazing hot already, and his watch read only nine twenty-seven. He crossed the street to 1201 Goedkoop, and entered the building, checking to see if there was a side or a back entrance. Nothing. Just the big brass doors through which he'd entered, and through which Augusta would have to pass when she left. He looked at his watch again, and then went across the street to take up his position.

She did not come out of the building until a quarter to eleven.

He had hailed a taxi five minutes earlier, and flashed the tin, and had told the cabbie he was a policeman on assignment and would want him to follow a suspect vehicle in just a few minutes. That was when he was still allowing Augusta at least twenty minutes to get to her next sitting, crosstown and uptown. Her calendar had listed it for eleven sharp; she would be late, that was certain. The cabbie had thrown his flag five minutes ago; he now sat picking his teeth and reading the *Racing Form*. As Augusta came out of the building, another taxi pulled in some three feet ahead of her. She raised her arm, yelled "Taxi!" and then sprinted for the curb, her shoulder bag flying.

"There she is," Kling said. "Just getting in that cab across the street."

"Nice dish," the cabbie said.

"Yeah," Kling said.

"What'd she do?"

"Maybe nothing," Kling said.

"So what's all the hysteria?" the cabbie asked, and threw the taxi in gear and made a wide U-turn in an area posted with NO U-TURN signs, figuring, What the hell, he had a cop in the back seat.

"Not too close now," Kling said. "Just don't lose her."

"You guys do this all the time?" the cabbie asked.

"Do what?"

"Ride taxis when you're chasing people?"

"Sometimes."

"So who pays for it?"

"We have a fund."

"Yeah, I'll just *bet* you have a fund. It's the *taxpayers* are footing the bill, that's who it is."

"Don't lose her, okay?" Kling said.

"I never lost nobody in my life," the cabbie said. "You think you're the first cop who ever jumped in my cab and told me to follow somebody? You know what I hate about cops who jump in my cab and tell me to follow somebody? What I hate is I get *stiffed!* They run out chasing the guy, and they forget to pay even the tab, never mind a tip."

"I won't stiff you, don't worry about it."

"Sure, it's only the taxpayers' money, right?"

"You'd better pick it up a little," Kling said.

The melodramatic chase (Kling could not help thinking of it as such) might have been more meaningful if Augusta's taxi hadn't taken her to 21 Lincoln Street, where Coopersmith Creatives had its studios—as he'd learned from the Isola directory the night before, while Augusta was still in the tub. Kling wanted nothing more than to prove his wife was innocent of any wrongdoing. Innocent till proved guilty, he reminded himself; the basic tenet of American criminal law. Beyond a reasonable doubt, he reminded himself. But at the same time, something inside him longed perversely for a confrontation with her phantom lover. Had the taxi taken her anywhere else in the city, her elaborate lie would have been exposed. Write down an appointment at Coopersmith Creatives for 11:00 a.m., and then fly off to meet some tall, handsome bastard at his apartment in a more fashionable section of town. But no, here she was at 21 Lincoln Street, getting out of the taxi and handing a wad of bills through the open window, and then dashing across the sidewalk to a plate-glass door decorated with a pair of thick diagonal red and blue stripes, the huge numerals 21 worked into the slanting motif. He handed the cabbie the fare and a fifty-cent tip. The cabbie said, "Will wonders never?" and pocketed the money.

Kling walked past the building, and glanced through the plate-glass door. She was no longer in the small lobby. He yanked open the door and walked swiftly to the single elevator at the rear of the building. The needle of the floor indicator was still moving, five, six, seven—it stopped at eight. He found the directory for the building's tenants on the wall just inside the entrance door. Coopersmith Creatives was on the eight floor. No need to call her again with a trumped-up story reminding her of a dinner date. She was exactly where she was supposed to be.

The sitting was a short one. She came out of the building again at a little past noon, and walked directly to a plastic pay-phone shell on the corner. Watching from a doorway across the street, he saw her fishing in her bag for a coin, and dialing a number. He wondered if she was calling the squad room. He kept watching. She was on the phone for what seemed a long time. When finally she hung up, she did not immediately step out of the shell. Puzzled, he kept watching, and then realized she had run out of coins and had asked the person on the other end to call her back. He did not hear the telephone when it rang, the street traffic was too noisy. But he saw her snatch the receiver from the hook and immediately begin talking again. She talked even longer this time. He saw her nodding. She nodded again, and then hung up. She was smiling. He expected her to hail another taxi, but instead she began walking uptown, and it took him another moment to realize she was heading for the subway kiosk on the next corner. He thought, protectively, Jesus, Gussie, don't you know better than to ride the subways in this city? and then he quickened his pace and started down the steps after her, catching sight of her at the change booth. A train was pulling in. He flashed his shield at the attendant in the booth and pushed through the gate to the left of the stiles just as Augusta entered one of the cars.

Someone had once told Kling that one of America's celebrity novelists considered graffiti an art form. Maybe the celebrity novelist never had to ride the subways in this city. The graffiti covered the cars inside and out, obscuring the panels that told you where the train was headed and where it had come from, obfuscating the subway maps that told you where the various station stops were, obliterating the advertising placards, the windows, the walls, and even many of the seats. The graffiti spelled out the names of the spray-can authors (maybe *that's* why the celebrity novelist considered it an art form), the streets on which they lived, and sometimes the "clubs" to which they belonged. The graffiti were a reminder that the barbarians were waiting just outside the gates and that many of the barricades had already fallen and wild ponies were galloping in the streets. The graffiti were an insult and a warning: we do not *like* your city, it is *not* our city, we *shit* on your city. Trapped in a moving cage of violent steel walls shrieking color upon color, Kling stood at the far end of the car, his back to Augusta, and prayed she would not recognize him if she chanced to glance in his direction.

On a normal subway tail, there'd have been two of them, one in each of the cars flanking the suspect's car, standing close to the glass panels on the doors separating the cars, a classic bookend tail. In recent years, you couldn't *see* too easily through the glass panel because it had been spray-painted over, but the idea was to squint through the graffiti, and keep your eye on your man, one of you on either side of him, so that you were ready to move out when he came to his station stop. Today, and curiously, the spray paint worked *for* Kling. Facing the glass panel in the door at the end of the car, he noticed that it had been spray-painted only on the outside, with a dark-blue paint that made through-visibility impossible but that served to create a mirror effect. Even with his back to Augusta, he could clearly see her reflection.

She had taken a seat facing the station stops, and she craned for a look through the spray-painted squiggles and scrawls each time the train slowed. He counted nine stops before she rose suddenly at the Hopper Street station and moved toward the opening doors. He stepped out onto the platform the instant she did. She turned left and began walking swiftly toward the exit steps, her high heels clicking; his wife was in a goddamn hurry. He followed at a safe distance behind her, reached the end of the platform, pushed through the gate, and saw her as she reached the top of the stairs leading to the street, her long legs flashing, the shoulder bag swinging.

He took the steps up two at a time. The sunlight was blinding after the gloom of the subterranean tunnel. He looked swiftly toward the corner, turned to look in the opposite direction, and saw her standing and waiting for the traffic light to change. He stayed right where he was, crossing the street when she did, keeping a block's distance between them. A sidewalk clock outside a savings-and-loan association told him it was already twelve-thirty. Augusta's next appointment was uptown, at 2:00 p.m. He guessed she planned to skip lunch. He hoped against hope that he was wrong. He'd have given his right arm if only she walked into any one of the delicatessens or restaurants that lined the streets in this part of the city. But she continued walking, swiftly, not checking any of the addresses on the buildings, seeming to know exactly where she was going. The area was a mélange of art galleries, boutiques, shops selling antiques, drug paraphernalia, sandals, jewelry, and unpainted furniture. She was heading toward the Scotch Meadows Park in the heart of the Hopscotch artists' quarter. He's an artist, Kling thought. The son of a bitch is an artist.

He followed her for two blocks, to the corner of Hopper and Matthews. Then suddenly, without breaking her stride for an instant, without looking up at the numerals over the door— she was surely familiar with the address—she walked into one of the old buildings that had earlier been factories but which now housed tenants paying astronomical rents. He gave her a minute or two, checked out the hallway to make sure it was empty, and then entered the lobby. The walls were painted a dark green. There was no elevator in the building, only a set of iron-runged steps at the end of the lobby, reminiscent of the steps that climbed to the squad room at the station house uptown. He listened, the way a good cop was taught to do, and heard the faint clatter of her heels somewhere on the iron rungs above. There was a directory of tenants in the lobby. He scanned it briefly, afraid Augusta might suddenly decide to reverse her direction and come down to discover him in the lobby.

He went outside again, and stood on the sidewalk. In addition to the street-level floor of the building, there were five floors above it. Four windows fronted the street on each of these upper stories, but he supposed most of the loft space was divided, and he couldn't even *guess* how many apartments there might be. He jotted the address into his notebook—641 Hopper

Street—and then went into a luncheonette on the corner across the street, and sat eating a soggy hamburger and drinking a lukewarm egg cream while he watched the building. The clock on the grease-spattered wall read 12:40 p.m. He checked the time against his own watch.

It was one o'clock when he ordered another egg cream. It was one-thirty when he asked the counterman for an iced coffee. Augusta did not come out of the building until a quarter to two. She walked immediately to the curb and signaled to a cruising taxi. Kling finished his coffee, and then went into the building again and copied down all the names on the lobby directory. Six of them in all. Six suspects. There was no rush now; he suspected the damage had already been done. He took the subway uptown to Jefferson and Wyatt, where his wife had a two o'clock appointment at Fashion Flair. He waited outside on the sidewalk across the street from the building till she emerged at a little past five, and then followed her on foot crosstown to her agency on Carrington Street. He watched as she climbed the steps to the first floor of the narrow building.

Then he took the subway again and went home.

Jonathan Newman was wearing only slacks when he admitted Carella and Genero to his penthouse suite at the Pierpoint Hotel. He told them he had just taken a cold shower, and was *still* suffocating from the damn *heat* in this city. The air conditioner seemed to be set very low; the apartment was actually chilly. But Newman was sweating nonetheless, and Carella thought he understood why. He had never seen such a hairy man in his life. Newman was slightly taller than Carella himself, perhaps six-one or six-two, with a head of unruly red hair, a shaggy red beard covering his upper lip, jowls, and chin, and a mat of thick red hair on his chest, back, and arms. He rather resembled an orangutan, with the same dense fur and the same coloration. He shambled across the room to where a drink was in a glass of melting ice cubes, and then asked the detectives if they'd care to have anything. Both declined.

"When's this heat supposed to break?" he asked.

"Next week sometime," Carella said. "Maybe."

"It was beautiful when I left San Fran," he said. "We call it the air-conditioned city, you know. Good reason for that.

Beautiful breezes all the time. How can anybody *stand* it here in the summer?"

"Well, you used to live here, didn't you?" Carella said.

"Only till I got old enough to know better," Newman said. "Actually, I got my Navy discharge out on the Coast, decided to stay there. Best decision I ever made in my life. You know what business I'm in out there?"

"No," Genero said. "What?" He actually had an intelligent look on his face; Carella assumed he was fascinated by his first talking ape.

"Coffins," Newman said.

"Coffins?" Genero said.

"Coffins," Newman repeated. "I was in advertising when I joined the Navy, enlisted to get out of sleeping in the mud someplace, knew damn well I'd be drafted anyway if I didn't make my move. Went in as an ensign, well, I was a graduate of Ramsey U here—do you know Ramsey U?"

"Yes," Carella said.

"Yes," Genero said, but he sounded doubtful.

"Got out of the Navy, and the first decision I made was to stay out there on the Coast. Then I asked myself what kind of business I wanted to go into. Advertising again? If I wanted to go back into advertising, I should've come back *East*, right? *This* is where advertising is. So I said No, not for me, not advertising again. So then I asked myself what it was that everybody sooner or later needed. You know what it was?"

"What was it?" Genero asked, even though he already knew the answer.

"Coffins," Newman said. "Sooner or later, we all go to that great big ad agency in the sky, am I right? And we all need a coffin to ride when we make the big trip. That's what I'm in out there. Coffins. I manufacture coffins."

Carella said nothing.

"So here I am on business—well, part-pleasure, I have to admit, you won't tell Internal Revenue, will you?—and my damn-fool brother kills himself and ends up in a coffin I didn't even *make*. Well, what're you gonna do?" Newman said, and drained his glass and went to the wall bar for a refill. "Are you guys sure?" he asked.

"We're on duty," Genero said.

"So what?" Newman said.

Genero seemed tempted.

"No, thanks, we can't," Carella said. "When did you get here, Mr. Newman?"

"Twentieth of July. It was nice then, do you remember? Damn heat didn't start till later. I can't stand this heat. I really can't *stand* it," he said, and plopped four ice cubes into his glass.

"Been here since?"

"Yeah," Newman said. He lifted a bottle of tonic water and splashed some of it over the gin and the cubes.

"Did you see your brother before his death?"

"Nope."

"How come?"

"Didn't like him very much."

"Lots of people don't like their brothers," Genero said. He looked at Carella, and then shrugged.

"Not since he became a lush anyway," Newman said.

"After your father died," Carella said.

"Two years ago, right. Used to be a fairly decent guy before then, I mean if you can excuse what he did to Jessica."

"What was that?"

"Well, you know. Married to her for such a short time, and then ditched her for Annie. Listen, Annie's a better-looking broad, I'll admit it. But you should never lose your head over a piece of tail, am I right? Jessica had it all over her, six ways from the middle. Have you met Jessica? She is *some* kind of woman, believe me. Captain in the Israeli Army—I think she's got a kill record of seventeen Arabs. Great tits besides."

"Yes," Genero said.

Carella looked at him.

"So my brother ditches the only good thing that ever happened to him and settles for the Great American Snow Queen instead. You probably met Annie. I'm sure you had to talk to her about my brother, didn't you?"

"Yes," Genero said, and quickly looked at Carella to see if he'd said the wrong thing again. "Well, Detective *Carella* did," he added.

"Coolest cucumber in the Western Hemisphere," Newman said. "Ice in her veins. She may be great in bed—or so my brother told me when he first fell head over heels—but you'd never know it just looking at her. Anyway, let's say she's the greatest lay in the world, so what? My brother was a fool to give up what he had for two inches of real estate slit vertically up the middle."

Genero looked as though he were trying to dope out the metaphor.

"Anyway, all water under the bridge. He's dead now, God rest him merry," Newman said, and raised his glass in a toast.

"I understand you saw Miss Herzog last week," Carella said.

"Yeah, last Wednesday. We had lunch together."

"And you were reminiscing about your brother's aversion to pills."

"Yeah."

"Didn't like to take pills of any kind, is that it?"

"That's putting it mildly."

"What do you make of his having swallowed twenty-nine of them?"

"*Bullshit* is what I make of it."

"You don't think he could've done it, huh?"

"No way."

"When did you learn about his death, Mr. Newman?"

"Mom called me. Friday, it must've been. There was a message when I got back to the hotel—call Susan Newman, urgent. I knew right off it was my brother. It had to be dumb fucking Jerry falling out the window or something, dead-drunk. What *else* could be urgent in my mother's life?"

"So what happened when you called her back?" Carella asked.

"She told me my brother was dead."

"Did she mention that he'd died of an overdose of Seconal?"

"No, she didn't learn that till the next day. I guess they hadn't done the autopsy yet."

"What was your reaction?"

"When I found out he was dead? You want the truth?"

"Please."

"I thought good riddance."

"Uh-huh."

"He'd been nothing but a pain in the ass to all of us for the past two years. Me, my mother, Annie, *all* of us. Lorded it over all of us because he was the one who inherited that big chunk of money when my father died, thought he was better than—"

"What chunk of money?" Carella asked at once.

"Well, not *money* as such, not immediately after his death. But all those paintings, you know. He left all of them to Jerry. My father was one of the best abstract expressionists around. There had to be at least two hundred paintings stored in that big studio he used to work in. Jerry got all of them. That's why he could afford to piss away his life."

"What did he leave to your mother?"

"A farewell note," Newman said, and smiled grimly.

"And you?"

"Zilch. I was the black sheep. I was the son who left home to manufacture coffins. My dear brother, Jerry, was the *artiste*, you know, following in our father's footsteps. Churning out utter crap, as it was, but that didn't disturb my father, oh no. Jerry was carrying on the great family tradition."

"When you say a large chunk of money—"

"Millions," Newman said.

"Who gets that now, would you know?"

"What do you mean?"

"All that money. Now that your brother's dead."

"I have no idea."

"Did he leave a will?"

"I don't know, you'd have to ask Annie."

"I will. Thank you, Mr. Newman, you've been very helpful. When will you be going back to California?"

"In a day or so, few things here I've still got to wrap up."

"Here's my card, in case you need to get in touch with me," Carella said.

"Why would I need to get in touch with you?" Newman asked, but he accepted the card.

In the street outside, as they walked toward where Carella had parked the unmarked sedan, he wished this wasn't Kling's day off. The way the squad room schedule broke down, a man often found himself partnered with different detectives at any given time of the month. Carella would have settled for any one of them today. Even Parker, who was not Carella's notion of an ideal cop, had years of experience, and could bring to any case the kind of street smarts often necessary to break it.

Police lore held that a good partner was a man you could count on in a shoot-out. That was why so many uniformed motor-patrol cops objected to having a woman officer riding with them; they figured she couldn't be depended on if it came to going up against a heavy with a shotgun in his hands. But Carella had seen women on the range who could dot an *i* with a .38-caliber pistol. Sheer brute strength didn't amount to a hill of beans in a shoot-out. Jessica Herzog had been a captain in the Israeli Army and, according to her brother-in-law, had killed seventeen men in combat. Would any cop on the force have objected to Jessica as a partner? He doubted it. But a partner was more than that, much more.

Genero—whose value in a shoot-out was debatable anyway; the man had once accidentally put a bullet in his own foot—simply did not provide the necessary "bounce" essential to an investigatory give-and-take. The bounce, Carella thought. That's what I miss. The bounce.

"*He* noticed, too," Genero said.

"What's that?" Carella said.

"Her tits," Genero said.

"Yeah," Carella said.

He was thinking about the millions of dollars Jeremiah Newman had realized when he'd sold the paintings he'd inherited from his father. He was wondering whether a will had been filed with Probate, and was wondering further what the directives of that will might be. He was thinking a partner was somebody off whom you could bounce the facts, back and forth, mulling them, gnawing at them till they yielded a meaningful picture of what might have happened. He was thinking a partner was someone you could trust not only with your life but also with your wildest speculation. He was thinking a partner was someone who could risk telling you he suspected his wife was playing around. He was thinking a partner was someone who could openly sob in your presence, without fear you would laugh at him. He was wishing Kling was with him on this third day after the body of Jeremiah Newman had been found by his wife in an apartment as hot and as stinking as the corridors of Hell.

At dinner that night with Meyer and his wife, Kling and Augusta listened to Meyer telling two jokes, both of them about immigrants to this city. The first one was about a Russian immigrant who changed his name almost immediately after he arrived here. One day, he ran into a friend from his old village, and the man was surprised to learn that his former countryman was no longer Boris Rybinski but was now C. R. Stampler. "So from vhere did you gat this new name?" he asked. The newly arrived immigrant shrugged and said, "Tzimple. I am liffink now on Stampler Stritt, so dot's from vhere I got the name." His friend thought about this for a moment, and then said, "So vot does it stend for the C.R.?" The immigrant smiled broadly and said, "Corner Robertson."

The second joke was perhaps the definitive story about this city, which had never been celebrated for its friendliness or warmth, and which in fact had a reputation for abruptness bordering on rudeness. It was a very short story, a one-liner. An immigrant stops a stranger on the street and says, "Excuse me, can you tell me where the Municipal Life Building is, or should I go fuck myself?"

Augusta laughed louder than anyone else.

Kling remembered that between the hours of twelve-thirty and one forty-five, she had been inside a building on Hopper Street, corner Matthews. When they left the restaurant at ten, Meyer offered to give them a lift, but they were only a few blocks from where they lived, and so they all said good night on the sidewalk outside.

As they moved past the restaurant, a man stepped out of a doorway across the way, and began walking parallel to them on the other side of the street.

He was a huge man with the broad, powerful shoulders of a weight lifter. His dark eyes were shadowed by the brim of a hat pulled low on his forehead and covering his black hair. He followed Kling and Augusta all the way home, and after they went inside he stood on the sidewalk across the street and watched the lighted windows on the second floor of the brownstone. He did not leave until the lights went out at a little past eleven.

Then he went uptown to look for a gun.

SIX

It was worse up here than it was anywhere else in the city.
Even in the Marine Tiger section of Riverhead, there was sometimes a breeze coming in off the River Dix and rushing through
the comparatively higher plateau of what had once been fertile
farmland. But here in Diamondback, at the farthermost reaches
of the city's central island, the heat was insufferable—even at
ten past midnight, when Halloran came up out of the subway.

The heat had been baking into the brick walls and the tarred
roofs of the buildings all day long. The buildings themselves
stretched row upon row, block after block, six and seven stories
high, forming a grid that trapped the heat and held it motionless,
a giant stifling canopy of heat. The windows in the apartments
were open, but the air was still and the heat within was equally
balanced with the heat outside, so that the people who lived
here felt they were moving through a vast, viscid, impenetrable,
virtually blinding force field. They sat on the fire escapes hung
with clothing that refused to dry because of the humidity. They

sat on the front stoops of buildings eroded by time and abuse.
They lounged listlessly on the street corners. They played
checkers in the light of the streetlamps. It was past midnight
in Diamondback, but it could just as well have been high noon.
The streets were thronged. There would be no sleeping tonight,
not with this heat. Tomorrow morning, many of the residents
here would travel downtown to work in air-conditioned offices,
restaurants, shops, and stores. But tonight, there was only the
heat, and the roaches, and the rats.

Halloran could hear the rats foraging in the empty lots as
he walked along the avenue toward the address Jimmy Baker
had given him. He could see their eyes gleaming in the dark.
He could hear their teeth gnawing. The lots were piled with
garbage. It was easier to throw your garbage out the windows
in this neighborhood, into an empty lot, than to pack it neatly
in plastic bags at the curb. The Sanitmen weren't as particular
about Diamondback as they were about some of the city's better
sections. The garbage would sit outside the buildings for days,
waiting for collection. The rats would gnaw through the plastic.
In packs, the rats would cover the sidewalks instead of the
empty lots. It was safer to throw your garbage into the lots.
You kept the rats off the sidewalks that way. You created little
pockets of rat zoos, the rats waiting for feeding time, chewing
up the scattered garbage instead of the faces of infants in cribs.

Halloran was only one of a very few white men abroad in
Diamondback that night. It was an axiom of urban survival
that if you were white you did not walk the streets of Diamondback after dark. The white men up there after dark were
either junkies looking for a fix or out-of-towners looking for
black pussy. Either was fair game to many of the people who
lived here. The ones who went to work downtown each morning
would sit on their fire escapes and look down into the streets
where a man was getting rolled or mugged, and they would
shake their heads in despair, and curse the accidental skin
coloration that caused honest men and women to be equated
with thieves, prostitutes, and pimps. They would sigh deeply,
recognizing forlornly that this was a condition of life, however
unfair, and in the morning they would dress in the clothing
they had purchased in any one of the better stores downtown,
and be ready at nine sharp to take dictation or to sell a negligee
or to drive a passenger from the airport to his apartment in

Stewart City on the River Dix, where a doorman in livery would open the door of the taxi and say, "Good morning, sir, sorry about this heat, sir." That would be in the morning. This was the night.

Halloran was a big man who looked like he might have been a detective out of the Eight-Three up here, and this was in his favor. Moreover, there was a sense of menace about him, a certain emanation that this man was street-smart, and it would not be wise to tangle with him. There were easier marks, it wouldn't pay to jump a honkie who might turn out to be either a cop or some cocksucker wanted for murder in fourteen of the fifty states. Halloran walked the crowded midnight streets unmolested.

Jimmy Baker had been his cellmate up at Castleview, until last October anyway, when Jimmy was paroled after serving ten on an armed robbery rap. Together, he and Jimmy had shared some of the choicest young meat inside the prison. The way they worked it, they would pick out a baby-faced little doll riding up, and then Halloran would put the muscle on the kid, coming on like the big bad wolf about to eat him alive, and Jimmy—who was slender and slight—would stand up for the kid, facing Halloran down, telling him he'd cut off his balls if he didn't leave the kid alone. The kid in gratitude would sidle up to Jimmy, who'd be fucking him before the week was out, threatening to throw him to the beast who was Halloran if he didn't put out. A classic Mutt-and-Jeff situation. But by the end of the second week, *both* of them would be alternating with the kid, who by then had realized he'd been conned, but who figured two stir-wise operators like Halloran and Jimmy would keep all the *other* animals away. There were as many animals up at Castleview as there were rats foraging in the lots of Diamondback.

The pool hall Jimmy Baker owned and operated was in the middle of the block, set between a storefront Baptist church and a beauty parlor advertising hair-straightening and skin-lightening. There were two dozen young black guys shooting pool when Halloran walked through the front door at a quarter past midnight. Fuckin' niggers got nothing to do but shoot pool in the middle of the night, Halloran thought. My fuckin' daughter's married to a nigger, he thought. Oddly, he did not think of Jimmy Baker as a nigger. Jimmy Baker was simply his cellmate, and a nicer guy you'd never want to meet in your life. The exception to the rule, Halloran thought. Enjoyed more damn two-on-ones with Jimmy up there at Castleview. Jimmy was okay. Black or white, he was okay. In his presence, Halloran never used the word "nigger." Even if he was one.

The guys shooting pool all looked up when he came in. Their eyes caromed off each other's like the balls on the tables. They were figuring him for a cop. Next few minutes, there'd be an "Up against the wall, mother-fuckers." A fat black guy reading the early edition of the city's tabloid newspaper looked up from where he was sitting behind a high counter just inside the entrance door. A sign behind his head advised what the hourly rates were for a table. He was chewing on a cigar. He went back to his newspaper, deciding to ignore Halloran. If he was fuzz, he'd make his intentions known soon enough.

"I'm looking for Jimmy Baker," Halloran said without preamble.

"Who wants him?" the black man asked.

"Jack Halloran."

"What for?"

"We celled together at Castleview," Halloran said.

"Just a sec," the man said, and lifted the receiver of a phone on the counter. He dialed a single number and waited. "James," he said, "they's a man named Jack Halloran out here, wants to see you." He listened, nodded, and then put up the phone. "Go right on back," he said. "Red door there, far end of the room."

"Thanks," Halloran said.

The man went back to chewing his cigar and reading his newspaper. All around the room, billiard balls clicked. There was the low murmur of conversation, "Three ball in the side . . . Nice shot, man . . . Bank the four down here."

Halloran walked to the red door and opened it.

Jimmy Baker was sitting behind a desk cluttered with papers. There were two phones on the desk. He had put on a little weight since Halloran had last seen him, but he was the same old Jimmy, big white teeth gleaming in his mouth as he grinned across the desk, and then came around it, both hands extended, his hair cut in an Afro now instead of the closer prison-cut, still grinning, shaking his head in wonder. He was wearing tailored jeans, a black silk shirt unbuttoned to the waist, and a gold medallion hanging from a gold chain around his neck.

"Hey, man," he said, and took both Halloran's hands in his own. "Man, man, you a sight for sore eyes, I gotta tell you."

"What's this James shit?" Halloran asked, grinning, really happy to see him.

"I'm the big honcho here," Jimmy said. "Anybody calls me anything but James—or sometimes *Mr*. James," he said, rolling his eyes, "I kick his ass for him. When was you sprung, man?"

"A week ago today. What's today?"

"By the feel of it, or the clock?" Jimmy asked. "By the clock, it's Tuesday, the twelf' of August. By the feel, it's still Monday night, man, till the sun comes up, at least. Sit down. You want somethin to drink? Hey, man, you look terrific, I gotta tell you. A week ago today, huh? You want a beer? I got some cold beer. You want somethin stronger? Name it, man. Jee-*sus*, it is *good* to see you!"

"It's good to see you, too, Jimmy," Halloran said. He was still grinning. "How's it treatin' you out here?"

"*Comme-çi, comme-ça,*" Jimmy said. "I got the pool parlor, I got me a little numbers runnin, I got me a little dope dealin, it ain't been too bad a'tall. I'm still lookin aroun for a big score someplace, just bidin my time, somethin'll come along sooner or later. How about you?"

"Well, I just got out, you know. Lots of business to take care of, you know."

"Sure, gettin adjusted. It's a big motherfuckin hassle out here, ain't it? Times I wisht I was back inside, where evythin's taken *care* of for you. You want some beer? Lissen, have a bottle of beer, okay?"

"Yeah, sure," Halloran said.

Jimmy went to a small refrigerator set under a counter against the far wall. He pulled out two bottles of beer and uncapped them.

"Here's to the fuckin Castle," he said.

"Cheers," Halloran said, and took only a sip. He didn't want to get piss-eared drunk the way he'd been yesterday when that whore picked him up.

"How you like this fuckin heat?" Jimmy asked. "City arranged a nice big welcome for you, dinn it? Reg'lar *home-comin* celebration. Fuckin heat you could die in."

"Yeah," Halloran said.

"So you come up here to see old Jimmy, huh?" he said, grinning again. "Man, it is *so* good to *see* you, man."

There was a long silence.

"I need a piece," Halloran said.

"Uh-huh," Jimmy said, and his eyes narrowed.

"I figured you might know where I could get one."

"What've you got in mind? Anythin might interest me?"

"I don't think so."

"'Cause, like I said, I been lookin for some kind of score."

"No, this isn't anything like that."

"So why you need a piece, man? I mean, I'll hep you *get* one, shit, we'll get one for you in a *minute*. But whut you need it for?"

"Some guy I have to see."

"Need a piece for it, huh?"

"Yeah."

"What kinda weapon you have in mind?"

"Something he won't walk away from," Halloran said.

"Who's the lucky dude?" Jimmy asked, and laughed.

"Well, maybe I shouldn't tell you," Halloran said. "Be safer for you that way."

"Whut I doan know won't hurt me, huh?"

"That's what I mean."

"Well, sure, man, we goan get you a piece put a big hole in the motherfucker. Put a *monstrous* hole in the man. Let me jus' make a few calls, all right? See whut the market looks like this fine summer night. Finish your beer, man, this won't take but a minute."

The market that fine summer night looked bullish.

Before they left the pool hall, Jimmy made three phone calls, and by one that morning, they were sitting with a short black man who looked like an accountant, the sleeves of his white shirt rolled up over his forearms, the collar of the shirt open, his face sweating behind thick, rimless eyeglasses. Jimmy introduced him simply as Sam. On the table before Sam was an arsenal of some forty automatics and revolvers.

They were in a third-floor apartment on Carlton Street. Years ago, during the Depression, the building had housed a speakeasy on the ground floor. Next door, there used to be a jazz joint frequented by whites who would drift uptown in their diamonds and furs. That was during the Depression. Now the building was a rat-infested tenement. Sam sat under a naked light bulb in the kitchen of his apartment, the oiled weapons gleaming on the enamel-topped table in front of him. In the next room, Halloran could hear someone snoring lightly. Sam's wife, he guessed. Sweat glistened on Sam's face and on his exposed forearms.

"What kind of job you hope to do with this piece?" he asked.

"Well, that don't matter," Jimmy said at once.

"'Cause if it's something where you need to keep the gun out of *sight* when you walk in, then I'd recommenn maybe the .38 here, with the snub-nose."

"He needs a piece'll do the job," Jimmy said.

"I was only tryin to fine out—"

"The *whole* job," Jimmy added.

"Then you want somethin with lots of power, is that it?"

"Yes," Halloran said.

"An' it don't matter whether the piece'll show under your coat, or nothin like that?"

"No."

"You be doin this job durin the day or at night?"

"I don't know yet."

"'Cause if it's durin the day, then you got to keep the piece *hid,* man, and some of these bigger mothas, like the Ruger Magnum there, they gonna stand out like a hard-on under your clothes."

"Well, maybe I'll do it at night then."

"You can't beat the Ruger for power," Sam said.

"Which one is the Ruger?" Halloran asked.

"This one right here."

"Looks like a fuckin cannon," Jimmy said.

"Shoots like one, too," Sam said. "Some states, they won't even 'low the *pigs* to use a Magnum. Pig shoots at some guy runnin out of a grocery store, bullet can go right *thu* the guy an' hit some preggint lady doin her shoppin besides. This gun is one mighty fuckin pow'ful pistol, man. You say you want to do the *whole* job, this gun'll do the whole job an' *then* some."

"How much would something like that cost me, that gun," Halloran asked.

"Give him a good price now, man," Jimmy said.

Sam figured they'd been asshole buddies in jail. Man gets in with a cellmate, ain't too long before they're behaving like man and wife. That's what Sam figured this relationship to be.

"I has to get a hun' fifty for that piece," he said.

"That's too high," Jimmy said at once.

"Cost you two hunnerd in a store," Sam said. "That piece is brand-new, ain't been fired once. I has to get at *least* a hun' fifty."

"Make it a hun' twenty-five," Jimmy said. "An' throw in whutever ammo the man's gonna need."

"The ammo ain't a problem," Sam said, shaking his head. "But I has to get a hun' fifty. James, the thing cost *me* a hunnerd, I swear on my mother's eyes. A fifty-dollar profit ain't hardly no profit at all."

"Whutchoo think, man?" Jimmy asked Halloran.

"I haven't got that kind of bread," Halloran said.

"How much you got, man?"

"About a hundred."

"Well, now, that's impossible," Sam said, and rose from where he was sitting, and stretched, signaling that the negotiations were over.

"You want that piece?" Jimmy asked.

"It looks like it could do the job," Halloran said.

"Blow a man's head off, that fuckin piece," Sam said.

"So you want it or not?" Jimmy asked.

"I haven't got a hun' fifty," Halloran said. He picked up the gun and hefted it on the palm of his hand.

"Fires either .44 Magnum or .44 Special cartridges," Sam said. "I got both in stock, you don't need to worry none."

"It's a nice piece," Halloran said.

"Seven-and-a-half-inch barrel on that motha," Sam said. "Beats the .357 Magnum all to shit. You got twice the killing power with this pistol that you got with the .357 Magnum."

"Yeah," Halloran said.

"They calls that gun there the *Super* Blackhawk," Sam said. "Same caliber as a *carbine,* that gun. Cost you two hunnerd dollars you try to buy it in any store. All I'm askin is a hun' fifty."

"I just haven't got that kind of bread," Halloran said.

"If you want the gun, you got it," Jimmy said. He turned to Sam. "You're thowin in the ammo, am I right?"

"However many rouns the man wants."

"Then you got yourself a deal, you fuckin thief," Jimmy said, laughing and reaching into his pocket. He pulled out a roll of bills fastened with a rubber band, slipped off the rubber band, pulling it onto his wrist, and then peeled off three fifties. Still laughing, he said, "You way too high, man. I shoulda taken him to Nicky Garters."

"Nicky ain't *got* no Rugers," Sam said.

"Jus' wait the next time you come in my pool parlor," Jimmy said, handing him the bills. "Coss you twenny dollars an hour nex' time you want to play."

"Man, a hunnerd of this is whut I already laid *out* for that piece."

Halloran hefted the gun again. His eyes met Jimmy's. Very softly, he said, "Thank you, Jimmy."

Asshole buddies, Sam thought. Just like he figured.

The air conditioner was humming in the second-floor bedroom of the brownstone. The room was cool, but Kling could not sleep. It was two in the morning, and he wasn't due back at work till four this afternoon, but he'd hoped to get up early again in the morning, in time to leave the apartment when Augusta did. He wanted to see if she visited her pal on Hopper Street again. Wanted to see if visiting her pal was a regular lunch-hour thing with her, quick matinee every day of the week when she wasn't out screwing around instead of eating in a Chinese restaurant. He was tempted to confront her with it now, tell her he'd followed her to Hopper Street, tell her he'd seen her go into the building at 641 Hopper Street, ask her what possible business she could have had in that building. Get it over with here and now. He remembered what Carella had advised him.

"Augusta?" he whispered.

"Mm."

"Gussie?"

"Mm."

"You awake?"

"No," she said, and rolled over.

"Gussie, I want to talk to you."

"Go t'sleep," Augusta mumbled.

"Gussie?"

"Sleep," she said.

"Honey, this is important," he said.

"Shit."

"Honey..."

"Shit, shit, *shit,*" she said, and sat up and snapped on the bedside lamp. "What is it?" she said, and looked at the clock on the table. "Bert, it's two o'*clock,* I have a sitting at eight-thirty, can't this wait?"

"I really feel I have to talk to you now," he said.

"I have to get up at *six*-thirty!" she said.

"I'm sorry," he said, "but, Gussie, this has really been bothering me."

"All right, what is it?" she said, and sighed. She took a pack of cigarettes from beside the clock, shook one free, and lighted it.

"I'm worried," he said.

"Worried? What do you mean?" she said.

"About us," he said.

"Us?"

"I think we're drifting apart."

"That's ridiculous," she said.

"I think we are."

"What makes you think so?"

"Well, we... for one thing, we don't make love as often as we used to."

"I've got my period," Augusta said. "You know that."

"I know that, but... well, that didn't used to matter in the past. When we were first married."

"Well," she said, and hesitated. "*I* thought we were doing fine."

"I don't think so," he said, shaking his head.

"Is it the sex, is that it? I mean, that you think we don't have enough sex?"

"That's only part of it," he said.

"Because if you, you know, if you'd like me to..."

"No, no."

"I thought we were doing fine," she said again, and shrugged, and stubbed out the cigarette.

"You know this girl who's with the agency?" he said. Here it is, he thought. Here we go.

"What girl?"

"Little blond girl. She models junior stuff."

"Monica?"

"Yeah."

"Monica Thorpe? What about her?"

"She was out there at the beach that night of the party. On the Fourth. Do you remember?"

"So?"

"We got to talking," Kling said.

"Uh-huh," Augusta said, and reached for the pack of cigarettes again. Lighting one, she said, "Must've been fascinating, talking to that nitwit."

"You smoke an awful lot, do you know that?" Kling said.

"Is that another complaint?" Augusta asked. "No sex, too much smoking, are we going to go through a whole *catalogue* at two in the morning?"

"Well, I'm only thinking of your health," Kling said.

"So what about Monica? What'd you talk about?"

"You."

"Me? Now *there's* a switch, all right. I thought Monica never talked about anything but her own cute little adorable self. What'd she have to say? Does *she* think I smoke too much?"

"She said she's seen you around town with a lot of guys," Kling said in a rush, and then caught his breath.

"What?"

"She said—"

"Oh, that rotten little *bitch!*" Augusta said, and angrily stubbed out the cigarette she'd just lighted. "Seen me *around*, seen me—"

"One guy in particular," Kling said.

"Oh, *one* guy in particular, uh-huh."

"That's what she said."

"Which guy?"

"I don't know. You tell me, Gussie."

"This is ridiculous," Augusta said.

"I'm only repeating what she said."

"And you believed her."

"I . . . listened to her. Let's put it that way."

"But she couldn't tell you *which* guy, in *particular,* I'm supposed to have been seen around town with, is that it, Bert?"

"No. I asked her, but—"

"Oh, you *asked* her. So you *did* believe her, right?"

"I was listening, Gussie."

"To a juvenile delinquent who's only been laid by every photographer in the entire city, and who has the gall—"

"Calm down," he said.

"—to suggest that *I'm*—"

"Come on, Gussie."

"I'll kill that little bitch. I swear to God, I'll *kill* her!"

"Then it isn't true, right?"

"Right, it isn't true. Did you think it *was?*"

"I guess so."

"Thanks a lot," Augusta said.

They were silent for several moments. He was thinking he would have to ask her about 641 Hopper Street, about why she'd gone this afternoon to 641 Hopper Street. He was thinking he'd done what Carella had suggested he should do, but he still wasn't satisfied, he still didn't have the answers that would set his mind at ease. He had only opened the can of peas, and now he had to spill them all over the bed.

"Gussie . . ." he said.

"I love you, Bert," she said, "you know that."

"I thought you did."

"I do."

"But you keep going places without me . . ."

"That was *your* idea, Bert, you know it was. You *hate* those parties."

"Yeah, but still . . ."

"I won't go anywhere else without you, okay?"

"Well . . ."

What about during the day? he wondered. What about when I'm out chasing some cheap thief, what about then? What about when I have the Night Watch? What will you be doing *then?* he wondered. The parties don't mean a damn, he thought, except when you tell me you had dinner at a Chinese restaurant with a whole bunch of people, and Mr. Ah Wong himself tells me there was no redhead in Miss Mercier's party. You should have been a brunette, Gussie, they don't stand out as much in a crowd.

"I promise," she said. "No place else without you. Now lie down."

"There are still some things . . ."

"Lie down," she said. "On your back."

She pulled the sheet off of him.

"Just lie still," she said.

"Gussie . . ."

"Quiet."

"Honey . . ."

"Shh," she said. "Shh, baby. I'm gonna take care of you. Poor little neglected darling, Mama's gonna take good care of you," she said, and her mouth descended hungrily.

When you're working a homicide, or what may turn *out* to be a homicide, the schedule doesn't mean a damn. You go to the office, and you nag the thing to death, around the clock sometimes, because the killer has an edge you do not have, and time only hones that edge to razor-thin sharpness.

Carella wasn't due back at the office till four that Tuesday afternoon, but he came in at ten in the morning, and nobody working the Day Tour was surprised. Carella had caught a suicide last Friday, and almost every cop on the squad was experienced enough to know that a suicide without a suicide note was like a pastrami sandwich without a pickle. Carella had briefed Lieutenant Byrnes on the persistent problem of the *heat* in that damn apartment, and Byrnes had filled in the other men on the squad, just in case any of them might come up with a brilliant idea about why an air conditioner had been turned off during the middle of the hottest week that summer. None of them had any brilliant ideas.

They did, however, have a great deal of sympathy for Carella, who was here at the office at 10:00 a.m. on a day when he wasn't supposed to arrive till four. They had all been in his boots before. They had all worked cases that drove them bananas, catching a few hours' sleep at night on one of the Swing Room cots, working the damn case like a terrier with a half-dead rat, shaking it and shaking it and shaking it till it lay still and lifeless and ready to be buried as CLOSED. They talked softly to Carella, and offered to bring him coffee from the Clerical Office. They knew he was extremely troubled. They thought he was only troubled about the absence of a suicide note and the further absence of air conditioning in an apartment as hot as the Sahara. They did not know, because Carella had not yet told Byrnes, and Byrnes had not in turn briefed the others on it, that Carella was *also* troubled about an apparent suicide victim who was supposed to have swallowed twenty-nine Seconal capsules when the man wouldn't have been caught dead within a hundred yards of an *aspirin*.

The first call Carella made that morning was to the Police Lab downtown on High Street. The man he spoke to there was the technician who'd been in charge of the team that had gone through the Newman apartment. He was a Detective Third/Grade and his name was John Owenby. He started Carella's day with a bang by telling him they weren't ready with their reports yet.

"What do you mean?" Carella said. "This is *Tuesday*, you were there Friday morning, what's the delay?"

"The heat is the delay," Owenby said.

"What's the heat got to do with...?"

"What have you got here, Carella?" Owenby said. "What does it look like you've got here."

"A suicide," Carella said.

"Right, a suicide."

"Although there are circumstances—"

"Don't give me with circumstances," Owenby said, "this ain't a court of law. You've got what looks like a suicide, you've got an empty bottle of Seconal—"

"*Almost* empty," Carella said.

"On my block," Owenby said, "if there's only a single capsule left in a bottle, and a guy swallowed the *rest* of them, then the bottle is empty."

"So what's taking you so long up there? The M.E.'s already given us a cause of death, he had to carve up a whole damn *corpse* to—"

"Priorities," Owenby said. "Maybe the M.E.'s got different priorities than we got up here. Let me tell you something about priorities, Carella. When we get—"

"Instead, why don't you tell me whether you found any wild prints in that apartment?"

"We found a great many latents, and they are now with the Fingerprint Section. I spoke to them just this morning, and they haven't had a chance to compare them yet against the dead man's and the ones you sent down for his wife. It's priorities, Carella. A homicide takes precedence over a suicide, an armed robbery takes precedence over a burglary, an assault takes precedence over spitting on the sidewalk. You know how many damn homicides we've got with this heat? This heat is bringing them out of the woodwork. And there's supposed to be a full moon this Friday night. You know what *that'll* do, don't you? It'll bring out every bedbug in the city. We'll be jammed up here with more shootings, knifings, axings, stranglings, and suffocations than you can shake a stick at. You know what you can do with your measly suicide, don't you? I'll call you when the report is ready."

"Where's Captain Grossman?" Carella said. "I want to talk to him."

"Going over my head isn't going to—"

"Where is he?"

"In court. He'll be in court the rest of the week, Carella. Testifying on a homicide. Which takes precedence over a suicide. Priorities, Carella."

"When do you think I can have your report?"

"In a day or so."

"Make it tomorrow morning."

"I said in a day or so. We're working on what we vacuumed up, we're running our tests on that capsule—"

"The M.E.'s *already* identified the drug—"

"We have to do it here, too. As soon as we get the package together—"

"Shoot for tomorrow, okay?"

"I'll do the best I can," Owenby said, and hung up.

The manila envelope from the telephone company was hand-delivered not ten minutes later. The patrolman who brought it up to the squad room waited while Carella signed for receipt, and then tossed it onto the desk, where it landed on a pile of junk that included a mimeographed sheet announcing the PBA's annual Labor Day picnic and dance, a flyer from the Three-One asking for information regarding any shooting involving a Smith & Wesson .38-caliber revolver, a BOLO from the cops in Sarasota, Florida, and a stack of eight-by-ten glossies the Photo Unit had enlarged from the ones they'd taken in the Newman apartment last Friday.

Carella opened the envelope.

There were four photocopied pages in it, listing all the calls made from the Newman apartment since the last billing in July. In this city, as in most American cities, a telephone-company bill was broken down into columns that recorded the date of any long-distance call, the city to which that call had been made, the number called in that city, the time the call was made, the duration of the call in minutes, and finally the charge for the call.

Carella started with the last page first.

Anne Newman had left the Silvermine Oval apartment at a quarter to nine on the morning of August first, and had not returned home till the eighth. Presumably, then, any calls made from the 765-3811 number during that time span had been made by Jerry Newman himself, while he was still alive.

The last listing read:

DATE	LONG DISTANCE CALLS	TIME	MIN	AMOUNT
8/7	BVRLY HILLS CA 213 275 4282	621P	3B	85

On the seventh of August, then, Jerry Newman had placed a call to Beverly Hills at 6:21 p.m., local time, which would have made it 3:21 p.m. on the Coast. He had spoken for three minutes and the call had cost him eighty-five cents. Carella didn't know what the "B" following the "3" in the minute column meant, but the number Newman had called seemed familiar to him. He dialed California Information, and asked for the number of the Beverly Wilshire Hotel. The operator read it off to him: 213-275-4282. He thanked her, and then dialed the Business Office, hoping he would not get either Miss Corning or Miss Shulz. He spoke to a nameless operator, instead, who told him that the "B" following the "3" simply meant the call had been placed either in the evening or on the weekend, when the rates were lower. He thanked her and hung up.

Jerry Newman had presumably been alive at 6:21 p.m. on the night before his body was discovered. He had called the Beverly Wilshire Hotel and had presumably spoken to his wife at 3:21 p.m. Pacific Daylight Saving Time. Carella took out his notebook. At 5:00 p.m. Pacific Daylight Saving Time, that same day, Anne Newman had called her mother-in-law to tell her she was contemplating divorce. She had then presumably packed and had later gone to the airport to catch a ten-thirty plane scheduled to arrive here the next morning at six-thirty. But if she'd spoken to her husband on *Thursday*, why had she told Carella she'd spoken to him for the last time on *Tuesday*, when she'd called to give him her travel plans?

He lifted the receiver again, and dialed Susan Newman's number. He let the phone ring a dozen times, and was about to hang up when a breathless voice he recognized as Anne's said, "Hello?"

"Mrs. Newman?"

"Yes, just a moment, please."

He waited.

When she came back onto the line, she said, "I'm sorry, I was in the shower. Who's this, please?"

"Detective Carella."

"Oh, hello, how are you?"

"If this is an incovenient time for you . . ."

"No, that's all right," she said. "What is it?"

"Mrs. Newman, I have a phone bill here that indicates your husband placed a call to the Beverly Wilshire Hotel on August seventh—that would have been Thursday evening at six twenty-one our time, three twenty-one on the Coast."

"Yes?" she said.

"When I talked to you last Friday, you told me the last time you'd spoken to your husband was on Tuesday, August fifth, isn't that correct?"

"Yes, that's exactly when I *did* speak to him."

"But apparently he called the Beverly Wilshire on Thursday, the seventh."

"At what time, did you say?"

"Three twenty-one in California."

"I was out," she said.

"You were out."

"Yes, I was out walking."

"I see. What time did you get back to the room?"

"It must have been a little before five."

"Just before you called your mother-in-law, is that right?"

"Yes. I'd been doing a lot of thinking that afternoon, I wanted to talk to her about what I'd decided."

"I see. Was there a message that your husband had called?"

"If there was, I didn't get it."

"Then you didn't know he'd tried to reach you."

"Not until just now. Are you *sure* he . . . ?"

"Well, I have the telephone bill right here," Carella said.

"Then he was still alive on Thursday," Anne said.

"It would seem so, yes."

"God," she said.

"Well," he said, "thank you, I just wanted to check this, I'm sorry to have bothered you."

"Not at all," she said, and hung up.

Carella debated whether or not the city would start screaming about the number of long-distance calls he was making, decided the hell with the city, and dialed the Beverly Wilshire Hotel in Los Angeles. The desk clerk he spoke to informed him that one copy of any telephone message was placed in a guest's box within minutes of its receipt, and another copy was slipped under the guest's door shortly thereafter. He could see no reason why a guest coming back to the hotel at a little before five would not have seen at least *one* copy of a message received at three twenty-one.

Carella thanked him and hung up.

The call from Probate came a half hour later. The clerk with Probate Division was a woman named Hester Attinger, who at Carella's request yesterday had checked to see whether any attorney had filed a will following Jeremiah Newman's death. In this state, the law required that a will be filed within ten days after knowledge of a death. Most attorneys kept a daily watch on the newspaper obituary columns to see if any of their clients had kicked the bucket overnight. And whereas most laymen did not know about the law's requirements, chances were that if they were in possession of a will, or even if they had been witnesses to the signing of a will, they would call their *own* attorney to ask what they were supposed to do. Most wills—except for those hidden at the bottom of a well or under the floorboards of a house—found their way to Probate. Jeremiah Newman's will had been filed there yesterday.

"The will is now a matter of public record," Miss Attinger

said, "so you can come down here anytime you want to look at it."

"Do you think you could read it to me on the phone?" Carella asked.

"Well . . ." she said.

"This is a homicide I'm working," he said, forgiving himself the lie. In his own mind, he had already begun classifying it as a homicide. "You'd save me a lot of time."

"I've only scanned it," Miss Attinger said. "Without going into detail, I think I can tell you the will leaves everything to a man named Louis Kern."

"As sole beneficiary?"

"Yes."

"Any alternate beneficiaries."

"Kern's wife and two children."

"Who filed the will, would you know?"

"Someone named Charles Weber, I'm assuming he's an attorney. The will's in a blue binder, and the name of the firm on the binder is Weber, Herzog and Llewellyn. That's a double L in—"

"*Herzog*, did you say?"

"What?"

"Is one of the partners named *Herzog?*"

"Yes, Herzog."

"Can you spell that for me, please?"

"H-E-R, Z-O-G," Miss Attinger said.

"Is there an address?"

"There is an address. 847 Hall Avenue, here in Isola."

"Thank you kindly," Carella said.

"No trouble at all," Miss Attinger said, and hung up.

The law offices of Weber, Herzog and Llewellyn were on the twenty-eighth floor of a building in the heart of midtown Isola. The building was delightfully cool inside, its windows sealed shut, the entire forty-two-floor structure air-conditioned from top to bottom. This was very convenient when there were no power failures. It became inconvenient only when the electric company experienced an overload at any of the upstate plants servicing the city, a common occurrence during the dog days of summer. Whenever that happened, it was impossible to open any of the windows, and the building became a forty-two-story steam bath. It was also somewhat difficult to commit suicide by defenestration in the edifice at 847 Hall.

Carella had called Charles Weber at a little past ten, and was told the busy lawyer could spare only a half hour before lunch that day. When Carella arrived, Weber was with a client. He did not buzz his secretary and ask her to show Carella in until almost a quarter to eleven. He was a portly man, in his early fifties, Carella guessed, with graying brown hair and penetrating blue eyes. He was wearing a pale-blue tropical that matched the color of his eyes, a darker-blue silk tie fronting his white shirt. The monogrammed initials C.P.W., in navy against the white, peeked from under the left-hand lapel of his suit jacket. He sat behind a large, uncluttered desk in a vast two-window office overlooking both the avenue and the western end of Grover Park, smiled pleasantly, glanced at his watch to remind Carella that this would have to be brief, and then said, "What can I do for you, Mr. Carella?"

"Mr. Weber, I'm investigating the apparent suicide of Jeremiah Newman, and I understand—"

"Apparent?" Weber said.

"Yes, sir, apparent."

"It was my understanding that he'd died of an overdose of barbiturates."

"Yes, that's true, sir. But the case hasn't yet been officially closed out as a suicide."

"I see."

"Mr. Weber, I understand you filed his will with Probate yesterday."

"I did."

"Were you the attorney who prepared the will?"

"I was."

"If I'm correct, the will leaves everything to a man named Louis Kern?"

"It does."

"Who *is* Mr. Kern, sir?"

"The owner of the Kern Gallery."

"An art gallery?"

"A very important and influential one."

"Where?"

"Here in the city. Right up the street, in fact."

"Can you tell me how much Mr. Kern stands to inherit?"

"I don't believe I'm obliged to do that, Mr. Carella."

"I already know Mr. Newman inherited several million dollars' worth of paintings when his father died. That was only two years ago. Can I safely assume...?"

"I don't want to be difficult," Weber said, and smiled. "I think you can assume, if you wish, that the estate is worth at *least* two million dollars, yes."

"And Mr. Newman left all that to Louis Kern."

"Yes."

"Why?"

"*Why?* I don't understand your question, Mr. Carella. A man is certainly entitled to decide upon his own beneficiary."

"To the exclusion of his wife? Or his mother? Or his brother?"

"His wife is adequately taken care of in an insurance policy."

"What's the face amount of the policy?"

"A hundred thousand dollars."

"So he left a hundred thousand to his wife and in excess of two million to a stranger."

"Mr. Kern isn't what you would call a *stranger*. When Lawrence Newman was alive, he exhibited all his work at the Kern Gallery. It was Mr. Kern, in fact, who appraised the paintings after he died, and later handled the sale of them for Jerry."

"So Jerry was grateful, naturally."

"Yes."

"To the tune of two million dollars."

"We only prepared the will," Weber said. "We had nothing to do with any of its directives. Mr. Newman chose his own beneficiaries. We executed the will as per his wishes. I wasn't *pleased* with what he asked us to do, but—"

"Why not?"

"Well, I don't know if you're familiar with the statutes regarding inheritance in this state..."

"No, I'm not."

"I'll explain them to you as simply as I did to Mr. Newman. In this state, if a man changes his will to exclude his wife, she's *still* entitled to a share of his estate not *less* than it would have been if he'd died intestate. Intestate means—"

"Yes, without leaving a will."

"Exactly. In other words, even if he changed his will to

exclude her, she'd *still* be entitled to half his estate if she chose to assert her right of election."

"And you explained all this to Mr. Newman?"

"Yes."

"What was his reaction?"

"He seemed intent on a punitive course of action."

"Punitive?"

"Yes. He insisted on eliminating her as beneficiary of his will. Considering his vehemence on the subject, I suggested an alternate possibility."

"And what was that?"

"A circumventive maneuver, if you will. A minimum amount *could* have been settled on his wife to satisfy her elective right. If her share of the estate would have come to more than twenty-five hundred dollars—as of course it would have, in this case— then it would have been within the law for him to have left her twenty-five hundred in cash, with half the remainder of the estate put in trust for her and providing an income for life."

"But he chose not to accept this alternative."

"He said he didn't want to leave her a *penny*. He told me he'd have to take his chances on her not asserting election. He insisted that his entire estate go to Louis Kern."

"And that's the way you drew the will."

"That's the way I drew it. A lawyer's responsibility is to advise. A client, of course, isn't obligated to accept the advice. I believe he made a mistake. Under my suggested alternative, she'd have got only the same half she'll *now* get if she asserts her elective right. Besides, it would have been more in keeping with the punitive action he had in mind."

"In what way?"

"Well, the money would have been doled out over the years, you see. The income from the trust. She would never have seen it in a lump sum of cash. Of course, asserting her right now will entail legal fees and delays and whatnot, and perhaps that was what he had in mind. Causing her as much trouble as he possibly could."

"Why would he have wanted to cause her trouble, Mr. Weber?"

"I have no idea."

"You didn't ask him?"

"I'm not a marriage counselor."

"Was the marriage in trouble?"

"Mr. Newman was a drunk."

"I know that. But from what I understand, Anne Newman was a devoted and loving wife who—"

"I did not ask Mr. Newman why he wanted to change his will. I simply advised him on the law, and then followed his wishes."

"When did he make this new will, Mr. Weber?"

"Last month sometime."

"In July?"

"Yes."

"Can you let me have the exact date?"

"Certainly," Weber said, and pressed a toggle on his intercom. "Miss Whelan," he said, "can you get me the execution date of Jeremiah Newman's will, please?" He clicked off without waiting for a response.

"Does Louis Kern know he's about to inherit such a large sum of money?" Carella asked.

"I'm sure he's been informed."

"Who informed him?"

"The Trust Department of First Liberal, I would guess. The bank that was named executor of the will."

"When would that have been?"

"Yesterday. I called them yesterday to inform them of Mr. Newman's death and to remind them they'd been named as executor."

"And you believe they, in turn, would have called Louis Kern."

"That's my belief. You're thinking of the movies, Mr. Carella, where everyone sits in a lawyer's office while a will is being read. In actual practice, that rarely ever happens. The beneficiary is usually informed by letter, or sometimes by telephone. Even in a case such as this, where Mr. Newman instructed that the will be kept confidential until after his death—"

"*Was* it kept confidential?"

"Of course."

"Mr. Weber, is someone named Herzog a member of your firm?"

"Yes, he's one of our senior partners."

"What's his first name?"

"Martin."

"Martin Herzog."

"Yes."

"Any relation to Jessica Herzog?"

"She's his sister."

"I see."

"It was Martin who introduced her to Jerry, in fact. Oh, this was many years ago." Weber suddenly smiled, "Is that a conflict-of-interest look I see on your face, Mr. Carella? There was none, believe me. A man who was a client asked that we prepare a will for him. The fact that he was once married to the sister of one of our firm's partners had no bearing on either the will's directives or our determination to see that our client's needs were served."

"Uh-huh," Carella said.

"We have a standing rule here, in fact, that neither the firm itself nor any individual working for the firm may be named as executor of any will we prepare. The rule was designed *precisely* to avoid even a *suggestion* of conflict."

"It's your belief, then, that Miss Herzog knew nothing at all about this will."

"That's my firm belief."

"You don't think Mr. Herzog might have mentioned it to his sister."

"Of course not."

The buzzer on the intercom sounded. Weber flipped the toggle.

"Yes?" he said.

"I have that execution date, sir," a woman's voice said.

"Yes, Miss Whelan?"

"It was the eighteenth of July, sir."

"Thank you," Weber said, and clicked off. "The eighteenth of July," he said to Carella.

"Exactly three weeks before he was found dead in his apartment," Carella said.

"Yes, it would seem so," Weber said.

"Well, thank you very much," Carella said. "I appreciate your time."

"Not at all," Weber said, and looked at his watch.

SEVEN

When Jessica Herzog opened the door for them at three that afternoon, she did not much resemble a captain in the Israeli Army. Carella thought she looked like a dancer in a thirties backstage movie. Kling thought she looked like an under-dressed tennis player. She was wearing very short white shorts that hugged her thighs and called stark attention to her long, magnificently tanned legs. She was also wearing, or *almost* wearing, a shirred white tube top that emphasized her exuberant breasts; Carella immediately thought of Genero's lost oppor-tunity. White high-heeled, ankle-strapped sandals added at least two inches to her already substantial height. There was a thin sheen of perspiration on her face and naked shoulders. She apologized, insincerely it seemed to both of them, for her appearance—she had been out on the terrace taking some sun—and then asked them to come in, please.

"Would you care for some iced tea?" she asked. "I have just made a pitcher."

"Yes, thank you," Carella said.

"Thanks," Kling said, and nodded to her as she went out to the kitchen.

The walls of the apartment were hung with paintings Carella automatically assumed were valuable. He knew very little about art, but he had read an article in which the wheelings and dealings of the art world made the price-fixing of the big-business cartels seem like the trading kids did for bubble-gum cards. He had come away with the understanding that even minor artists could be maneuvered into positions of status and wealth by powerful dealers and critics, and he wondered now whether Lawrence Newman, who had left his son two million dollars' worth of paintings when he'd died, had been the grateful recipient of such manipulation. The room was similarly adorned with pieces of sculpture standing on pedestals or resting on tabletops, some of them representational nude studies in bronze, most of them abstract; Carella guessed the unfathomable ones were the ones worth real money. A large metal mobile hung from the ceiling just inside the sliding glass doors that led to the terrace— Right where someone can bang his head on it, Carella thought.

"Shall we go outside?" Jessica said.

She was carrying a tray upon which were three glasses of iced tea with lemon wedges in them. The deeper brown color of the tea, the floating paler hint of yellow, the white shorts, top, and shoes all seemed designed to complement Jessica's superb tan, the way the white walls of the apartment itself had been designed to enhance the paintings that hung on them, the pieces of sculpture that floated in the space they enclosed. Floating in the space that enclosed her, Jessica moved fluidly to the sliding glass doors, waited while Kling opened one of them for her, and then led the detectives out onto the terrace, where she put the tray down on a small round table flanked by two lounge chairs.

From up here, the city that spread below them looked almost benign.

"So," she said, "please, help yourselves. I did not put sugar, did you wish sugar?"

"No, thank you," Carella said.

"No, thanks," Kling said.

"It is so hot, truly," she said, dabbing with a crumpled Kleenex at the cleft above the shirred tube top. "Will you sit down, please? I'll get another chair."

She slid open the door, went into the living room again, and returned not a moment later with a straight-backed chair that she placed against the low terrace wall. Neither of the detectives had yet seated themselves.

"Please," she said, and indicated the lounge chairs.

They both sat.

"So," she said, "what is it you wish to talk about? You said on the phone that some information had come to light."

"Yes, Miss Herzog," Carella said. "I learned this morning from your former husband's attorney that he left his entire estate to a man named Louis Kern. Something in excess of two million dollars."

"Well, I am not surprised," Jessica said. "His father's paintings, you know, were worth quite a bit of money."

"Miss Herzog, the law firm that made the will for Mr. Newman is a firm named Weber, Herzog and Llewellyn."

"Yes?"

"Your brother works for that firm."

"Yes?"

"Mr. Newman changed his will on the eighteenth of July, three weeks before he was found dead in the apartment on Silvermine Oval."

"But what has this to do with me or my brother?"

"Did you know Mr. Newman had changed his will?"

"No, of course not."

"Your brother never mentioned it to you?"

"Certainly not. In any event, what would that have to do with me? Am I inheriting something?"

"Not that I know of. Are you?"

"Of course not."

"Do you know Louis Kern?"

"No. Who is he?"

"He owns the Kern Gallery here in Isola."

"I do not know him."

"But you were familiar with the art world..."

"Yes?"

"...when you were still married to Jerry?"

"Yes, I was."

"Didn't you know that your father-in-law exhibited his paintings at the Kern Gallery?"

"I may have known it."

"Yes or no?"

"Why do I have to answer these questions?" Jessica asked. "Is this Nazi Germany?"

"No, ma'am, it isn't," Carella said. "But what's so difficult about answering a simple question about an art gallery?"

"You are saying that I knew about Jerry's will. You are saying the will may have had something to do with his death."

"I'm simply asking whether you knew your father-in-law exhibited his paintings at the Kern Gallery."

"No, you are asking whether my brother told me anything about Jerry's will. And I have already told you no. Why then do you persist in . . . ?"

"Miss Herzog," Carella said slowly, "this isn't Agatha Christie."

"What?" she said.

"I'm a civil-service employee with a job to do. I don't *like* shlepping all over the city in this heat, I don't *like* checking out a brother-sister relationship that may or may not have led to a breach of confidentiality, I really don't. I would much prefer sitting here on a nice terrace, sipping iced tea, and getting myself a suntan. But your former husband ended up dead three weeks after he changed his will. If anyone had prior knowledge of that will—"

"I had no prior knowledge of it."

"I'm not suggesting you had anything to do with—"

"I certainly did not."

"But if you *did* know of the will, and if you mentioned it to anyone who might have *benefited* from the terms of the—"

"I do not know this Louis Kern. I had no knowledge of the will. Are you forgetting that I am the one who suggested to you that Jeremiah could not have voluntarily taken those pills?"

"No, Miss Herzog, I haven't forgotten."

"But now you suspect that *I*, or my brother, may have had something to do with his death. Because of his will. When it was *I* who came to you in the first place, Detective Carella, to tell you he could not possibly have committed suicide by—"

"Yes, Miss Herzog, I know that."

"I do not have to answer your questions."

"Miss Herzog—"

"This is not Nazi Germany," she said, and suddenly she was weeping.

The tears startled them both.

"I should not have come to you in the first place," she said. "I thought I would be doing my duty as a citizen, but instead—" She groped blindly for the crumpled tissue in the shirred tube top, dabbed at her eyes with it. "Now there will be trouble for all of us. I should have stayed away from you entirely, I should have minded my own business."

"All of us?" Carella said.

"Yes, yes," she said, weeping, drying her eyes "Me, Louis, *all* of us."

The detectives looked at each other.

"Louis Kern, do you mean?"

"Yes, Louis," she said. "Oh God, I should not have come to see you. Now there will be only trouble."

"What kind of trouble, Miss Herzog?"

"He is married, he has two children."

They waited.

"We have been lovers," she said.

Still, they waited.

"For many years now. And when my brother told me he was to inherit such a large sum of money, I naturally . . . we are lovers. I told him."

"Then you *did* know about the will."

"Yes."

"When did your brother give you this information?"

"Only last week."

"And you told Mr. Kern?"

"Yes."

"When?"

"Last Thursday. When I was with him last Thursday."

Carella nodded.

"Now there will be trouble," Jessica said. "I know it."

The Kern Gallery was on the wide cross street running arrow straight between the Majesta Bridge on the south shore of Isola, and the docks lining the River Harb on the north. The two street-floor windows of the gallery were crowded with French impressionist paintings, and a printed placard informed any passersby that the current show had started on August sixth and would continue through the end of the month. Carella and Kling stopped at the desk just inside the entrance door, and asked a blond receptionist where they might find Mr. Kern. She directed them to an office on the second floor of the gallery.

They took the elevator up, and found themselves in an open room the size of Guadalcanal and littered with what appeared to be the wreckage of half a dozen World War II bombers. A poster on the wall, featuring a photograph of one of the crashed B-29's, informed them that this was the work of a sculptor named Manfred Wills. They walked past what looked like a smashed rear turret with a gnarled machine gun poking out of its plastic bubble, and followed a discreet sign lettered OFFICES, a small arrow under the word directing them to turn left through an arched doorway. At the end of the corridor, Carella showed his shield to a young brunette sitting at a desk there.

"We'd like to see Mr. Kern, please," he said.

"Who shall I say is here, sir?"

"Detectives Carella and Kling, Eighty-seventh Squad."

The girl rose from behind the desk. She was taller than she'd appeared sitting, and she was wearing tight-fitting tailored slacks that emphasized the long, slender look of her. She was gone only a moment. When she came back, she told Carella that Mr. Kern was on the phone and would be with them shortly.

"Could I see that again?" she asked. "Your badge?"

Carella showed her his shield and the lucite-encased I.D. card.

"Gee," she said, "that's the first time I ever saw one of those. It actually says 'Detective,' on the badge, doesn't it?"

"Yes," Carella said.

"Gee," the girl said. The phone on her desk buzzed. She lifted the receiver, listened, and then said, "You can go in now."

Louis Kern was sitting behind a white modern desk. The walls of his office were covered with abstract paintings, a riot of primary colors that overwhelmed the singularly drab man himself. He was wearing a dark gray flannel suit—with the heat outside standing at ninety-nine degrees—and a white button-down shirt with a black wool knit tie. He had graying tufts of hair over each ear, but he was bald otherwise, and his pale, almost ghostly face indicated that he was not an avid beachgoer. Carella guessed his age at seventy or thereabouts.

"Mr. Kern," he said, "we're investigating the suicide of Jeremiah Newman, I wonder if you can spare us a little of your time."

"Yes, certainly," Kern said.

He had the thick, rasping voice of a heavy smoker. An ashtray on his desk was brimming with butts, and he reached for a package of unfiltered cigarettes now, and offered them to Carella and Kling—who both shook their heads—before lighting one himself. A cloud of smoke, the color of the wisps of hair around his ears, hovered above his head.

"Mr. Kern, do you know that you're the beneficiary of Mr. Newman's will?" Carella asked.

"I do," Kern said.

"When did you learn that, sir?"

"Yesterday. I got a call from the bank."

"Did they tell you how much you might expect to inherit?"

"Yes. Something more than two million dollars."

"Were you surprised?"

"By the sum? No, I knew Jerry was well-off."

"By the fact that you were named as sole beneficiary."

Kern hesitated.

"Well, no," he said at last. "I can't truthfully say I was surprised."

"Then you knew about it before the bank called."

"Yes, I knew."

"Would you have found out about the will from Jessica Herzog?"

Kern looked startled.

"Mr. Kern?"

"Yes," he said, and nodded. "Jessica told me about it last week."

"How would you define your relationship with her, sir?"

Again Kern hesitated. Then he sighed and said, "We have been keeping steady company for the past five years now."

The expression "steady company," in this day and age, sounded singularly old-fashioned to Carella, a term the elderly Kern might have used when there were still horses and buggies in the streets of Isola. But there was nothing old-fashioned about two million dollars in a city where murder was often done for a couple of bucks, the contents of a mugging victim's wallet. Two million dollars was definitely not popcorn. Jerry Newman had signed his new will on the eighteenth of July, and Louis Kern had known about it on the Thursday before Newman was found dead.

"Mr. Kern," Carella said, "I wonder if you can give me a rundown on your whereabouts for Thursday, the seventh of August."

"What?"

"I said I wonder if you can—"

"I heard what you said, but why should I provide you with such information?"

"Because I'm a police officer diligently pursuing an investigation, and I would appreciate your cooperation."

"You're suggesting, aren't you, that since I *knew* I was to inherit a large sum of money..."

"No, sir, I'm not."

Kern shrugged. "I have nothing to hide," he said, and shrugged again.

"Fine, sir. Then can you tell me...?"

"I'll get my calendar," Kern said.

In the afternoon stillness of the stark white office, Carella and Kling pored over Kern's appointment calendar for the week preceding the discovery of the body, zeroing in on Thursday, the seventh of August, when Jerry Newman had made a phone call to California at 6:21 p.m.

Kern's calendar for that day showed appointments at ten, eleven, and twelve. He identified the people in chronological order as a painter, a gallery-owner from Palm Beach, and the trustee of a private art collection in Boston. His luncheon date, at twelve-thirty that afternoon, was with someone identified on his calendar only as J.H., who Kern now admitted was Jessica Herzog. He had gone back to her apartment after lunch, there to enjoy—among other things—the good news that he would inherit two million dollars when Jerry Newman died. At four that afternoon, he'd met with a man wanting to sell a vast collection of pre-Columbian art to the gallery.

Drinks at six that night and dinner at six-thirty had been with his wife and a few friends whom Kern identified by name, after which they'd all gone on to the opening of a musical titled *Caper*, another hopeless attempt—according to the review the next morning—to weld music with mystery. As they looked at the calendar entry now, Kern gave his own capsule review; music terrific, book rotten. He also mentioned that he had gone afterward to the opening-night party at Baffin's, a midtown restaurant catering to theatrical people, and had remained there until close to one in the morning, by which time all the newspaper reviews were in; the television critics had already been heard from, and the show seemed doomed.

"My wife was with me," he said. "So were five hundred other people."

"Where'd you go when you left Baffin's?" Kling asked.

"Directly home."

"And where's that, Mr. Kern?"

"1241 South McCormick."

"Is there a doorman there?"

"There is. He saw my wife and me when we got back to the apartment."

"What time would that have been?"

"One-thirty or thereabouts."

"What time did you leave the next morning?"

"Nine-thirty."

"And went where?"

"I came directly here to the gallery."

Kern looked as clean as the bald pate that glistened between the bookend fringes of his hair. The detectives thanked him for his time, and went downstairs to the cauldron of the street again. Carella had forgotten to turn down the visor with its POLICE DEPARTMENT VEHICLE placard clipped to it. An overzealous patrolman had stuck a parking ticket under the windshield wiper on the driver's side of the car.

"Great," he said, and unlocked the door, and then leaned into the car to yank up the lock-button on the passenger side. As he started the engine, he asked, "Have you talked to Augusta yet?"

"Yeah," Kling said. "Last night."

"And?"

"We worked it out." He hesitated. "It was nothing."

Carella looked at him. "Well, good," he said.

"Nothing at all, like you said."

"Good," Carella said, but he glanced again at Kling before easing the car out into the steady stream of traffic.

At ten minutes to nine that night, Kling stood outside the building on Hopper Street and looked at its façade. Ground floor, first floor, second, third, fourth, fifth. Four windows on each of the stories above the street-level floor. The windows on the third and fourth floors were dark now. Businesses, he thought. Maybe she'd been there on a business appointment, after all. But why had none of the six names he'd copied from the directory sounded like business firms? He went to the front door of the building and shook the knob. Locked. He found a bell button marked SERVICE in the doorjamb, and pressed it. A loud ringing sounded inside someplace. He rang the bell again.

He heard footsteps within, approaching the door, and then a man's voice saying, "I'm coming, I'm coming."

He waited.

"Who is it?" the man asked from behind the door.

"Police," Kling said.

He heard a lock being turned, the tumblers falling. Good secure lock, he thought, looking at the keyway. The door opened a crack. An eye and a narrow slice of face appeared in the wedge.

"Let's see it," the man said.

Kling held up his shield. "Detective Atchison," he said.

There was no Detective Atchison on the Eight-Seven. He had not used his own name because Augusta's phantom lover would undoubtedly know it, nor had he used the name of any other detective on the squad, on the assumption that Augusta may have dropped it in her casual pillow talk with the son of a bitch she was seeing. He had no intention of showing his I.D. card. His name was not on his shield. Beneath the Police Department legend and the city's seal, there was only the word DETECTIVE and his serial number.

The man opened the door wide.

He was a white man in his sixties, wearing only a tank top undershirt and baggy cotton trousers. He looked Kling over, and then said, "I'm Henry Watkins, superintendent of the building. What's the violation this time?"

"No violation," Kling said. "Okay to come in?"

"What'd you say your name was?"

"Atchison."

"Like Atchison, Topeka, and Santa Fe?" Watkins said.

"That's it," Kling said.

"Used to be a railroad man," Watkins said, and stepped aside to allow Kling entrance. "So what is it?" he asked, closing and locking the door again.

"Looking for a runaway," Kling said. "I have information she may be living in the building here."

He normally carried, stuffed into the back of his notebook, a dozen or more photographs of teenage runaways who might have found their way uptown to the headier narcotic climate of the Eight-Seven, where the grass was presumably greener and more easily obtainable than it was elsewhere in the city. He took his notebook from his hip pocket, and leafed through the pictures, selecting a graduation photo of a chubby seventeen-year-old-girl beaming at the camera, black-rimmed eyeglasses perched on her freckled nose, blond hair neatly combed, eyes sparkling. He wondered what she looked like now. If she'd come to this city—

He showed the photograph to Watkins.

"This is the girl," he said. "Her name's Heather Laughlin. Have you seen her in the building at any time?"

"Get a lot of traffic here," Watkins said, looking at the picture. "Two photographers in the building, we get girls coming and going all the time."

Photographers, Kling thought. Maybe Augusta *had* been here on business, after all. He took out the list of names he'd copied from the directory.

"Which one of these would be the photographers?" he asked.

Watkins scanned the list.

"Well, there's Peter Lang on the third floor and Al Garavelli on the fourth. They're both photographers."

"How come they don't list themselves as such in the directory?" Kling asked.

"If you're a cop, you should know that."

"What should I know?"

"Lots of burglars check out a lobby directory, spot a listing for a photographer, come back that night and try to rip off the studio. Lots of cameras in a photographer's studio—pretty easy items to fence. Also, lots of them work with music going, you know. Expensive stereo equipment. Photographers are easy marks for burglars. You should know that."

"Now I know it," Kling said, and smiled. "Do these people *live* here as well? Lang, is it? and Garavelli?"

"No, they just got their studios here. Nine to five. Well, usually later than that. I got their home addresses inside, you want them. Case of emergency, you know. Got to know where I can reach my tenants. You should know that."

"How about the rest of these people?" Kling said, and showed him the list again.

"Yeah, they're residents."

"Any of them home right now?"

"Well, I'm not obliged to check on the comings and goings of any of my tenants. You should know that. They all got keys to the outside door here, they come and go as they please, same as anywhere else in this city."

"I'll have to talk to them," Kling said.

"Then I'd better put on a shirt, come up with you."

"I don't want to inconvenience you," Kling said.

"That's what I'm paid for. Tenants wouldn't want me letting people in to wander around the building without my—"

"But I'm a police officer," Kling said.

"Well, yes, so you are."

"I'm sure they wouldn't expect you to—"

"Well, maybe not," Watkins said. "Third and fourth floor're dark, that's where Lang and Garavelli work. You can take the steps up, try your luck with the others." He looked at his watch. "It's almost ten o'clock, people don't like cops banging on their doors in the middle of the night, you should know that."

"Sorry, but my information indicates—"

"Sure," Watkins said. "Knock on my door when you're finished, if it ain't too late, I'll give you those addresses. And be sure you explain I offered to come with you, will you? When you talk to the tenants."

"Yes, I will," Kling said. "Thanks."

"Sure," Watkins said.

Kling took the iron-runged steps up to the first floor. Below, he could hear Watkins closing and locking the door to his own apartment. The steps and the first-floor landing were badly lighted. There was only one door on the landing. He went to it. No bell. He knocked on the door. Silence. He knocked again.

"Yo?" a voice inside said. A man.

"Police," Kling said.

"What?" the man said.

"Police," Kling said again.

"Just a second," the man said.

Kling waited.

The door opened a crack, held by a night chain.

"What is it?" the man said.

"May I come in a moment, please?" Kling said, holding up his shield. "I'm Detective Atchison, Isola Police, I'd like to ask a few questions, sir." He had not mentioned the precinct for which he worked. He put the shield in its leather case back into his pocket almost at once.

"Yeah, just a second," the man said, and took off the night chain and opened the door.

He was wearing running shorts and track shoes, nothing else. He was perhaps five feet, eight inches tall, a spare, balding white man with dark-brown eyes and a thin nose under which there was a mustache the color of the black hair curled on his naked chest. A fan was going somewhere in the apartment. Kling could hear the whir of its blades and could feel the faint breeze it stirred.

"Well, come in," the man said. "Kind of late to be making a visit, ain't it?"

"I'm sorry, sir, but we have to follow leads whenever we get them."

"What kind of lead are you following?" the man asked. "Come in, come in."

"I'm sorry, sir," Kling said, stepping into the apartment. "Are you . . . ?" He consulted the list of names he'd copied from the directory downstairs. Apartment 11, Lucas, M. "Mr. Lucas?"

"Michael Lucas, yes," he said, and closed and locked the door, and then put on the night chain again.

The apartment was a converted loft that obviously served now as a combined living space and artist's studio. An easel was set up near the windows to the north, the sky outside black beyond them, a large abstract painting shrieking its colors into the room. A cot was set up against one wall, a table-top burner and a refrigerator against another. The loft was vast. The wooden floors were paint-spattered. A rack against the third wall supported at least a dozen huge canvases that seemed to have been spattered in the same haphazard fashion as the floor had been.

"So, what's so urgent?" Lucas asked.

"We're looking for a runaway," Kling said, and took the picture from his notebook. "We have information she may be living in this building. Ever see this girl?"

Lucas looked at the picture.

"No," he said at once.

"Do you live here alone, Mr. Lucas?" Kling asked.

"What's that got to do with anything?"

"I was wondering if anyone *else* living in the apartment might have seen her."

"I live here alone."

"Got the whole floor, right?"

"The whole floor, right."

"You're an artist, I see."

"I try to be."

"That's a nice painting," Kling said, nodding toward the easel.

"Thanks."

"Do you use models for that kind of stuff?"

"*What* kind of *stuff?*" Lucas said.

"You know, this . . . uh . . . nonrepresentational, do you call it?"

"I call it abstract expressionism," Lucas said. "We *all* call it abstract expressionism."

"Are you familiar with the work of Lawrence Newman?" Kling asked.

Lucas looked surprised. "Yes," he said. "How come you know Newman's work?"

"Well, you know," Kling said, and smiled. "I drop into the Kern Gallery every now and then."

"Uh-huh," Lucas said, and was silent for a moment. "What's this *really* about?" he asked suddenly. "Larry's son killing himself?"

"What?" Kling said.

"His son committed suicide last week, it was in all the papers. Is that why you're here?"

"I don't know about that case," Kling said.

"It was in all the papers."

"Well, I'm looking for a runaway." Kling said, and smiled. "You haven't seen her, huh?"

"No," Lucas said.

"Are you here all day long?" Kling asked.

"Why do you want to know?"

"Because if she really *is* living in the building . . ."

"I'm here all day, this is where I work," Lucas said.

"She was seen here yesterday, that's what our informant told us. Were you here yesterday?"

"I was here yesterday."

Kling made a show of consulting his notebook. "Between the hours of twelve-thirty and one forty-five?"

"I didn't see her."

"Maybe your model . . ."

"I don't use a model."

"Did you have *any* visitors at all between those hours?"

"What's that to you?"

"I'm trying to locate a girl who's been missing from her home in Kansas for almost two years, Mr. Lucas. This is the first fresh lead we've had. I'm trying to find out if *somebody*, for Christ's sake, might have *seen* her. I know this is a little late to be making the rounds this way, but I'd appreciate your help, sir, I really would. Her parents—"

"I was alone during that time," Lucas said.

"No visitors?"

"None."

"And you haven't seen her?"

"I haven't seen her."

"Thank you, Mr. Lucas. I'd appreciate it if you took another look at the photo, and if you *do* happen to see her—" He cut himself short just in time. He'd been about to follow normal procedure, give the man his card, ask him to call him at the Eight-Seven if anything came up.

"Yeah, what?" Lucas said.

"I'll be back in a few days, you can let me know then."

"I thought this was urgent," Lucas said. "If it's so fuckin' *urgent*—"

"I'll give you my card," Kling said, "with a number where I can be reached." Again, he made a show of looking through his notebook, even though he kept his cards in the slipcase of the leather folder containing his shield and his lucite-enclosed identification card. "I'm all out," he said. "If you've got a piece of paper, I'll jot it down for you."

"Just give it to me," Lucas said, "I'll remember it."

Kling knew he had no intention of remembering it. He reeled off the number for the Headquarters building on High Street, thanked Lucas for his time, and then went out into the hall again. He should not have brought up Lawrence Newman's name. He

had done so only to crack Lucas's hostile façade, show him he
was familiar with the world of abstract expressionism, but he'd
only succeeded instead in arousing suspicion about his cover story.
He would not make that mistake again. He climbed the dimly
lighted stairway to the second floor of the building. Two doors
here, one at either end of the hallway. He pressed the bell button
outside the door to the right of the stairwell. Apartment 21. Healy,
M., and Rosen, M. A buzzer sounded inside.

"Who is it?" a woman's voice called.

"Police," he said.

"Police?" The voice sounded totally astonished. He waited
until she opened the door for him, and then he went through
the routine of identifying himself as Detective Atchison, and
giving her a brief glimpse of his shield and then asking her if
he might come in and show her a picture of the runaway he
was looking for.

The woman's name was Martha Healy.

She was tall and angularly built, wearing black tights and
a yellow halter top that matched the color of the hair massed
and pinned on top of her head. Her eyes were green—like
Augusta's. She had wiry legs and arms, and he suspected she
was a dancer even before she told him she was. There was
another woman in the apartment, a small, dark-eyed brunette
in her twenties, wearing only panties and a T-shirt. The T-shirt
was lettered with the words SQUEEZE ME. She was lying on a
sofa against one of the walls, leafing through a magazine and
smoking. She looked up when Kling came in, and then went
back to the magazine.

The apartment had obviously been one section of a loft,
now divided to form the two living units on this floor of the
building. Mirrors lined one entire wall of the room, from floor
to ceiling. "For when I practice," Martha explained. There were
no proper walls dividing the living spaces; many of these converted lofts tried to maintain the feeling of openness that had
been there originally. Living room melted into bedroom and
kitchen and then a small area lined with bookshelves. Kling
smelled marijuana on the air, and realized that what the girl
on the sofa was smoking was pot. Nobody bothered flushing
a joint when the Law arrived these days; he had been in movie
theaters where the cloud of marijuana smoke was enough to

produce a high if you just inhaled deeply. Augusta smoked marijuana. So did Kling himself, on occasion.

"Have you seen her around?" he asked, and handed Martha the photograph.

"No," Martha said. "How about you, Michelle?"

"What?" the brunette said.

"You see this kid around anyplace?" she asked, and moved to the couch, a dancer's walk, somewhat stiff-legged and duck-footed. She handed the photograph to Michelle, who studied it through a marijuana haze.

"No," Michelle said. "Don't know her."

"Are you both here most of the time?" Kling asked.

"In and out," Martha said.

"How about yesterday, between twelve-thirty and one forty-five?"

"I was in class. Michelle?"

"I was here."

"Alone?" Kling asked.

"Alone," she said, and looked at him, and smiled suddenly and radiantly. She had Bugs Bunny teeth.

"Because if you had any visitors, one of them might've seen—"

"We save our visitors for the nighttime," Martha said. She looked at Michelle, who was still smiling. The women exchanged a glance. Kling thought he saw Martha nod, almost imperceptibly.

"No one here then, huh?" he said. "Between twelve-thirty and one forty-five?"

"Just little old me," Michelle said, still grinning like Bugs Bunny.

"So they send you out on this kind of thing at night, huh?" Martha said, and sat Indian-fashion on one of the throw pillows scattered on the floor.

"Well, whenever we get something that looks like real meat, we usually—"

"Real meat, huh?" Martha said.

"Yes, that's what we—"

"Real meat, Michelle," Martha said.

"So how late do they keep you working?" Michelle asked. She had put down the magazine, and was sitting up cross-

legged on the couch now, the same way Martha was sitting on
the throw pillow. Her panties were blue.

"Well, this is on my own time, actually," Kling said.

"They make you work on your own time, too, huh?" Martha
said.

"Yes. Sometimes."

"What time do you think you'll be quitting?" Martha said.

"Whenever I get done with the building," Kling said. "Few
more people to see here."

"Just the fifth floor," Michelle said. "Peter and Al are only
here during the day."

"Yes, I know that. The photographers, you mean."

"Yeah, the faggot photographers," Michelle said. "And
there's only one apartment on the fifth, shouldn't take you long
up there."

"But there's another apartment on *this* floor, isn't there?"
Kling said.

"Yeah, Franny next door in twenty-two," Martha said.

"She's never here," Michelle said. "She's usually uptown
with Zooey."

"Zooey?"

"Her boyfriend. His name's Frank Ziegler, we call him
Zooey."

"Is he ever here during the daytime?" Kling asked.

"Zooey? No, he works for an advertising agency someplace
on Jefferson."

"How about Franny?"

"I don't know what she does," Martha said. "Michelle thinks
she's a hooker. Oops," she said, "I keep forgetting you're a
cop."

"You don't look like a cop, though," Michelle said.

"He looks like an actor or something, doesn't he?" Martha
said.

"Yeah," Michelle said. "Or a ballplayer. A baseball player,
you know?"

"An actor, I thought," Martha said.

"Some kind of athlete," Michelle said.

Again, the glance passed between the two women. This
time, Kling was positively certain about Martha's small nod.

"Would you like a drink or something?" she asked.

"No, thanks, I'm not allowed to—"

"You said this was your own time."

"It is, but technically—"

"How about some grass then?" Michelle asked.

"No, no," Kling said, and smiled.

"Listen," Martha said, "why don't you come back down when you're through?"

Kling looked at her.

"If you'd be interested in a two-on-one, that is," Michelle said matter-of-factly.

"Thanks," Kling said, "but—"

"That's a water bed over there," Martha said.

"King-size," Michelle said. "What's your first name?"

"Jerry," he said, thinking he was picking the name out of the air until he realized, not a second later, that Jerry Newman was the name of the man who'd been found dead uptown on Friday morning.

"Come back down later, Jerry," Martha said.

"Well, I'll see," Kling said, and began moving toward the door.

"Listen, we mean it, Jerry," Michelle said.

"Thanks, I'll see," Kling said. "And thanks for your—"

"What time do you have to go to work in the morning?" Martha said.

"I'm due in at eight."

"Nice long night, Jerry," Michelle said.

"Shouldn't take you long to do the fifth floor, should it?" Martha said.

"Ten minutes or so, right?" Michelle said.

"Well . . ." he said, and smiled again, and went to the door and opened it. "Good night," he said.

"See you later," Martha said.

"Ten minutes," Michelle said.

He closed the door behind him. He heard the lock tumblers falling, and then the night chain rattling into place. He put his ear to the door.

"You think he'll be back?" Martha said.

"Oh, sure," Michelle said.

Silence.

"That was a bunch of bullshit, wasn't it?" Martha said. "The runaway bit."

"Oh, sure," Michelle said. "He's lookin' to get laid."

He waited. Silence. He kept waiting. Nothing more. He went to the door at the other end of the hall, and knocked on it. Franny's apartment. That would be Harris, F. in the directory downstairs. Franny who was never home. Franny who was maybe a hooker. He knocked again. Still no answer. He knocked once more, to be certain, and then took the steps up to the third floor. There was only one door on the landing, marked with a white-on-black plastic nameplate: PETER LANG. One of the faggot photographers. He continued on up to the fourth floor. The light was out on the landing there. He picked his way through the dark and up the stairs to the fifth floor.

The man who opened the door to apartment 51 could have been an idealized mirror-image of Kling himself, slightly taller, six-two or -three, Kling guessed, with a shock of blond hair not unlike his own, brown eyes set in a handsome, rough-hewn face, a nose any male model in New York would have pillaged and killed for, a cleft chin, and a petulant mouth. He was wearing designer jeans and nothing else. He'd lifted weights when he was younger, Kling was certain of that. His shoulders were enormous, his chest and his arms were bulging with muscle.

"Detective Atchison," Kling said, "Isola Police."

"Let me see that again," the man said.

Kling held the shield up again.

"What precinct is that?" he asked.

"The Three-Two," Kling lied.

"Where's your I.D. card?"

"We're getting new ones issued," Kling said.

"So, where's your *old* one?"

"Had to turn it in so I could get the new one," Kling said. "Why? What's the problem? Would you like to call my lieutenant to verify I'm a bona fide cop."

"You're supposed to have an I.D. card," the man said.

"You can't buy this shield in the five-and-ten," Kling said. "Forget it, I'll come back next week, when I get the new card. Thanks for your cooperation, mister. There's nothing a man likes better on a night like this than to climb up all these stairs—"

"Come in, calm down," the man said. "What is it you want?"

"I'm looking for a runaway," Kling said.

"There're lots of burglaries in this neighborhood." the man

said, closing and locking the door behind them. "You learn to be careful."

"I can understand that. I'm sorry about the I.D., it's just one of those stupid departmental—"

"Don't sweat it," the man said.

"Ever see this girl anywhere in the building?" Kling asked, and showed him the picture. "I'm sorry, I didn't get your name."

"Bradford Douglas," he said, taking the picture.

Bradford Douglas. Douglas, B. in the directory downstairs, apartment 51.

"Recognize her?" Kling said.

"No, I don't know her," Douglas said, and handed back the picture.

"Do you live here, or work here, or what?" Kling asked.

"I live here."

"What kind of work do you do, Mr. Douglas?"

"What's that question got to do with your runaway?"

"I'm trying to find out whether you were here in the building yesterday between—"

"Why do you want to know that?"

"Because the girl was seen here sometime between twelve-thirty and one forty-five yesterday . . ."

"I was only here till noon."

"You left at noon?"

"Yes. I was waiting for a friend of mine . . ."

"What time did your friend get here?"

"At a little past twelve. What the hell can *that* have to do . . . ?"

"A visitor might've seen her," Kling said. "If somebody came to visit, he . . . or she . . . might've seen the girl." He hesitated. "Who was here, can you tell me?"

"No."

"Why not?"

"Let's say it would be indiscreet of me, okay?"

"In what way?"

"Let's say marriage is a delicate arrangement, okay?"

"Oh, are you married, Mr. Douglas?"

"No."

"Then your visitor—"

"End of conversation," Douglas said.

"I wish you'd help me, Mr. Douglas. Because, you see, this girl's been missing for two years now, and if there's anyone who might've seen her—"

"End of conversation," Douglas said again.

"You left here at twelve, huh?"

"A lttle after twelve, yes."

"Left your visitor here alone, huh?"

"I don't want to talk about any visitors," Douglas said.

"Where'd you go? When you left here."

"To work."

"What kind of work do you do?"

"I'm a model," Douglas said.

"Photographer's model?"

"Yes."

"Fashion or what?"

"Mostly fashion, occasional beefcake."

"Uh-huh," Kling said.

"Will *that* help you find your runaway?" Douglas asked.

"No, but—"

"I didn't think it would. If you'll excuse me now, I've got company."

"Company?"

"In the other room."

"Could *she* possibly have seen . . . ?"

"Is that a trick question?"

"What?"

"The *she*. Are you trying to find out if my company's a woman?"

"Well, no, I'm—"

"She *is*, okay?"

"Fine," Kling said.

"That it?"

"Could she possibly have seen the girl I'm looking for?"

"No."

"How do you know that?"

"Because she wasn't here yesterday afternoon when you say your runaway was spotted."

"Ah, okay then," Kling said. He's playing the field, he thought. If this is the guy, you picked yourself a fine one, Gussie.

Douglas led him to the door.

"Hope you find her," he said.

"Yes, thanks a lot," Kling said.

The door closed behind him. He waited until Douglas had locked it and chained it, and then put his ear to the wood.

"It's okay," he heard Douglas call. "He's gone now."

EIGHT

The drug bust was scheduled to go down at ten forty-five that Wednesday night. At a meeting in the lieutenant's office at a little before noon, Byrnes offered the opinion that perhaps Meyer Meyer wasn't yet physically fit enough to lead the team in. Meyer had been shot in the leg on Christmas Day, and although this was already August, he was still limping a little. "It's the humidity," he kept telling everyone in the squad room. He told that to Byrnes now.

"I was thinking a position behind the others," Byrnes said.

The lieutenant was a man with the compact head of a bullet, his iron-gray hair clipped short and parted on the left, his blue eyes moving first to Meyer's left thigh and then to the area just below Meyer's kneecap, drilling the leg in question as surely as the .38-caliber slugs had done last Christmas.

The "others" to whom he'd referred were draped around the lieutenant's office in various postures of inattentiveness, Hal Willis half-sitting on the window ledge, Cotton Hawes sitting in a chair near the lieutenant's bookcase with the bound law books he rarely consulted anymore, Arthur Brown leaning against the closed door, his arms folded across his chest. The four-man team, because they'd been conducting the six-month long stakeout, was supposed to enter the suspect apartment first, six patrolmen from the Eight-Seven behind their flying wedge, and two brave Narc cops bringing up the rear.

"How you gonna kick in the door?" Byrnes asked.

"With my right leg," Meyer said. "I *always* use my right leg."

"How's your *left* leg gonna support you?"

"It'll support me," Meyer said. "It's just the humidity, Loot."

The lieutenant looked dubious.

"You miss that lock on the first kick, there's gonna be a hail of bullets coming through the wood," he said.

"How can I possibly miss the lock?" Meyer asked. "I'm not *blind*, Pete, it's only my *leg* got shot."

"I mean kick it *open*," Byrnes said. "You don't bring enough force against it, those guys inside'll start shooting."

"Have we got our warrant?" Willis asked.

He was the shortest man on the squad, measuring five-feet eight inches in his stockinged feet, and having barely cleared the Department's height requirement at a time when inches used to count. That was before a five-foot-six former bartender brought suit against the city—for refusing even to *look* at his application for a job with the Police Department—on grounds that he was being discriminated against because of his size. After the man won his case, the joke running through all the precincts was that pretty soon there'd be jobs on the force for three-foot tall midgets, who could close any illegally opened fire hydrant without having to stoop over. Willis hadn't found the joke comical.

"We've got the warrant?" Meyer said.

"With a No-Knock?"

"With a No-Knock."

"Are we wearing vests?" Hawes asked.

He was six feet two inches tall, and his long legs were sprawled out halfway across the lieutenant's small office. Sunlight streaming through the window touched his red hair, setting it aglow; the white streak of hair over his left temple resembled a puff of sifted ashes against a bed of embers. He was very hungry. As he waited for the lieutenant's answer, his stomach grumbled, and he glanced at Brown as though accusing *him* of the indiscretion.

"Damn vests are more trouble then they're worth," Meyer said. "What do you think?"

"If there's gonna be shooting . . ."

"There might be."

"Then let's use the vests." Hawes said simply, and shrugged. His stomach growled again.

"I'm asking for a volunteer," Byrnes said flatly.

"Pete, it's *my* team," Meyer said. "If anybody's gonna kick in that door . . ."

"I'll walk point," Brown said.

He was the only black man on the squad, a Detective 2nd/ Grade who was taller and broader than Hawes, measuring six feet four inches and weighing in at two hundred and twenty pounds. When Arthur Brown kicked in a door, it *really* got kicked in. When Arthur Brown kicked in a door over in Calm's Point, it sailed over the bridge and landed in the river, near Bethtown.

"We put you on point, Caroline may become a widow," Hawes said. "Let me take it, Pete."

"Listen, what the hell *is* this?" Meyer said. "I'm all of a sudden a cripple? Maybe I should put in for a disability pension."

"I don't want to risk that door," Byrnes said.

"You want me to demonstrate for you?" Meyer said heatedly. "Lock your fuckin' door, Loot, I'll kick it open for you."

"This has nothing to do with—"

"What *has* it got to do with, okay?" Meyer said. "Tell me what—"

"It has to do with risking the *team*, okay?" Byrnes said.

"Then why don't I stay home in bed? I mean, what the hell *is* this?" Meyer said.

"He wants to be a hero," Willis said.

"Let the man be a hero," Brown said.

"I'm a hero *already*," Meyer said. "I've been *shot* already, I deserve a medal."

"Give the man a medal," Hawes said.

"Let the man kick in the door," Willis said.

"In a minute, I'll kick in the man's ass," Byrnes said.

"Maybe I ought to transfer to the Sanitation Department," Meyer said angrily. "You think I can lift a garbage can, Loot?"

"Meyer . . ."

"Don't 'Meyer' me. It's my team, I lead it in."

"Let's get one of the *Narcs* to lead it in," Willis said.

"Yeah, fat chance," Brown said.

Byrnes sighed. "With a *vest,*" he said.

"With a vest, all right," Meyer said.

"What time's it going down?"

"Ten forty-five."

"Why so early?"

"They've been assembling right after dinner, nine, nine-thirty. We hit them a little before eleven, they'll all be there, we should find the dope *and* the money all laid out for us."

"Will the Frenchman be there?"

"Both of them, we hope."

"You've seen them at the building?"

"Not since last month. But Artie's been sitting a wire . . ."

"They called?"

"Two days ago," Brown said. "They'll be there tonight, Loot, no question."

"Did they talk money?"

"The one with the deep voice said he was prepared."

"In English?"

"In English."

"Was that the exact word he used?"

"Prepared," Brown said, and nodded. "That's the word he used last month, too. Prepared."

"Meaning to make the sale," Meyer said.

"We *hope,*" Byrnes said.

"What else could he have meant? Prepared to dance the tango?"

"Who knows with thieves?" Byrnes said philosophically. "Have you picked your patrolmen?"

"The captain's giving us six of his best men."

"Six of the city's finest," Hawes said drily.

"Who's the Narc Squad sending?"

"Miller and Gerardi," Meyer said. "I don't know them."

"I don't, either," Byrnes said, and shrugged. "What time will they be here?"

"I told them an hour before the bust."

"Good," Byrnes said, and nodded. "Okay, anything else?"

"Nothing I can think of."

"I still wish—"

"And *I* wish I was a millionaire," Meyer said.

"I thought you were already," Willis said.

"All that graft," Brown said, and winked.

"Maybe you can rip off some of that shit tonight," Hawes said. "You're so eager to go in first, maybe you can grab a kilo and stick it in your pocket."

"Stick it up your ass," Meyer said cheerfully.

The meeting was over.

Dr. James Brolin's office was in a part of the city affectionately dubbed Shrink City, a stretch of real estate running for two blocks from the southern rim of Grover Park at Hall Avenue, past Jefferson, and terminating at Garden. The street, lined with analysts' offices, was the unofficial dividing line between the still-posh apartment buildings to the west and a Puerto Rican slum to the east. On the Puerto Rican side of the line, Carella could see fire hydrants open and wasting the city's precious water supply, kids in swim trunks doing their Gene Kelly numbers under the spray, stomping their feet in the puddles, grinning broadly, shouting to each other. Carella wished he could join them.

He had made the appointment for 1:50 p.m., to take advantage of Brolin's ten-minute break between patients. He was there five minutes early. A man with an umbrella was sitting in Brolin's small waiting room. He was wearing gray flannel trousers, and a heavy wool overcoat under which Carella could see a tweed sports jacket and a V-neck sweater. The man looked exceedingly cool. Carella wondered if he'd tipped to some kind of secret way to beat the heat. A woman came out of Brolin's inner office at exactly ten minutes to one. She looked at the man in the overcoat, looked at Carella, and then went into what Carella assumed was a small toilet off the waiting room. He heard the lock on the door click.

"Peeing," the man in the overcoat said. "She always pees."

"Mr. Carella?"

"Yes?" Carella said, turning from the man in the overcoat. "Dr. Brolin?"

"Won't you come in, please?"

"I thought *I* was next," the man in the overcoat said.

"Yes, Mr. Garfield, this won't take a moment," Brolin said.

"You're not supposed to use names," the man in the overcoat said, and turned his back to Brolin. The doctor smiled pleasantly, led Carella into his office, and closed the door behind them.

He was a man of about Carella's height, give or take a few inches, perhaps an even six feet, perhaps six-one. He was heftier than Carella, though, with broader shoulders and a thicker neck. The hair on his head was white, as was the small Vandyke beard that decorated his chin. Carella guessed he was somewhere in his late forties or early fifties.

"So," Brolin said. "This is about Mr. Newman?"

"Yes," Carella said. He still hadn't taken a seat. There was a leather couch angled out from a single chair beside the desk, and there was also a leather armchair facing the desk.

"The armchair," Brolin said.

Carella sat.

"What did you want to know?" Brolin asked. "I'm sorry this has to be so brief, but I have a full caseload. . . ."

"I understand," Carella said. "Dr. Brolin, I know it would be unethical to discuss anything a patient says here in this office . . ."

"It would," Brolin said.

"But what I have to ask today doesn't concern Anne Newman, per se, except as it relates to her husband."

"Uh-huh," Brolin said.

"So if you can answer some of my questions . . ."

"I'd have to hear the questions first."

"Of course," Carella said. "First, can you tell me whether Mrs. Newman ever mentioned the possibility of her husband committing suicide."

"Yes," Brolin said.

His immediate response surprised Carella; he had half-expected a lengthy discourse on confidentiality. Taken aback, he blinked, and then said, "She did?"

"Yes," Brolin said again.

"When was this, Dr. Brolin?"

"On several occasions."

"Said she was afraid her husband might commit suicide."

"Said he had *threatened* suicide."

"Did she say why?" Carella asked.

"Well, the man had a drinking problem," Brolin said, and rested his elbows on the desk, and tented his hands in front of his face, and peered over them. His eyes were an intense blue, Carella noticed. "He was finding it increasingly difficult to cope. His occupation didn't help much, I'm sure. He was a commercial artist, free-lancing out of the apartment, and was alone much of the time. Without the normal give-and-take of a so-called community relationship—the sort of camaraderie one might normally enjoy in the atmosphere of a business office or a shop or what-have-you—his problems must have appeared insurmountable. I'd suggested to Mrs. Newman, on more than one occasion, that he seek help. But apparently—"

"By help . . . ?"

"Psychiatric help."

"What was his reaction to this?"

"He refused. He told her he was perfectly capable of handling his own life. And now . . ." Brolin sighed. "The way he handled his own life was to end it."

Carella nodded, and then said, "Dr. Brolin, these suicide threats, would they have predated the drawing of his will?"

"What will is that?" Brolin asked.

"Mr. Newman had a new will drawn last month."

"Oh my, he'd been threatening suicide for almost as long as I've been treating Mrs. Newman."

"Then this wasn't something new."

"Not at all."

"Dr. Brolin, had Mrs. Newman ever discussed divorce with you?"

"I'm not sure I wouldn't be breaching a patient's confidence if I answered that question."

"Then again," Carella said, "you just answered it, didn't you?"

"I suppose so," Brolin said, and smiled. "Yes, she explored the possibility of divorce."

"What did you advise her."

"It's not a psychiatrist's role to *advise*, Mr. Carella. I'm here to help my patients find a way of dealing realistically with their problems."

"When did she first discuss the possibility of divorce?"

"Last month sometime."

"Dr. Brolin...do you believe Mrs. Newman had any knowledge of her husband's new will?"

"The first I've heard of any will is when you mentioned it a few minutes ago." His reference to time seemed to alert him to the patient waiting outside. He glanced at his watch.

"Just a few more questions," Carella said, and looked at his own watch. "When Mrs. Newman discussed divorce with you, did she indicate it might have had anything to do with her husband's will?"

"I just told you—"

"I'm referring to the fact that Mr. Newman left all of his estate to an art dealer named Louis Kern."

"That name has never been mentioned here in this office."

"What I'm trying to learn, Dr. Brolin, is whether Mrs. Newman may have felt any resentment—"

"Resentment?"

"Yes, over the fact that her husband named her as beneficiary of a relatively small insurance policy, whereas in his *will*—"

"If she knew about such a will, she never mentioned it here."

"Dr. Brolin, in your...?"

"Mr. Carella, I'm really very sorry, but I have a patient waiting."

"Just this one last question."

"Please."

"In your professional opinion, would someone with a severe aversion to medication of any kind have willingly ingested a fatal dose of Seconal?"

"I have no way of answering that without knowing the case history of the person in question."

"The person in question, I'm sure you realize—"

"Yes, is Mr. Newman. But I know nothing more about him than what his wife has told me in this office. That's not sufficient empirical evidence upon which to base a professional judgment."

"I see," Carella said, and rose. He extended his hand across the desk. "Thank you, Dr. Brolin," he said, "I appreciate your time."

"Glad to be of help," Brolin said.

The man in the overcoat was still sitting in the small waiting room outside. As Carella passed him, he looked up and said, "Are you going to pee now?"

"Later," Carella said.

The men on the team had all gone down the hall to pee.

The clock behind the muster-room desk read 10:10 p.m. as they came downstairs to pick up their equipment in the small supply room to the right of the iron-runged steps. The hand-held, battery-powered radios were Police Department property, and marked as such. The vests had been privately purchased and were privately owned by any detective who thought he might have cause to need one. In this city, only Emergency Squad cops were issued bulletproof vests; any other cop who wanted one had to pay for it with his own hard-earned bucks. The vests bore the names of the various cops stenciled across their backs. The cops often loaned their vests to other cops less affluent than themselves when something heavy was going down and they would be sitting the back of a liquor store instead. Not all of the detectives on the Eight-Seven owned bulletproof vests, but normally there were always more than enough to go around.

The vests were bulky and uncomfortable and often limited movement to such an extent that many detectives preferred taking their chances without them. There wasn't a cop in the world who thought he was faster than a speeding bullet, but mobility was sometimes vital in a shoot-out, and if a vest caused you to move too clumsily, a bullet in the head might easily result; there was no vest that covered a cop's head. Tonight, the men would not put on their vests until they were approaching the building on Culver Avenue; this would have been nor-mal procedure even when it *wasn't* so damn hot. The two detectives from the Narcotics Squad hadn't brought along any vests. They wanted to know now if they could borrow a couple from the Eight-Seven.

There were four 87th Precinct detectives and six 87th Pre-cinct patrolmen working the bust. There were only eight vests. Willis decided he didn't want to wear one. The six patrolmen, as part of the family, drew straws to see who would get to wear the remaining five vests. One of the patrolman and both Narcs were left out in the cold. Gerardi, the older of the Narc Squad cops, complained that the Eight-Seven ought to learn some common courtesy. Miller, the other Narc, said this wasn't even their bust; the Eight-Seven would get credit for the bust, and they'd be risking their asses without vests. Meyer told them both to go home to their knitting. The men all went to pee again before leaving the station house.

The police van posing as a bakery truck was parked across the street from 1124 Culver when the unmarked sedans pulled up. The men had put on their vests when they were three blocks away from the building, and had sat in silent, cramped discomfort on the approach. The moment the cars angled into the curb, they piled out gratefully onto the sidewalk, and moved swiftly toward the front door of the building, guns drawn. Meyer was in the lead. Immediately behind him in the triangular wedge were Brown and Hawes, and behind them Willis and a patrolman named Roger Higgins, who was scared out of his wits. The men went up the steps as quietly as they possibly could, considering the number of them. Their main interest was speed. Get up to the third floor, kick in the door, nail them cold with the dope and the money, make the arrest. On the second-floor landing, one of the Narc cops tripped and muttered "Shit," and one of the patolmen shushed him, and then suddenly all of them were on the third floor, and Higgins wasn't the only one who was scared. As Meyer approached the door to the suspect apartment, he felt a familiar pounding in his chest, the anticipated reaction to fear of the unknown. He thought he knew who would be behind the door he was about to kick in, but he didn't know what kind of arsenal was inside there.

In the state for which these men worked, it was necessary to obtain a search warrant from either a Criminal Court judge, or a Superior Court judge—a justice of the Supreme Court, as it applied to Isola—in order to enter any suspect premises. The form and content of the search warrant were defined by law. If the investigating officers felt there might be contraband materials on the premises, they would *also* request that the warrant carried a No-Knock provision, which would allow them to enter without announcing themselves. Meyer's warrant, signed downtown at the Criminal Courts building yesterday, contained just such a provision. But being legally sanctioned to go in unannounced did not dissipate that persistent fear of the unknown, the possible sudden death that lurked behind an alien door. He was sweating as he braced himself against the wall

opposite the door, and then jack-knifed his right leg and re-
leased a flat-footed kick at the lock.

The jamb splintered, the door sprang open.

"Police!" Meyer shouted. "Don't move!"

There were two people in the room.

They both sat at a long table.

One of them was a woman wearing only a slip. The other
was a man in his undershorts. The woman was white, the man
was black. The woman was thin to the point of emaciation.
The man looked relatively robust, but his eyes were as glazed
as hers, and there was a syringe on the tabletop, and a book
of matches, and a soot-blackened tablespoon, and two torn,
empty glassine packets. The man and the woman looked up as
the detectives and the uniformed policemen swarmed into the
room. Neither of them said a word. The cops fanned out,
throwing open doors to other rooms, closets, a small toilet.
The apartment was empty except for the man and the woman
who sat at the table, stoned, watching them silently.

"Anybody else here?" Meyer asked.

The woman shook her head.

"What's your name?" he asked.

"Mary," she said.

"Mary what?"

"What's my name?" she asked the black man.

The black man shrugged.

"How about you?" Meyer asked him.

"Jefferson Hill."

"Where'd you get this shit?" one of the Narc cops asked,
picking up an empty glassine packet.

"Mary?" Hill said. "Where we get this?"

"Good shit," Mary said, and nodded.

"Where're the guys running this place?" Brown asked.

"Where're the guys, Mary?" Hill asked.

"Yeah," Mary said, and shrugged.

"All this for a couple of fuckin' junkies," the other Narc
cop said.

Some you win, some you lose.

Augusta had told him they'd be shooting outdoors tonight,
at Long General downtown, something to do with juxtaposing
the new line of ski fashions with the stark, monolithic archi-

tecture of the hospital and the starched white uniforms of the staff nurses they'd be using as background extras. The commercial would not appear on television till December sometime, Augusta explained, they worked very far in advance. She was not looking forward to the assignment. Modeling ski parkas, in the stifling heat under bright lights was not her idea of an ideal way to spend a summer night.

Kling hadn't believed a word of it.

A call to the senior security officer at the hospital informed him that no plans had been made for anyone to take pictures in or around the place that night. "This is a *hospital*," the security man said somewhat testily, "there are *sick* people here, we don't allow such shenanigans here."

Marveling at the blatancy of her lie, Kling thanked the man politely, and then sat at his desk in the squad room, staring at the windows, listening to the lost sounds of summer outside. In a little while, he said good night to Carella, and went downstairs, and told Murchison on the muster desk that he was checking out, and then walked the two blocks to the kiosk on Grover, and took the subway downtown.

The lights on the first floor of the building on Hopper Street, in the apartment occupied by the painter Michael Lucas, were out. So were the lights on the second floor; Martha and Michelle were most likely prowling the town, and God knew where Franny the possible hooker was. He expected the photographers' studios on the third and fourth floors to be dark, and they were. But the fifth-floor apartment—the one rented or owned by the man who modeled "Mostly fashion, occasional beefcake," the man named Bradford Douglas with his bulging muscles and his flowing blond hair—*his* apartment was ablaze with light across the entire top floor of the building. Kling was tempted to go up there and kick in the door, no search warrant with a No-Knock provision, just kick the damn thing in and find Augusta there.

He stood across the street, in the shadows, thirty feet or more away from the single lamppost on the corner. The shops and restaurants lining the street were closed for the night; this was now a little past eleven, and Augusta had left for her imaginary shoot at a quarter to nine. He looked up at the lighted windows. In his mind, they became multiple screens flashing pornographic movies, Augusta scantily clad, Douglas bare-

chested, Augusta in his arms, Augusta accepting his embrace
and his kisses, Augusta opening herself to—

The first shot took him completely by surprise.

He heard the roar of the gun somewhere off to his left,
beyond the circle of light cast by the street-corner lamppost,
heard the slug as it whacked home against the brick of the
building, saw from the corner of his eye the brick a foot away
from his head shatter with the impact of the bullet, throwing
flying pieces of soot-stained red into the air. By the time the
second shot came, he was flat on his belly on the sidewalk,
his pistol in his hand, his heart beating wildly, his eyes scanning
the darkness beyond the circle of light. There was a third shot,
triggered off in haste, and then the sound of footsteps pounding
away into the darkness. As he scrambled to his feet, he
saw the running man cross a pool of light under another lamppost.
Dark windbreaker and fedora. Gun flailing in his right hand as
he pumped the air like a track star. He disappeared around the
corner just as Kling began chasing him, and was gone when
Kling reached the lamppost.

Out of breath, he walked back to where he thought the shots
had come from. On his hands and knees, he began searching
the pavement, touching, feeling with his palms and his fingers,
looking for spent cartridge cases. All he got was dirty hands.
Either this wasn't the exact spot or else the man had been firing
a revolver rather than an automatic. He went back to where
he'd been standing when the shooting started. The hole in the
brick wall was at least six inches in diameter; his assailant had
been using a high-powered gun. The area was dark. He looked
up and down the street, hoping to find a radio motor-patrol
car; the patrolmen would be carrying torchlights. The street
was empty of traffic. Never a cop around when you needed
one. He got down on his hands and knees again, in the dark,
and began feeling the sidewalk, searching for bullets. He found
only one, in pretty good shape, not too badly deformed. He
pocketed the slug, debated phoning this in to the local precinct,
and decided against it. Instead, he walked up to the lighted
avenue two blocks away, hailed a taxi, and told the driver to
take him to Long General. There were no photographers and
no models outside the hospital. He gave the driver his home
address, and then nervously took a cigarette from the package
he'd bought that morning, and lighted it, his hands trembling.

The last time he'd smoked was on his wedding night, almost four years ago, when Augusta, his bride, was abducted by a lunatic who'd then held her captive for three days.

The cabbie said, "Would you mind putting that out, please? I'm allergic to cigarette smoke."

"What?" Kling said.

"There's a sign back there, can't you see the sign?" the cabbie said.

Kling put out the cigarette.

Back at the ranch, they were dicussing the abortive raid.

"They must've been tipped," Gerardi, the older of the Narc Squad cops said.

"I don't think so," Meyer said.

"Then how come we find only two junkies with track marks running from their shoulders to their assholes?"

"It must've been called off," Brown said, "Maybe the shipment was delayed."

"Delayed, my ass," Miller, the other Narc said. "Somebody tipped them."

"You should tighten your security up here," Gerardi said.

"What've you got up here?" Miller asked. "Some cop on the take?"

Brown glared at him and said nothing. Brown's glares were often more meaningful than a thousand words.

"Where's the son of a bitch sitting that bakery truck?" Gerardi asked. "I thought he was supposed to come up here."

"He's clearing it with Photo," Willis said.

"What?" Gerardi said.

"He's with Photo, he's got to clear it with his command."

"Clear *what* with his command? Coming up here to tell us what the hell *happened* tonight?"

"He'll be here," Willis said.

"When? It's half-past eleven already."

"As soon as he clears it."

"He's trying to save his ass, is what he's trying to do," Miller said. "How come *we* weren't tipped?"

"What do you mean?" Hawes asked.

"How come the guy in that van, who's sitting there day and night taking pictures, didn't radio in to say there was nobody up there but a coupla hopheads?"

"You want *my* opinion," Gerardi said, *"he's* the one on the take."

"Almost broke my neck on those fuckin' stairs," Miller said.

"Two junkies stoned out of their minds. Place as empty as a hooker's heart," Gerardi said. "Somebody tipped them, I'm telling you."

"Here he is," Meyer said, and walked swiftly to the slatted rail divider. "Al," he said, "come on in. You clear it okay?"

"Don't know why I needed clearance in the first place," the man said, He was wearing a brightly patterned, short-sleeved sports shirt, pale-blue cotton trousers, and sandals. He had clipped his plastic-encased I.D. card to his shirt pocket before coming into the muster room downstairs, as though he were entering Headquarters or something.

"This is Al Rodriguez," Meyer said. "Gerardi and Miller from the Narc Squad. I think you know the others."

"Yeah, hi," Rodriguez said.

"You the guy been sitting that van?" Gerardi asked.

"Yeah," Rodriguez said.

"So what happened tonight?"

"What do you mean?"

"We go up there, there's only two junkies. Where's the guys in all those pictures you took?"

"How the hell do I know?"

"You been *sleepin'* inside that fuckin' truck?"

"I been takin' pictures," Rodriguez said.

"So what pictures did you take tonight? Two junkies going up there for a private little party?"

"I don't know who went up there or who didn't go up there," Rodriguez said. "I focus the camera on the front door, the camera takes the pictures. The camera clicks empty, I change the reel. I don't know what's on that film till it's developed downtown. I sometimes don't even know what's on it *after* it's developed."

"Who turns on the camera?"

"I turn it on."

"When?"

"Whenever somebody goes near that front door."

"So who went near that front door tonight?"

"Lots of people."

"Did lots of people go inside that building?"

"Sure," Rodriguez said.

"So where'd they disappear to?"

"How the fuck do I know? Maybe they went up the roof to fly pigeons. I ain't supposed to *tail* them, I'm only supposed to *photograph* them."

"You recognize any of the people who went in that building?"

"Some of them looked familiar."

"Did the two Frenchmen go in?"

"How the fuck do I know which of them is French or which of them ain't?"

"You can tell a Frenchman," Gerardi said.

"You shoulda called," Miller said.

"What for?"

"To tell us what was happening there."

"How the fuck do *I* know what was happening there? It looked the same as it does every month. Whole stream of guys going in, same guys as usual. I'm supposed to call to tell you it's business as usual?"

"You shoulda called," Miller said again.

"Listen, I'm tired," Rodriguez said. "Is this why you dragged me up here? To hear a lot of bullshit about what I shoulda done or shouldn'ta done? I mean, tell it to my lieutenant, okay? You got a beef, go bend *his* ear. *I'm* goin' home to sleep."

"We're gonna be looking at that film," Gerardi warned.

"So look at it," Rodriguez said heatedly. "Have a good time."

"Take it easy," Meyer said.

"Fuckin' Narcs got nothing to do but *squawk* all the time," Rodriguez said. "Why don't you go find an honest job?" he said to Gerardi. "So long, Meyer," he said, "you know where to reach me." He walked to the railing, shoved his way through the gate, and went angrily downstairs, his footsteps sounding heavily on the iron-runged steps.

"So what now?" Miller asked.

"We try again next month," Meyer said.

"Those guys'll be in *China* by next month," Gerardi said. "I'm telling you somebody tipped them. They know we're bringing heat to bear, and they're smart enough to stay far, far away from it. We can forget this bust, it'll never come off."

"We'll call you when it won't be coming off," Meyer said.

"That's supposed to be humor," Gerardi said to his partner.

She came into the apartment at a little after midnight. He was sitting before the television set watching the beginning of an old movie.

"Hi," she said from the front door, and then took her key from the lock, and came into the living room, and kissed him on top of his head.

"How'd it go?" he asked.

"It was called off," she said.

"Oh?"

"Some trouble with the hospital. They didn't want us shooting outside. Said it would disturb the patients."

"So where'd you end up shooting?" Kling asked.

"We didn't. Had a big meeting instead. Up at Chelsea."

"Chelsea?"

"Chelsea TV, Inc. Would you like a sandwich or something? I'm famished," she said, and walked out to the kitchen.

He watched her as she went, kept watching her as she unwrapped a loaf of sliced bread at the kitchen counter. He could remember the first time they'd met, could remember all of it as if it were happening here and now, the call from Murchison on the desk downstairs, a Burglary Past at 657 Richardson Drive, Apartment 11D, see the lady.

The lady had long red hair and green eyes and a deep suntan.

She was wearing a dark-green sweater, a short brown skirt, and brown boots. Her legs were crossed, she was staring bleakly at the wall. His first impression of her was one of total harmony, a casual perfection of color and design, russet and green, hair and eyes, sweater and skirt, boots blending with the smoothness of her tan, the long sleek grace of crossed legs, the inquisitively angled head, the red hair cascading in clean vertical descent.

She had high cheekbones, the lady, eyes slanting up from them, fiercely green against the tan, tilted nose gently drawing the upper lip away from partially exposed, even white teeth. Her sweater swelled over breasts firm without a bra, the wool cinched tightly at her waist with a brown, brass-studded belt, hip softly carving an arc against the nubby sofa back, skirt revealing a secret thigh as she turned.

He had never seen a more beautiful woman in his life.

"Who are they?" he asked.

"What?" Augusta said from the kitchen.

"Chelsea TV."

"The ad firm shooting the commercial."

"Oh," he said. "So what was the meeting about?"

"Rewriting, rescheduling, picking a new location—the same old jazz." She licked the knife with which she'd been spreading peanut butter and said, "Mmm, you sure you don't want some of this?"

"They needed you for that, huh?"

"For what?"

"Rewriting, and rescheduling, and—"

"Well, Larry wants me for the spot."

"Larry?"

"Patterson. At Chelsea. He wrote the spot, and he's directing it."

"Oh, yeah, right."

"So we had to figure out my availability and all that."

He found himself staring at her as she came back into the living room, the sandwich in her hand, just the way he'd stared at her on their first date so long ago, couldn't stop staring at her. When finally she'd told him to stop it, he was forced to admit he'd never been out with a girl as beautiful as she was, and she simply said he'd have to get over it, he could still remember her exact words.

"Well, you'll have to get over it. Because I think you're beautiful, too, and we'd have one hell of a relationship if all we did was sit around and stare at each other all the time. I mean, I expect we'll be seeing a lot of each other, and I'd like to think I'm permitted to sweat every now and then. I do sweat, you know."

Yes, Gussie, he thought, you do sweat, I know that now, and you belch and you fart, too, and I've seen you sitting on the toilet bowl, and once when you got drunk with all those flitty photographer friends of yours, I held your head while you vomited, and I put you to bed afterward and wiped up the bathroom floor, yes, Gussie, I *know* you sweat, I *know* you're human, but Jesus, Gussie, do you have to...do you have to *do* this to me, do you have to behave like...like a goddamn bitch in heat?

". . . thinking of going down to South America to do it," Augusta said.

"What?" Kling said.

"Larry. Shoot the spot down there. There's snow down there now. Forget the *symbolic* mountain, do it on a *real* mountain instead."

"What symbolic mountain?"

"Long General. Have you ever seen it? It looks like—"

"Yeah, a mountain."

"Well, you know what I mean."

"So you'll be going to South America, huh?"

"Just for a few days. If it works out."

"When?"

"Well, I don't know yet."

"When do you *think* it might be?"

"Pretty soon, I guess. While there's still snow. This is like their winter, you know."

"Yeah," Kling said. "Like when? This month sometime?"

"Probably."

"Did you tell him you'd go?"

"I don't get many shots at television, Bert. This is a full minute, the exposure'll mean a lot to me."

"Oh, sure, I know that."

"It'll just be for a few days."

"Who'll be going down there?" he asked.

"Just me, and Larry, and the crew."

"No other models?"

"He'll pick up his extras on the spot."

"I don't think I've met him," Kling said. "Have I met him?"

"Who?"

"Larry Patterson."

"No, I don't think so," Augusta said, and looked away. "You sure you don't want me to fix you something?"

"Nothing," Kling said. "Thanks."

NINE

Manfred Leider was a police psychologist who had once helped Carella while he was investigating the murders of several blind victims. He was a man in his fifties, sporting a gray beard that he thought made him look like a psychiatrist. In this state a psychiatrist had to go through four years of college, four years of medical school, one year of internship, three years of residency, and another two years of clinical practice before taking the written and oral examinations he had to pass for a license to practice. That was why psychiatrists charged a minimum of fifty dollars an hour for their services. Leider was only a psychologist. That was why he was working for the Police Department at an annual salary of $36,400.

When Carella called him early Thursday morning, he was in with a patient, a patrolman who'd suddenly developed conversion hysteria symptoms about drawing and firing his pistol should the need arise. You did not have to be a psychiatrist or even a psychologist to know what a pistol symbolized. Leider's secretary told Carella that the doctor (he *was* a doctor, if only a lowly Ph.D.) would call him back when he was free. He returned the call at a quarter past eleven.

"Dr. Leider here," he said.

"Hello," Carella said, "how are you? I don't know if you remember me, this is Detective Carella at the Eighty-seventh Precinct. We had a talk not too long ago about—"

"Yes, involving a screen memory, wasn't it?"

"Yes, the nightmares and the—"

"Yes, I remember. How'd that one work out?"

"Well, we got the guy."

"Good," Leider said, "glad to have been of help."

"I've got a very simple question this time," Carella asked.

"Mm," Leider said. He was used to very simple questions that required marathon explorations.

"I've got an apparent suicide victim, overdose of Seconal. The man's former wife and his brother tell me he was averse to taking medication of any kind."

"Phobic about it?"

"Had a reaction to penicillin when he was a teenager, wouldn't go near even an *aspirin* since."

"I would say that might be termed phobic."

"The question: Would such a person have voluntarily swallowed twenty-nine Seconal capsules?"

"Mm," Leider said.

Carella waited.

"The problem with asking a psychologist such a question," Leider said at last, "is that I can think of circumstances in which he *might* have, yes."

"What circumstances?"

"Well, there are two ways of dealing with a phobia," Leider said. "The first way is to avoid whatever it is that's causing the fear. If you're phobic about open spaces, for example, you stay in your apartment, you simply refuse to go outside, where the phobia will cause extreme anxiety."

"And the second way?"

"You confront the fear, you rush at it headlong. Many war heroes, for example, were terrified of battle. They conquered their fear, well, that's too strong a word, *'conquered.'* They *dealt* with it by volunteering for dangerous missions, which for them proved more effective in dealing with the phobia than simply sitting still and shaking with terror every time a grenade exploded. Do you understand what I'm saying?"

"I think so."

"There's what we call phobic avoidance, and then there's the reverse mechanism, counterphobic confrontation. Rushing into the fear itself. When I was in private practice, oh, this was many years ago, I treated an airline pilot who'd become a flier because he was afraid of heights. That was his way of overcoming the phobia."

"That's very reassuring," Carella said.

"Yes, well," Leider said.

"I mean, for airline passengers," Carella said.

"Yes," Leider said, and Carella realized he was dealing with a totally humorless human being. "So," Leider said, getting immediately back to the point, "your man *could* have attempted to overcome his phobia to medication by deliberately ingesting *more* of the barbiturate than was needed as a soporific. When we consider what he was about to do—"

"About to do?"

"You did say this was an apparent suicide?"

"Yes."

"Well then, the man was about to *kill* himself—"

"Yes."

"—which may have been his way of finally submitting to the phobia, rushing into its embrace, so to speak, surrendering to the phobia and to death at the same time. His final solution, so to speak."

"I see," Carella said.

"I'm sorry if I've disappointed you," Leider said.

"No, no, I've got to consider all the—"

"I understand," Leider said.

But Carella *was* disappointed.

He had hoped for a conclusive professional opinion unlike the one he'd received from James Brolin only yesterday: *I have no way of answering that without knowing the case history of the person in question.* Perhaps psychologists were wont to venture where psychiatrists feared to tread, but couldn't Leider just as easily have said "No, no way. This man definitely would *not* have taken pills of any kind to commit suicide"? It would have been so easy then. Oh, so very easy. All Carella would

have had to do then was find a murderer. There did not seem
to be many murderers lurking in the bushes these days.

He knew you couldn't run a case by intuition alone. He'd
known too damn many cops who—obsessively following a
wrong lead because they'd *felt* something about a case—were
left holding an empty bag. Maybe it was only intuition that
caused him to discount the fragile gallery owner and the former
Israeli captain as suspects in a murder that may or may not
have been committed, maybe he should have put a team of
men on them, have them followed day and night now that the
barn door was open and the horse was loose, maybe he was
giving up on them too soon. But whereas in this line of work
you didn't always know who was lying, you *always* knew who
was telling the truth. The truth had a ring like an ax hitting an
oak. He felt intuitively—yes, *felt*, yes, *intuitively*—that both
Louis Kern and Jessica Herzog had told him the complete and
unblemished truth, and he thought it would be a waste of
precious time to hassle them any further. Nonetheless, and
because he wanted to make certain he'd touched all the bases,
he made the obligatory call to Rollie Chabrier in the D.A.'s
office.

Chabrier was used to all sorts of odd calls from the detectives
of the Eight-Seven. Today, with the temperature outside stub-
bornly refusing to budge from the ninety-nine-degree mark,
the air conditioning in the Criminal Courts Building had decided
to quit, and Chabrier was sitting behind his desk in his shirt-
sleeves when the telephone rang. The moment Carella identified himself, he expected the worst. Bad things always came
in threes; the heat, the busted air conditioning, and now a call
from one of the dicks up there on Grover Park.

"What can I do for you, Steve?" he asked warily.

"I'm investigating a suspicious death," Carella said, "and
I'd like some information."

"This is a homicide?" Chabrier asked.

"An apparent suicide."

"Uh-huh."

"But there's a two-million-dollar will involved, and I want
to know something about the laws of inheritance in this state."

"Like what?"

"Like if I kill a guy because I'm going to inherit two million
bucks from him, do I get the money anyway?"

"There are no statutes regarding such instances," Chabrier said.

"What does that mean?"

"It means the law relies solely on judicial decision. Historically, anyone who slays a decedent has been barred from taking under the will or intestacy of the person slain."

"Decedent means—"

"Dead man."

"And taking under the will?"

"Inheriting. You know what intestacy means, don't you?"

"Yes. Dying without a will."

"Right. So to answer your question, if you decided to kill me because you know I'm leaving you a whole barrel of money, and if later it's proved that you did *indeed* kill me, you wouldn't stand a chance of inheriting."

"Okay," Carella said.

"Do you need chapter and verse on this? Try *Riggs* vs. *Palmer*, Citation 115—"

"No, that's okay," Carella said. "Thanks a lot."

He put the phone back on the cradle. It rang while his hand was still on the receiver, startling him. He picked it up again.

"Carella," he said.

"This is Dorfsman, at Ballistics," the voice said. "Is Kling there?"

"He's out just now," Carella said.

"Well, you can save me another call if you'll take this down and pass it on to him," Dorfsman said. "I promised I'd get back to him by noon."

"What's it on?" Carella asked.

"A bullet he brought down here this morning."

"Fast turnaround."

"Priorities," Dorfsman said. "This is an attempted murder. You got a pencil?"

"Go," Carella said.

"Nice easy one this time. Tell him it's a Remington .44-caliber Magnum, soft point. I won't *bore* you—that's a pun, Carella—with all the sordid details regarding lands, twist, groove diameter, and so on, but it's my learned opinion that the slug was fired from a Ruger .44-caliber Magnum Blackhawk. If you want to dress it up a little, you can tell Kling the average velocity of such a bullet is something like seventeen hundred feet, with a resulting paper energy of almost fourteen hundred foot-pounds. That's enough to stop a grizzly bear in his tracks."

"I'll tell him. Listen, can you transfer me to Grossman's office?"

"He's still in court," Dorfsman said.

"Then how about Owenby?"

"Just a second."

There was a clicking on the line. As Carella waited for the call to be transferred, he tried to recall any recent attempted murder Kling was working. As far as he knew—

"Owenby."

"Hello," Carella said, "how's my report coming along?"

"Should be on the captain's desk by the end of the day."

"So when will he get to it?"

"He's in court, I don't know when he'll be back. He's supposed to be finished over there today."

"Will he see the report today?"

"If he gets to it."

"Why don't you send me a copy at the same time?"

"Against regs," Owenby said.

"Then tell me what's *in* it, will you?"

"I can't do that. We've had too many foul-ups on verbal—"

"Okay, I'll come down there to look at it."

"It isn't typed yet. I told you it'd be on his desk the end of the day. Why don't you call him around four, four-thirty?"

"Thanks a lot," Carella said, and hung up.

He had deliberately chosen Ah Wong's downtown on Boone Street for three reasons: first, Augusta had told him she'd been working that morning at Tru-Vue, a photography studio close to the restaurant; second, it was here that she was *supposed* to have been last Saturday night, and when he baited his trap he wanted her to remember, if only unconsciously, that she was a woman involved in an affair, a woman searching for opportunities to deceive; and, lastly, the restaurant was close to the various courthouses downtown, where he hoped to go for his search warrant the moment he got Dorfsman's promised quick report on the bullet.

They met a little after noon.

She looked so radiantly beautiful that he almost forgot his resolve.

She complained about having to work all morning under the hot lights, and he told her all about what a hard day it had been in court all morning, where'd he'd been testifying on a burglary arrest he'd made two months back; he did not mention that he had gone to the lab first, to drop off the bullet that had been fired at him the night before. Gingerly, he approached the trap he had carefully constructed.

"Damn thing is," he said, "I've got Night Watch again tonight."

Every cop on the squad drew Night Watch once a month, for two nights running, the first night from 1600 to 0100, the second from 0100 to 0900, followed by two days off. Augusta knew this. She also knew that he'd drawn the duty not two weeks ago.

"How come?" she asked.

"Parker's sick," he said.

He had deliberately chosen Parker because he was one of the few cops they did not see socially; he did not want to risk using Meyer or Brown or any of the other cops Augusta knew; a call from a wife or a girlfriend could blow the whole scheme.

"He had the sixteen-hundred yesterday," Kling said, "and came down with a cold. I think he's faking, but who can tell with Parker? Anyway, Pete asked me to sub for him tonight."

"So what does that mean?"

"One to nine in the morning."

Augusta said nothing. He thought he noticed her chopsticks hesitating on the way to her mouth. Her eyes were lowered, she kept looking at her plate.

"A dozen guys from squads all over town," Kling said. "You know how it works."

"So where will you be?" she asked.

"At Headquarters. The office they let us use there, up on the third floor, in case you need to reach me," he said, and was immediately sorry. He did not want her calling Headquarters to check on him. "But we'll be out on the street most of the time," he added.

"I thought we were going to a movie tonight," Augusta said.

"Yeah, well. what can you do?"

"Actually, we could *still* go, couldn't we? If you don't have to be downtown till one?"

"I'll be in the squad room till then, hon," he said. "Paperwork on this suicide we're working."

"The Seconal case," she said, and nodded.

"That's the one. Only nice thing about pulling Parker's duty is it's air-conditioned downtown."

"Well, that's a plus, I suppose," Augusta said, and hesitated. "Maybe I'll go to the movies alone, would you mind that?"

"Why would I?" he said.

"Well, after what that twerp Monica told you . . ."

"I've forgotten all about that," Kling said.

"She'll be wearing a wig next time we meet," Augusta said. "Pull out all her *hair*, that bitch."

"Don't do anything I'd have to arrest you for," Kling said, and forced a smile.

"I *still* can't get over her, I mean it."

"She was drunk," Kling said.

"Even so . . ."

"Why don't you put it out of your mind?" he said, and covered her hand with his own. *"I have."*

"Are you sure?"

"Positive."

"Well, good," she said, and smiled.

"What time do you have to be back up there?" he asked.

Augusta looked at her watch. "I still have a few minutes," she said. "So will we be going out to dinner tonight, or what?"

"I planned on catching a sandwich in the squad room."

Augusta pulled a face. "Great," she said. "That means I won't be seeing you till nine tomorrow morning."

"Nine-thirty, by the time I get uptown."

"Terrific. My first *sitting's* at nine-thirty."

"Honey, I didn't *ask* Parker to get sick. If he really *is* sick."

"It's because you're the youngest guy on the squad . . ."

"No, Tack Fujiwara is."

". . . that you get all the shit jobs."

"Honey, that's not the way it works."

She looked at her watch again. "I've got to run," she said. "Before they start screaming up there." She pushed back her chair, came around to where he was sitting, kissed him on the cheek, and said, "Be careful tonight, okay?"

"You, too," he said.

"I'll be home with the door locked," she said, "you won't have to worry."

"I mean, on the way home from the movies."

"I might not even go. I'll see what's on television. Call me when you get home tomorrow morning, okay?" she said. "I'll be at Tru-Vue again, the number's in our book."

"I will."

"I'll be there at nine-thirty sharp."

"Okay."

"'Bye, darling," she said, and kissed him again on the cheek, and then walked swiftly to the front door, her shoulder bag swinging, and turned at the door to throw a kiss to him before she went out. He sat at the table for several moments longer, and then paid the check and went to the telephone booth near the doors to the kitchen. He dialed the squad-room number directly, bypassing the muster desk. Carella picked up on the third ring.

"I was just going down to lunch," he said. "Where are you?"

"Downtown here," Kling said. "I just got out of court. Did I get a call from Dorfsman at Ballistics?"

"Yeah, he said it was a Remington .44 Magnum. Which case . . . ?"

"Did he say what kind of gun?"

"A Ruger Blackhawk."

"Okay, thanks," Kling said, "I'll see you later," and hung up before Carella could ask him anything more.

For the first time in his capacity as a police officer sworn to uphold the laws of the city, state, and nation, Kling lied on an official application. Moreover, he lied both in writing and later orally to a supreme court magistrate. Kling's affidavit read:

1. I am a detective of the Police Department assigned to the 87th Detective Squad.

2. I have information based upon my personal knowledge and belief and facts supplied to me at the scene by the victim that an attempted

murder occurred outside 641 Hopper Street at 1:10 p.m. this Wednesday past, August 13.

3. I have further information based upon my personal knowledge and belief and facts disclosed to me by the victim of the attempted murder that several shots were discharged during the attempt.

4. I have further information based upon my personal knowledge and belief that the firearm used in the murder attempt was a .44-caliber Ruger Blackhawk firing Remington .44-caliber Magnum cartridges, as confirmed by Michael O. Dorfsman of the Ballistics Unit this day, August 14, working from a bullet I personally recovered from the sidewalk outside 641 Hopper Street.

5. I have further information based upon my personal knowledge and belief, and on information supplied to me, that a tenant named Bradford Douglas is in possession of a pistol of the same caliber and answering the description of the pistol used in the attempted murder.

6. Based upon the foregoing reliable information and upon my personal knowledge, there is probably cause to believe that the pistol in possession of Bradford Douglas would constitute evidence in the crime of attempted murder.

Wherefore, I respectfully request that the court issue a warrant in the form annexed hereto, authorizing a search of the person of Bradford Douglas and the premises at 641 Hopper Street, apartment 51. No previous application in this matter has been made in this or any other court or to any other judge, justice, or magistrate.

The judge to whom Kling presented his signed affidavit read it over carefully, and then looked up over the rims of his eyeglasses.

"What were you doing all the way down there, son?" he asked.

"Your Honor?"

"Long way from the Eighty-seventh, isn't it?"

"Oh, yes, Your Honor. I was off-duty. Just coming from a restaurant when I heard the shooting."

"Did you see the perpetrator?"

"No, Your Honor."

"Then you only have the victim's word that a murder attempt was made."

"I heard the shots, Your Honor, and I recovered a spent bullet from the pavement, which would seem conclusive evidence that a pistol had been fired."

"But not necessarily in a murder attempt."

"No, Your Honor, not necessarily. The victim, however, has described it as such."

"As a murder attempt?"

"Yes, Your Honor. The gun was fired at him point-blank."

"And you believe the gun used in that attempted murder might be in this apartment you want to search?"

"Yes, Your Honor, that's my firm belief."

"Where'd you get this information?"

"From the super of the building, a man named Henry Watkins. He's seen the pistol, Your Honor."

"When did you plan to conduct this search?"

"Tonight, Your Honor, As soon as I can ascertain that Mr. Douglas is at home."

"Mm," the judge said.

"Your Honor, I would also like a No-Knock provision."

"On what basis?"

"Information and belief that there is a lethal weapon in that apartment, Your Honor. A .44-caliber Magnum is a high-powered—"

"Yes, yes," the judge said. "All right," he said, "I'll grant the warrant. *And* the No-Knock."

"Thank you, Your Honor," Kling said, and took his handkerchief from his pocket, and wiped his brow.

The lie, as he rationalized it, was only a partial falsehood.

An attempted murder *had* taken place, and the weapon he'd described was the one used last night. But neither Henry Watkins nor anyone else had told him Bradford Douglas was in possession of such a gun; if indeed he found it in Douglas's apartment tonight, that would be strictly a bonus. He would be going there tonight looking for Augusta. The No-Knock provision gave him the right to kick in the door, no hiding in a closet or a bathroom, catch her there dead to rights.

As he came down the broad white steps of the courthouse, the heat enveloping him like a shroud, he felt a glommy certainty that tonight would be the end of it. And he longed for it to be the beginning instead, when he and Augusta were both fresh and new and shining with hope.

Hope is the thing with feathers.

Halloran watched him as he came down the courthouse steps.

He wondered what he'd been doing up there. Went to court this morning, met the redhead for lunch at twelve, then went back to the courthouse again. Busy with his little cases, the bastard. The redhead had to be his wife, or else some cheap cunt he was living with. She'd be living with a corpse tomorrow morning.

He had missed last night, but he wouldn't miss again.

Tonight, he wouldn't miss.

Tonight, he'd shove the gun in that bastard's face and do the job right, make that bastard eat the barrel and chew on the slug before it ripped off the back of his head.

Tonight.

At four that afternoon, Carella called Grossman's office. A woman answered the phone. She identified herself as Mrs. Di Marco, one of the lab assistants.

"The captain's not here," she said. "Who's this?"

"Detective Carella, Eighty-seventh Squad. When will he be back, do you know?"

"He just left. He's been in court all week, a man's entitled to go home when he's been in court all week."

"Then he's gone for the day, is that it?"

"He's gone for the day, yes."

"Would you know if he had a chance to look over any papers on his desk?"

"He looked at some papers, yes. He even took some papers home with him."

"Thanks," Carella said, "I'll call him at home then."

"He didn't *go* home."

"You just said—"

"That was figurative. He was taking his wife to dinner."

"All right, I'll call him later tonight then."

"Why don't you call him tomorrow morning instead? People don't like to be disturbed at home."

"Good-bye, Mrs. Di Marco," Carella said, and hung up.

It would have to wait, after all.

The city succumbed to the night with a sigh of gratitude.

It was not that the temperature dropped all that much. Neither did the humidity. But the night brought with it a semblance of relief, the false impression that darkness could be equated with coolness. At least the sun was gone from the sky, its blistering assault only an unmourned memory.

Now there was the night.

TEN

He wanted to make sure he'd given her enough time to get here.

She had called him at the squad room at nine o'clock, to say she was going to the movies after all, if he wouldn't mind, and would be catching the 9:27 show, just around the corner, he didn't have to worry about her getting home safe, the avenue was well-lighted. She had then gone on to reel off the name of the movie she'd be seeing, the novel upon which it was based, the stars who were in it, and had even quoted from a review she'd read on it. She had done her homework well.

It was now a little past ten.

The windows on the first floor of the Hopper Street building were lighted; Michael Lucas, the painter, was home. On the second floor, only the lights to the apartment shared by Martha and Michelle were on; Franny next door was apparently uptown with her Zooey. The lights on the third and fourth floors were out, as usual. Only one light burned on the fifth floor, at the northernmost end of Bradford Douglas's apartment— The bed-room light, Kling thought.

He waited.

In a little while, the light went out.

He crossed the street and rang the service bell. Henry Wat-kins, the superintendent he'd talked to this past Tuesday, opened the door when he identified himself.

"What's it now?" Watkins asked.

"Same old runaway," Kling said. "Have to ask a few more questions."

Help yourself," Watkins said, and shrugged. "Let yourself out when you're finished, just pull the door shut hard behind you."

"Thanks," Kling said.

He waited until Watkins went back into his own ground-floor apartment, and then he started up the iron-runged steps. On the first floor, a stereo was blaring rock and roll music behind Lucas's closed door. On the second floor, he heard nothing as he passed the door to the apartment shared by the two women. He walked past the studio belonging to Peter Lang, the photographer on the third floor, and then took the steps up to the fourth floor. The light was still out in the hallway there. He picked his way through the dark again, and went up the stairs to the fifth floor.

His heart was pounding.

Carella did not reach Sam Grossman at home until a quarter past ten that night. The first thing Grossman said was, "I've got a good one for you."

He was about to tell a joke. Carella could virtually *feel* over the telephone wires the contained glee in his voice. Grossman was a tall and angular man, who'd have looked more at home on a New England farm than in the sterile orderliness of a police laboratory. He wore glasses, his eyes a guileless blue behind them. There was a gentility to his manner, a quiet warmth reminiscent of a long-lost era, even though his voice normally rapped out scientific facts with staccato authority. Except when he was telling a joke. When he was telling a joke, he took his time.

"This shyster attorney is scheduled for a court appearance

downtown," Grossman said, "the Criminal Courts Building downtown. You know how tough it is to park down there?"

"Yes," Carella said. He was already smiling.

"So he circles the block, and he circles the block again, and the time is ticking away, and the judge who's going to hear the case is a stickler for punctuality. So finally the lawyer parks in a No Parking zone, and he writes a little note. The note says, 'I'm an attorney with a criminal case to try, and I'm late, and I've been circling this block for the past twenty minutes, and finally I had to park here. Forgive us our trespasses.' And he takes out a five-dollar bill, and folds it neatly inside the note, and sticks the bill and the note under the windshield wiper."

"'Forgive us our trespasses,'" Carella said, still smiling.

"Yes, and a five-dollar bill," Grossman said. "So he comes down again four hours later, and his note and the five-dollar bill are still under the windshield, but there's *also* a summons for the parking violation and a note from the patrolman who wrote the ticket. And the *cop's* note says, '*I've* been circling this block for the past twenty *years*. Lead us not into temptation.'"

Carella burst out laughing. Cops loved nothing better than jokes about foiled bribery attempts.

"Brighten your day?" Grossman said, chuckling.

"Immeasurably," Carella said. Whenever he was talking to Grossman, he found himself using vocabulary he rarely used otherwise. "But—what have you got for me on the Newman case?"

"Nothing," Grossman said.

"That's a big help," Carella said. "Owenby told me the report would—"

"Oh, I have the report, all right, it was on my desk when I got back from court this afternoon. Have it right here with me, in fact. How's that for conscientious?"

"Then what do you mean 'nothing'? I saw the techs lifting prints all *over* the place."

"Oh, yes, plenty of prints. All the dead man's and his wife's."

"No wild prints at all?"

"None."

"How about on the thermostat?" Carella asked.

"I was coming to that, are you getting to be a mind reader? Considering the heat, the thermostat should have been getting a big play, am I right? Even under *normal* conditions, people are fiddling with thermostats all the time. It gets hot, they turn the temperature setting down. It gets cool again, they adjust it. So where are the his-and-her prints you'd normally expect? Nowhere. The thermostat was wiped clean. Did they live there alone?"

"Yes," Carella said.

"So where are the his-and-hers? We found plenty of them on the flush handle of the toilet tank, partials mostly, that's another place we look because nobody ever wipes off the flush handle, they just don't. Their asses they wipe, but not the flush handle. Good partial of the dead man's right middle finger, one of the lady's index finger, okay, fine. But the thermostat was clean."

"So what does that mean to you?" Carella asked.

"What does that mean to *you?*" Grossman said.

"Well, *maybe ...*"

"More than maybe," Grossman said.

"How so?"

"Let's say the lady's a compulsive housekeeper. She wipes off everything the minute anybody touches it. Let's say that. So she or her housekeeper—has she got a housekeeper?"

"A cleaning woman. But she's been away since the middle of July."

"Which would account for why we found only the his-and-hers. I'm assuming the apartment was cleaned at least once since the middle of July."

"I'd guess so," Carella said.

"So let's say the lady did her own cleaning since then. Would even a very neat person go running around the apartment tidying up every minute and polishing everything in sight? Including an almost-empty bottle of Seconal?"

"What do you mean?"

"It was wiped clean, Steve."

"Are you you telling me there were no prints on that bottle?"

"That's what I'm telling you."

"That's impossible."

"I'm telling you what we found. Or *didn't* find, as the case happens to be."

"If Newman handled that bottle, there *had* to be prints on it. A guy with twenty-nine Seconal capsules inside him doesn't get up off the floor to wipe his prints off a bottle."

"It was clean as a whistle, Steve."

Both men were silent for a moment.

"You think the lady could have wiped off those prints?" Grossman asked.

"The lady was in California while the man was being done in."

Grossman was silent again. Then he said, "Does the lady have a friend?"

"I don't know," Carella said.

"It might be something you'd like to ask her," Grossman said.

He stood outside the door to apartment 51 and listened.
Not a sound.

He took his gun from his shoulder holster. Holding it in his right hand, he backed away from the door, and then leveled a kick at the lock. The door sprang open, wood splinters flying. He moved into the room swiftly, slightly crouched, the gun fanning the air ahead of him, light filtering into the room from under a door at the end of the hall, to his left. He was moving toward the crack of light when the door flew open and Bradford Douglas came into the hall.

He was naked, and holding a baseball bat in his right hand. He stood silhouetted in the lighted rectangle of the doorway, hesitating there before taking a tentative step into the gloom beyond.

"Police," Kling said, "hold it right there!"

"Wh . . . ?"

"Don't move!" Kling said.

"What the hell? Who . . . ?"

Kling moved forward into the light spilling from the bedroom. Douglas recognized him at once, and the fear he'd earlier felt—when he'd thought a burglar had broken in—was replaced by immediate indignation. And then he saw the gun in Kling's hand, and a new fear washed over him, struggling with the indignation. The indignation triumphed. "What the hell do you mean, breaking down my door?" he shouted.

"I've got a warrant," Kling said. "Who's in that bedroom with you?"

"None of your business," Douglas said. He was still holding the bat in his right hand. *"What* warrant? What the hell *is* this?"

"Here," Kling said, and reached into his pocket. "Put down that bat."

Without turning, Douglas tossed the bat back into the bedroom. Kling waited while he read the warrant. The bedroom fronted Hopper Street, and there were no fire escapes on that side of the building. Unless Augusta decided to *jump* all the way down to the street below, there was no hurry. He looked past Douglas, into the bedroom. He could not see the bed from where he was standing, only a dresser, an easy chair, a standing floor lamp.

"Attempted murder?" Douglas said, reading from the warrant. *"What* attempted murder?" He kept reading. "I don't have this gun you describe, I don't have *any* gun. Who the hell said I . . . ?"

"I haven't got all night here," Kling said, and held out his left hand. "The warrant gives me the right to search both you and the apartment. It's signed by—"

"No, just wait a goddamn *minute,"* Douglas said, and kept reading. "Where'd you get this information? Who told you I've got this gun?"

"That doesn't matter, Mr. Douglas. Are you finished with that?"

"I *still* don't—"

"Let me have it. And let's take a look inside."

"I've got somebody with me," Douglas said.

"Who?"

"Your warrant doesn't give you the right to—"

"We'll worry about that later."

"No, we'll worry about it *now,"* Douglas said.

"Look, you prick," Kling said, and brought the pistol up close to Douglas's face, "I want to search that bedroom, do you understand?"

"Don't get excited," Douglas said, backing away.

"I *am* excited," Kling said, "I'm *very* excited. Get out of my way."

He shoved Douglas aside and moved into the bedroom. The

bed was against the wall at the far end of the room. The sheets were thrown back. The bed was empty.

"Where is she?" Kling said.

"Maybe the bathroom," Douglas said.

"Which door?"

"I thought you were looking for a gun."

"Which *door?*" Kling said tightly.

"Near the stereo there," Douglas said.

Kling went across the room. He tried the knob on the door there. The door was locked.

"Open up," he said.

From behind the door, he could hear a woman weeping.

"Open up, or I'll kick it in," he said.

The weeping continued. He heard the small oiled click of the lock being turned. He caught his breath and waited. The door opened.

She was not Augusta.

She was a small dark-haired girl with wet brown eyes, holding a bath towel to cover her nakedness.

"He's got a warrant, Felice," Douglas said behind him.

The girl kept weeping.

"Anybody else here?" Kling asked. He felt suddenly like a horse's ass.

"Nobody," Douglas said.

"I want to check the other rooms."

"Go ahead."

He went through the apartment, turning on lights ahead of him. He checked each room and every closet. There was no one else in the apartment. When he went back into the bedroom again, both Douglas and the girl had dressed. She sat on the edge of the bed, still weeping. Douglas stood beside her, trying to comfort her.

"When I was here Turesday night, you told me you'd had a visitor the day before," Kling said. "Who was your visitor?"

"Where does it say in your warrant...?"

"Mr. Douglas," Kling said, "I don't want to hear any more bullshit about the warrant. All I want to know is who was here in this apartment between twelve-thirty and one forty-five last Monday."

"I...I'd feel funny telling you that."

"You'll feel a lot funnier if I have to ask a grand jury to subpoena you," Kling said. "Who was it?"

"A friend of mine."

"Male or female?"

"Male."

"What was he doing here?"

"I told him he could use the apartment."

"What for?"

"He's . . . there's a girl he's been seeing."

"Who?"

"I don't know her name."

"Have you ever met her?"

"No."

"Then you don't know what she looks like."

"Larry says she's gorgeous."

"Larry?"

"My friend."

"Larry *who?*" Kling said at once.

"Larry Patterson."

Kling nodded.

"He's married, so's the broad," Douglas said. "He needed a place to shack up, I've been lending him the pad here. I do a lot of work for him. He's one of the creative people at—"

"Chelsea TV," Kling said. "Thanks, Mr. Douglas, I'm sorry for the intrusion." He looked at the weeping girl. "I'm sorry, Miss," he mumbled, and quickly left the apartment.

He had not called ahead to tell her he was coming. He'd been in bed when he placed the call to Grossman, and he'd dressed hastily afterward, and left the apartment without waking Teddy, who'd been asleep beside him. Now, as he walked past the smiling statue of General Richard Joseph Condon, he weighed the possibility that there might be a reasonable explanation for that bottle to have been wiped clean—and decided there could not be one.

He identified himself to the doorman in the lobby of Susan Newman's building on Charlotte Terrace, and asked the man not to announce him. The doorman balked, citing rules and regulations. Carella told him he would hate like hell to bring charges for Hindering Prosecution, Section 205.55 of the Penal Law, and began quoting, "A person renders criminal assistance when, with intent to prevent, hinder or delay the discovery or apprehension—"

"Criminal assistance?" the doorman said. "Huh?"

"Stay off the phone," Carella said, and started for the elevator.

He got off on the third floor, and walked swiftly to apartment 3G. He listened outside the door, and then rang the bell.

"Who is it?" a woman's voice asked.

Anne Newman.

"Police," he said. "Detective Carella."

"Oh." The single word, and then silence. He waited. "Just a minute," she said.

When she opened the door, she was wearing a long blue robe over a pink nightgown he could see in the V-necked throat. She was barefooted.

"I'm sorry to be bothering you so late at night but . . ."

"That's all right," she said. "Please come in."

He went into the small entrance foyer behind her, and waited while she locked the door again. As they moved together into the living room, he asked, "Is your mother-in-law home?"

"She's asleep," Anne said. "It's almost eleven, Mr. Carella, I was getting ready for bed myself."

"Yes, well, I'm awfully sorry, Mrs. Newman, but we're trying to close this out, and there are just a few more questions I'd like to ask."

"Yes, of course," she said. "But I have an early appointment in the morning—"

"I'll try to make it brief. Mrs. Newman, are you aware that your husband left a will?"

"Yes."

"When did you learn about it?"

"Monday morning. Our attorney called to inform me."

"By your attorney . . ."

"Charles Weber. At Weber, Herzog and Llewellyn."

"And this is the first you knew of it?"

"Yes."

"Do you know when the will was drawn?"

"No."

"Three weeks before your husband died, Mrs. Newman."

"Oh? Jerry never mentioned it."

"Are you familiar with the terms of the will?"

"Yes, Charlie spelled them out for me."

"You know then that your husband left more than two million dollars . . ."

"Yes, I know that."

"And that you weren't named in the will at all?"

"I'm the beneficiary of an insurance policy."

"Which leaves you a hundred thousand dollars."

"Yes, so I understand."

"How do you feel about that, Mrs. Newman?"

"About what?"

"Your getting a hundred thousand and a stranger getting two million."

"I don't *know* how I feel, actually," she said.

"Well, you must feel *something,*" Carella said.

"Disappointment?" she said, smiling wanly. "Sadness?"

"But not anger?"

"Anger? No, not anger. Only sadness and disappointment. I was a loving and loyal wife for almost fifteen years, Mr. Carella. To think that . . . well, it doesn't matter. What's done is done. I don't need two million dollars, I'm not an extravagant person, I have my own work, I can get by very nicely on what I earn, even without what the insurance policy will bring."

"Do you know Mr. Kern?" Carella asked.

"Yes. My father-in-law exhibited his work at the Kern Gallery. It was Louis, in fact, who appraised the paintings my husband inherited."

"Did you know that Mr. Kern was aware of the will's contents *before* your husband died?"

"No, I didn't know that. How . . . ?"

"He was informed."

"By whom?"

"Your husband's former wife. Jessica Herzog."

"How did . . . oh, I see, yes. Her brother works for the firm, doesn't he?"

"He's a partner there."

"Yes, of course. But I had no idea she even *knew* Louis."

"They're lovers," Carella said.

"Louis and Jessica? You're joking," she said, and smiled. "But that's too comical for *words!*"

"It's a fact," Carella said.

"Well, stranger things do happen, I suppose," Anne said, and shook her head. "Louis and Jessica. My, my."

"Could either of them have known you were leaving for California?"

"Louis, do you mean? Jessica?"

"Yes."

"No, of course not. I haven't seen Louis in years, and Jessica . . . well, surely you must understand there was no love lost between us."

"And you say you had no knowledge of the will before Monday morning, is that correct?" Carella asked.

"That's correct."

"Your husband never mentioned it to you?"

"Never."

"Isn't that a bit odd?"

"Jerry *was* a bit odd."

"What I'm saying," Carella said, "is that it seems strange for a man not to discuss his will with his own wife."

"Well," Anne said, "I guess if a man's wife isn't *in* his will, then he might be somewhat reluctant to let her know about it, wouldn't you agree?"

"Can you think of any reason why your husband may have decided to change his will?"

"No, I can't."

"Could he have had any reason to suspect you were considering divorce?"

"None."

"You *were* planning to ask him for a divorce?"

"Yes, but that was a recent decision."

"A decision you've been considering for some time, isn't that so?"

"Not that long a time."

"How long a time?" Carella asked.

"I couldn't say with any accuracy."

"Longer than last month? When your husband changed his will?"

"I didn't know he'd changed his will till just this Monday. Oh, I see," Anne said. "You're thinking that in a childish fit of pique, *after* I'd learned I was no longer in his will, I began thinking about divorce. I wish everything in life were as simple as that, Mr. Carella. No, I did not know about his new will, and no, it had nothing whatever to do with my wanting a divorce. I'd simply had enough. Enough of wiping up after him, and supporting his ego, and bolstering—" She shook her head again. "Quite enough. On the Coast, when I was out there last week, I finally knew without question that I wanted out. I wanted to breathe again. I called my mother-in-law and told her what I planned to do. She gave me her blessings. So, you see, it really doesn't *matter* to me that I'm not inheriting two million dollars. Two million dollars would be very nice, yes. But I don't *care* about that, I don't even care about the hundred thousand the insurance policy will bring. You may find that difficult to understand, but I really don't *care*. I feel no anger, none at all. I feel only disappointment and sadness, as I told you. I served him well for almost fifteen years. Disappointment, and sadness, and—I will admit this—tremendous relief. It will be good to be alive again. You cannot know how good it will be."

"Mrs. Newman, you told me you have a cleaning woman, isn't that right?" Carella asked.

"Yes. I have someone who comes in once a week."

"On what day?"

"Friday."

"You left for California on a Friday, didn't you?"

"Yes."

"Was your cleaning woman there on the morning you left?"

"No. She was in Georgia. I told you that."

"Was she there on the Friday you returned?"

"No."

"She was *still* in Georgia, am I right?"

"Yes."

"So if she wasn't there, she couldn't have done any cleaning that day."

"Mr. Carella, I'm sorry, but what . . . ?"

"Mrs. Newman, did *you* do any cleaning that day? Did you, for example, wipe off the thermostat?"

"What?"

"The thermostat."

"Wipe it off, did you say?"

"Yes."

"Why would I have done that?"

"I have no idea. Did you?"

"No, of course not."

"The lab techs were through with the apartment at about ten. That means they'd have dusted the therm—"

"Dusted?"

"For latent prints, the thermostat. And everything else. You got home at eight-thirty, you told me . . ."

"Yes."

"Would there have been anyone who—between eight-thirty and ten—might have wiped off that thermostat?"

"Well, I . . . I don't know."

"Or the bottle of Seconal?"

"The what?"

"The Seconal. The bottle your husband *had* to have handled if he committed suicide."

"Well, I . . . I . . . don't really . . ."

"You're sure *you* didn't?"

"Of course I am! Why would I have . . . of course I didn't! I went right downstairs to call the police. I wasn't in the apartment more than . . . a minute or two . . . no more than—"

She fell silent all at once.

Carella stood staring at her. When the voice came from behind him, he turned, startled, and saw Susan Newman standing in the doorway to her bedroom beyond. She was wearing a saffron-color quilted robe. There was a faint, forlorn smile on her mouth.

"Darling," she said, "I think the gentleman already knows."

"Oh my God," Anne said, and took a deep breath, and squeezed her eyes shut tightly.

So now it was all over.

Face her down when she got home tonight after the "movie" she'd gone to see, tell her he knew she'd been with this man named Larry Patterson last Monday, enjoying a quick roll in the hay in a borrowed apartment, tell her he knew all about her and her little married playmate, had seen through the lie about the never-scheduled television commercial outside Long General, confront her with the indisputable fact that the man she'd be accompanying to South America was this man Larry Patterson, her lover, tell her, get it over with, end it. End it.

It was almost eleven-thirty when he got back to the apartment.

He inserted his key into the lock, and then opened the door. The apartment was dark, he reached for the switch just inside the door, and turned on the lights. He was bone-weary and suddenly very hungry. He was starting toward the kitchen when he heard the sound in the bedroom.

The sound was stealthy, the sound a burglar might make when suddenly surprised by an unexpected arrival home, nothing more than a whisper really, a rustle beyond the closed bedroom door; he reached for the shoulder holster and pulled his gun. The gun was a .38 Smith & Wesson Centennial Model with a two-inch barrel and a capacity of five shots. He knew this was not a burglar in there, this was Augusta in there, and he also knew that she was not alone, and hoped he was wrong, and his hand began sweating on the walnut grip of the pistol.

He almost turned and left the apartment. He almost holstered the gun, and turned his back on that closed bedroom door, on what was beyond that closed bedroom door, almost walked out of the apartment and out of their life as it had been together, once, too long ago, almost avoided the confrontation, and knew it could not be avoided, and became suddenly frightened. As he crossed the room to the bedroom door, the gun was trembling in his fist. There could have been a hatchet murderer beyond that door, the effect would have been much the same.

And then the fear of confrontation gave way to something alien and even more terrifying, a blind, unreasoning anger, the stranger here in his own home, the intruder in his bedroom, the lover, who was Larry Patterson, here with his wife, the trap sprung, she thought he would be working the Night Watch, she knew she would be safe till morning, there hadn't been a movie at all, there was only the movie here in this bedroom, *his* bedroom, an obscene pornographic movie behind that closed door.

He took the knob in his left hand, twisted it, and opened the door. And he hoped, in that final instant, that he would be wrong again, he would not find Augusta in this room, not find Augusta with her lover but instead find a small, brown-eyed girl who went by the name of Felice or Agnes or Charity, a mistake somehow, a comedy of errors they would all laugh about in later years.

But of course it was Augusta.

And Augusta was naked in their bed, absurdly clutching the

sheet to her breasts, hiding her shame, protecting her nakedness from the prying eyes of her own husband, her green eyes wide, her hair tousled, a fine sheen of perspiration on the marvelous cheekbones that were her fortune, her lip trembling the way the gun in his hand was trembling. And the man with Augusta was in his undershorts and reaching for his trousers folded over a bedside chair, the man was short and wiry, he looked like Genero, with curly black hair and brown eyes wide in terror, he looked just like Genero, absurdly like Genero, but he was Larry Patterson, he was Augusta's lover, and as he turned from the chair where his trousers were draped, he said only, "Don't shoot," and Kling leveled the gun at him.

He almost pulled the trigger. He almost allowed his anger and his humiliation and his despair to rocket into his brain and connect there with whatever nerve endings might have signaled to the index finger of his right hand, cause it to tighten on the trigger, cause him to squeeze off one shot and then another and another at this stranger who was in that moment a target as helpless as any of the cardboard ones on the firing range at the Academy—do it, *end* it!

But then—and this was against every principle that had ever been drilled into him throughout the years he'd spent on the force, never give up your gun, hang on to your gun, your gun is your life, save the gun, keep the gun—he suddenly hurled it across the room as though it had become malevolently burning in his hand, threw it with all his might, surprised when it collided with a vase on the dresser top, smashing it, porcelain shards splintering the air like the debris of his own dead marriage.

His eyes met Augusta's.

Their eyes said everything there was to say, and all there was to say was nothing. He turned away swiftly and rushed blindly out of the bedroom, hurling open the front door to the apartment, and rushing for the stairway without closing the door behind him, his eyes burning with unshed tears, down the steps to the entrance foyer, opening the door there, the heat of the night striking him like a closed fist—and suddenly he was seized from behind and pulled back into the foyer.

The arm around his throat was thick and powerful, his hands came up at once, groping for the arm, and a voice whispered close to his ear, "Hello, punk," and he thought only *I threw away my gun.* And then, because he had been trained over the years to believe that a bad situation could only get worse, you make your move at once or not at all, he brought up his right foot instinctively, and smashed the heel of his shoe down hard on the man's instep, and shot his elbow back piston-hard at the same time, into the man's gut, and whirled into his embrace, knocking the pistol aside with his left hand and gouging at the man's eyes with the curled fingers of his right. The gun went off with a shockingly loud explosion, plaster falling from the foyer ceiling, the man screaming as Kling tore at his eyes and then brought his knee up into his groin and struck him across the bridge of the nose with the flat edge of his hand, going for the kill, hitting him hard enough to drive bone splinters into his brain. The man reeled away, the gun still in his hand, and Kling butted him with his head, driving it fiercely against the man's jaw, *Fall*, you bastard, the gun going off again, the shot reverberating like the roar of a cannon in the small hallway, the sudden stench of cordite on the sodden air. He pulled back his fist and drove it with all his might at the man's Adam's apple, and felt him yield at last, saw him go limp at last, and topple at his feet like a giant oak, the gun clattering to the floor beside him.

Breathing hard, Kling looked down at him.

He did not recognize the man.

He took his handcuffs from his belt, and braceleted the man's hands behind him, and then he sat down on the hallway steps, still breathing harshly, and clasped his own hands in front of him as though in prayer, and lowered his head, and allowed the tears to come at last.

ELEVEN

The formal Q and A took place in the lieutenant's office at the 87th Precinct at seven minutes past midnight on the morning of August 15, a week after the discovery of the body of Jeremiah Newman in his apartment on Silvermine Oval. Present were Detective/Lieutenant Peter Byrnes, Detective/Second Grade Stephen Louis Carella, and an assistant district attorney named Anthony Costanza. A police stenographer took down every word that was said. Costanza asked all the questions. The answers were supplied first by Anne Newman and subsequently by Susan Newman.

Q: Mrs. Newman, you've told the arresting officers that you were responsible for the death—

A: *Partially* responsible.

Q: For the death of your husband, Jeremiah Newman.

A: Yes.

Q: By partially responsible...

A: I was the one who first suggested it.

Q: Suggested what, Mrs. Newman?

A: That we kill him.

Q: To whom did you suggest this?

A: To my mother-in-law.

Q: When did you make this suggestion?

A: On the Fourth of July.

Q: That is the exact date?

A: The exact date.

Q: How do you remember the date so well?

A: There was a party, and Jerry got drunk again.

Q: Was your mother-in-law at this party?

A: The party took place in her apartment.

Q: And you say your husband got drunk?

A: Yes. As usual. We had to take him home shortly after dinner.

Q: By we...

A: Susan and I. My mother-in-law and I. We put him in a taxi and took him home. It was after we'd got him to bed that I first explored the idea of killing him.

Q: Why did you want to kill him?

A: I wanted to get out of a relationship that was suffocating me.

Q: Why didn't you simply ask for a divorce?

A: What makes you think I didn't?

Q: You asked your husband for a divorce?

A: On too many occasions.

Q: And what was his response?

A: He refused to give me one.

Q: So you decided to kill him?

A: Of course not, don't be absurd! I had grounds enough to divorce him six times over, the man was a hopeless drunk! All I had to do was walk out, or throw him out.

Q: Then what made you...?

A: Do you think I'd have been rid of him? Really? Even if he'd *given* me the divorce I wanted? *Really* rid of him? Who do you think he'd have called whenever he was vomiting all over himself? First me, to tell me what a worthless artist he was, and then Susan to ask her to come take care of him. What good would a divorce have done?

Q: Was your mother-in-law in sympathy with your desire for a divorce?

A: Entirely. But she realized as well as I did that a divorce wouldn't solve anything. He'd plague us for the rest of our lives.

Q: How did she react to your suggestion that you kill him?

A: She was in complete sympathy with it. She'd had her share of him over the years, believe me. Every time he got sick, he'd call Susan, ask her to come over to take care of him. Wouldn't trust me to do it, oh no, needed his *nurse*. She said we'd be well rid of him.

Q: Was it decided that night . . . the Fourth of July . . . that you would attempt to murder him?

A: I'd say it was explored.

Q: But no decision was made.

A: No.

Q: When did you and she decide . . .

A: Three weeks ago.

Q: You decided to kill him.

A: Yes.

Q: What prompted this decision?

A: He told me he was going to change his will. He told me he was going to cut me out of his will completely.

Q: Why was he doing that?

A: Because I didn't love him anymore.

Q: Were those his exact words?

A: Yes, he said he knew I didn't love him anymore. Because I'd asked him repeatedly for a divorce. He told me he would *never* give me a divorce because he didn't want to pay alimony, but neither would he see all his money go to me when he died. He told me I was stuck. He said it was a bad situation I just happened to be stuck with. And then he laughed.

Q: So you decided to kill him.

A: Yes. Before he changed the will.

Q: But, as you now know, he had *already* changed his will before—

A: Yes, but I didn't know that at the time. I thought it was something he planned to get around to. After all, what was the rush? I was *stuck,* as he put it, so what was the rush? We didn't know . . . *I* didn't know . . . that it was already a *fait accompli*. He'd changed the will the day before he told me he was *going* to do it.

A: Did you report this to your mother-in-law?

A: Yes. I told her Jerry was going to change his will. I told her he wasn't going to leave me a penny. The same as his father had done to her.

A: What was her response?

Q: She said we would have to kill him before he did that. I was sole beneficiary of the old will, you understand. I agreed to share everything with Susan if she'd help me do this thing, help me kill him. That was only fair. *Her* husband should have left those paints to her in the first place. Half of her son's estate seemed small recompense for the service she'd rendered *both* of them over the years.

Q: Did she agree to help you?

A: Yes. In fact, the way we would do it was her idea.

Q: Mrs. Newman, are you aware that in this state a husband cannot disinherit his wife?

A: What?

Q: I said—

A: No, I didn't know that.

Q: Are you further aware that a person who slays a decedent is barred from taking under the will of the person slain?

A: I don't know what that means.

Q: It means that even if you *had* killed your husband in time to have prevented the changing of his will, you would have been barred from inheriting whatever he'd left you.

A: I didn't know that.

A: I'd like to ask your mother-in-law some questions now, if you don't mind.

A: Yes, certainly.

Q: Mrs. Newman, you've heard everything your daughter-in-law just said to us...

A: I heard every word.

Q: Is it true that you and she conspired together to kill your son?

A: It's true.

Q: Your daughter-in-law said that the method of murder, the *way* you planned to kill him...

A: Yes, was my idea.

Q: It was your idea to administer a fatal dose of barbiturates?

A: Yes. It was also my idea to do it while Anne was in California. We decided that would be the best time. While she was away. So that no suspicion would fall on her.

Q: Mrs. Newman, did you in *fact* administer a fatal dose of barbiturates to your son?

A: I did.

Q: When would that have been?

A: Last Thursday night.

Q: That would have been the seventh of August.

A: Yes, whatever last Thursday night was.

Q: Can you tell us what happened that night?

A: I simply called him and told him I wanted to see him about an important matter.

Q: What was the important matter?

A: It was nonsense. Just an excuse to go over to the apartment. I told him his brother, Jonathan, was in town and wanted to borrow money from me. I pretended to be seeking advice on whether or not I should lend him the money.

Q: Did he believe your story?

A: Who knows what he believed? He was drunk. As usual. Getting him to take the Seconal was truly child's play.

Q: How did you get him to ingest a fatal dose of—

A: I told you. He was drunk. He'd been drinking before I got there, and he kept drinking steadily while I told him all about the imaginary loan his brother wanted. I didn't want him to pass out on me. I'm a registered nurse, an unconscious patient is incapable of swallowing. Nor did I want to force-feed him. There was the danger there of his choking to death. I wanted it to look like suicide, you see.

Q: So what *did* you do?

A: I mixed the next two drinks for him. He drank them within minutes of each other. He always guzzled his whiskey and water as though afraid the supply would run out momentarily.

Q: Did you mix those drinks in his presence?

A: No, I went to the bathroom, to use the water tap there. It wouldn't have mattered, he was blind-drunk anyway.

Q: Mrs. Newman, was there anything in those drinks besides whiskey and water?

A: Well, of course. There was the Seconal. I dissolved the contents of fifteen capsules in the first drink, and fourteen in the second. Seconal doesn't dissolve too easily in water, but it's easily soluble in alcohol. He never noticed anything at all, the drunken fool. It's odorless, you know, but there's a slightly bitter taste to it. He never noticed.

A: Why did you leave one capsule in the bottle?

A: To make it look like a suicide. I knew the fatal dose, I'm a nurse. I knew I'd given him enough to kill him. He went into coma shortly after he finished the second drink. And he died shortly after that.

A: Mrs. Newman was the air conditioner functioning while you were in the apartment?

A: Yes. That was an idea I had before I left.

Q: What idea?

A: To turn off the air conditioner. So that your people would have trouble determining the postmortem interval. We were cutting it very close, you see, I should have done it earlier in the week, actually. But somehow . . . well, I just couldn't muster the courage. And then, knowing Anne would be back early Friday morning, I went up there on Thursday night, determined to—

Q: What time would that have been, Mrs. Newman?

A: I went over to the apartment at four-thirty. *Cocktail* time, don't you know? He was already drunk when I got there. I mixed the two drinks for him, one after the other, and he was dead by six-twenty.

Q: How do you happen to recall the exact time?

A: Because I called Anne in California at exactly six twenty-one to tell her it was finished. She told me she'd call later to find out if I'd got home all right, if I'd managed to sneak out of the building without the doorman seeing me.

Q: What time did you leave the apartment?

A: It must've been about a quarter to seven. After I'd wiped everything clean of fingerprints, anything I'd touched, the glasses, the thermostat, of course, the telephone, the door-knob, everything. And then, on the way home, I remembered what I'd *forgotten* to wipe. The doorknob outside the apartment. I had pulled the door shut behind me, and then locked the door with the key Anne had given me—it's a deadlock, you see. And then, in the taxi on the way home, I remembered that I hadn't wiped off that outside knob, my fingerprints would be on the outside knob. So when Anne called at eight that night, I told her to make sure she wiped off that knob when she got home in the morning, before she touched it. It would be all right for *her* fingerprints to be on it, you see, she *lived* there. But mine? No, that would have been a mistake.

Q: Mrs. Newman...did you also wipe your fingerprints off the Seconal bottle?

A: Yes.

Q: Why did you do that?

A: Well, because they were *on* the bottle, I was the one who'd *handled* the bottle.

Q: But surely you realized—

A: Only later. But by then there was nothing we could do about it, the police had already been in the apartment. All I could do then was hope and pray...well...

Q: Hope and pray what, Mrs. Newman?

A: That I wouldn't be suspected.

Q: What do you mean?

A: Well, why would anyone suspect a *mother* of killing her own son?

He found Kling in the Swing Room downstairs shortly after the Q and A was concluded. The room was dark, Carella hadn't bothered to turn on the overhead lights because he was only on his way through to the back door of the building and the parking lot where he'd left his car. At first he saw only someone lying face downward on one of the cots. Then he realized that the person was crying. And then he recognized him as Bert Kling.

He went to the cot.

He sat on the edge of it.

He put his hand on his friend's shoulder.

"Tell me," he said.

ABOUT THE AUTHOR

ED MCBAIN has won fame as the author of the long-lived 87th Precinct police procedural novels, which has been popular reading since 1956, and as Evan Hunter for a number of strong novels, beginning with THE BLACKBOARD JUNGLE to the most recently published, LOVE, DAD. In addition, Ed McBain is currently writing a new mystery series featuring lawyer Matthew Hope whose most recent appearance is in RUMPLESTILTSKIN, also published by Ballantine.

HEAT is Ed McBain's newest 87th Precinct mystery. Mr. McBain lives in Connecticut.